P9-CRN-816

Forgotten Sea

VIRGINIA KANTRA

BERKLEY SENSATION, NEW YORK

THE BERKLEY PUBLISHING GROUP
Published by the Penguin Group
Penguin Group (USA) Inc.
375 Hudson Street, New York, New York 10014, USA
Penguin Group (Canada), 90 Eglinton Avenue East, Suite 700, Toronto, Ontario M4P 2Y3, Canada
(a division of Pearson Penguin Canada Inc.)
Penguin Books Ltd., 80 Strand, London WC2R 0RL, England
Penguin Group Ireland, 25 St. Stephen's Green, Dublin 2, Ireland (a division of Penguin Books Ltd.)
Penguin Group (Australia), 250 Camberwell Road, Camberwell, Victoria 3124, Australia
(a division of Pearson Australia Group Pty. Ltd.)
Penguin Books India Pvt. Ltd., 11 Community Centre, Panchsheel Park, New Delhi—110 017, India
Penguin Group (NZ), 67 Apollo Drive, Rosedale, Auckland 0632, New Zealand
(a division of Pearson New Zealand Ltd.)
Penguin Books (South Africa) (Pty.) Ltd., 24 Sturdee Avenue, Rosebank, Johannesburg 2196,
South Africa

Penguin Books Ltd., Registered Offices: 80 Strand, London WC2R 0RL, England

This is a work of fiction. Names, characters, places, and incidents either are the product of the author's imagination or are used fictitiously, and any resemblance to actual persons, living or dead, business establishments, events, or locales is entirely coincidental. The publisher does not have any control over and does not assume any responsibility for author or third-party websites or their content.

FORGOTTEN SEA

A Berkley Sensation Book / published by arrangement with the author

PRINTING HISTORY
Berkley Sensation mass-market edition / June 2011

Copyright © 2011 by Virginia Kantra.
Excerpt from Dare Island series by Virginia Kantra copyright © by Virginia Kantra.
Excerpt from *Delaney's Shadow* by Ingrid Weaver © by Ingrid Caris.
Cover art by Tony Mauro.
Cover design by Rita Frangie.
Interior text design by Laura K. Corless.

All rights reserved.
No part of this book may be reproduced, scanned, or distributed in any printed or electronic form without permission. Please do not participate in or encourage piracy of copyrighted materials in violation of the author's rights. Purchase only authorized editions.
For information, address: The Berkley Publishing Group,
a division of Penguin Group (USA) Inc.,
375 Hudson Street, New York, New York 10014.

ISBN: 978-0-425-24183-7

BERKLEY® SENSATION
Berkley Sensation Books are published by The Berkley Publishing Group,
a division of Penguin Group (USA) Inc.,
375 Hudson Street, New York, New York 10014.
BERKLEY® SENSATION and the "B" design are trademarks of Penguin Group (USA) Inc.

PRINTED IN THE UNITED STATES OF AMERICA

10 9 8 7 6 5 4 3 2 1

If you purchased this book without a cover, you should be aware that this book is stolen property. It was reported as "unsold and destroyed" to the publisher, and neither the author nor the publisher has received any payment for this "stripped book."

"An absolutely fantastic paranormal/fantasy read . . . Gorgeous, complex, and fascinating." —*Errant Dreams Reviews* (5 stars)

"What a refreshing and unique world Virginia Kantra has created for Children of the Sea! Full of sensual magic, intrigue, and compelling characters, *Sea Witch* is a book to be savored."
—*CK²S Kwips & Kritiques* (4½ klovers)

"A bestseller arises from the depths of the sea and floats to the top of the romance/paranormal list! *Sea Witch* is enthralling!"
—*A Romance Review* (5 roses)

Home Before Midnight

"Sexy and suspenseful . . . A really good read."
—Karen Robards, *New York Times* bestselling author

"Virginia Kantra is a sensitive writer with a warm sense of humor, a fine sense of sexual tension, and an unerring sense of place." —*BookPage*

Close Up

"Holy moly, action/adventure/romance fans! You are going to LOVE this book! I highly, highly recommend it."
—Suzanne Brockmann, *New York Times* bestselling author

"Kantra's first foray into single-title fiction is fast paced, engrossing, and full of nail-biting suspense."
—Sabrina Jeffries, *New York Times* bestselling author

"Honest, intelligent romance." —*Romance: B(u)y the Book*

Berkley Sensation Titles by Virginia Kantra

The Children of the Sea Novels

SEA WITCH
SEA FEVER
SEA LORD
IMMORTAL SEA
FORGOTTEN SEA

HOME BEFORE MIDNIGHT
CLOSE UP

Anthologies

SHIFTER
(with Angela Knight, Lora Leigh, and Alyssa Day)

OVER THE MOON
(with Angela Knight, MaryJanice Davidson, and Sunny)

BURNING UP
(with Angela Knight, Nalini Singh, and Meljean Brook)

“Virginia Kantra is one of my favorite authors.”
—Teresa Medeiros, *New York Times* bestselling author

PRAISE FOR

Immortal Sea

“Exquisite . . . The passion and heat in this story were enough to make me grab a glass of sweet tea twice. I needed a walk in the cool evening breeze just to make my heart stop pounding . . . I can’t recommend this series enough.”

—*Bitten by Books*

“This Children of the Sea story is entertainment at its finest.”

—*RT Book Reviews* (4½ stars)

“Virginia Kantra has given us another gem.” —*Fresh Fiction*

“Sexy, bold, and refreshingly unique paranormal romance . . . Absolutely wonderful reading.”

—*The Erotic Reader* (Highly Recommended)

“A fascinating story . . . I really enjoyed this book—a lot.”

—*Romance Reviews Today*

“Fantastic romantic fantasy.” —*Genre Go Round Reviews*

Sea Lord

“Oh, this was a marvelous coming-of-age story, and the best in a truly excellent paranormal romance series. This book had it all: passion, magic, conflict, and a truly amazing heroine.”

—*ParaNormal Romance* (Top Pick)

“Virginia’s selkies are some of the most fascinating paranormal creatures around . . . Epic and wonderfully intimate . . . *Sea Lord* really delivers—both on the emotional front and on the action front.” —*Dear Author*

continued . . .

"With lush writing, vivid descriptions, and smoldering sensuality, Kantra skillfully invites the reader into the heart of the selkie sanctuary and into the hearts and minds of her characters."

—*Romance Novel TV* (5 stars)

"Fast paced, tense, sizzling, and romantic! Much like the previous books, *Sea Lord* kept me absolutely enthralled."

—*Errant Dreams Reviews* (5 stars)

"Highly recommended!" —*The Erotic Reader*

"You will find yourself so engrossed in this story, you will hate to put it down until you have read the last page."

—*Night Owl Romance* (Top Pick)

Sea Fever

"An especially fine paranormal with strong characters, logical plotting, and a great sense of place . . . Don't go to the shore without this bit of selkie romance."

—*RT Book Reviews* (4½ stars)

"An exciting and spellbinding addition to this phenomenal paranormal series." —*Fresh Fiction*

"There's no second-novel slump for this trilogy . . . Moving, heartbreaking, and beautiful."

—*Errant Dreams Reviews* (5 stars)

Sea Witch

"A paranormal world that moves with the rhythm of the waves and the tide . . . Kantra tells Margred and Caleb's story with a lyric, haunting, poetic voice."

—Suzanne Brockmann, *New York Times* bestselling author

"Full of excitement, humor, suspense, and loads of hot, hot sex . . . Anyone who enjoys a good paranormal should NOT miss this one!" —*Fresh Fiction*

ACKNOWLEDGMENTS

Special thanks to my online community of writer buddies (you know who you are), who have mentored, supported, and inspired me, especially Susan Andersen, Heidi Betts, Suzanne Brockmann, Kate Douglas, Eileen Dreyer, Eloisa James, and JoAnn Ross; to my editor, Cindy Hwang, for her patience and support, and to the wonderful team at Berkley; and to Michael, for reminding me what it feels like to be young and in love.

The sea had jeeringly kept his finite body up,
But drowned the infinite of his soul.

—HERMAN MELVILLE

The cure for anything is salt water—
sweat, tears, or the sea.

—ISAK DINESEN

Foreword

IN THE TIME BEFORE TIME, WHEN THE DOMAINS of earth, sea, and sky were formed and fire was called into being, the elementals took shape, each with their element: the children of earth, the children of the sea, the children of air, and the children of fire.

After earth had flowered and life crawled from the sea, humankind was born.

Not all of the elementals were pleased with this new creation. The children of fire rebelled, declaring war on Heaven and humankind. Forced to cohabit with the mortals, the other elementals withdrew—the fair folk to the hills and wild places of earth and the merfolk to the depths of the sea.

Over the centuries, the children of fire have grown strong, while the children of the sea have declined in numbers and in magic. In recent years, a tentative alliance between merfolk and humans has subtly altered the balance of power. Yet the children of air, forbidden to interfere directly in mortal affairs, have continued to exist apart from both their fellow elementals and humankind.

Or mostly apart.

There are those among the angels who, in their zeal or frustration, cannot resist becoming involved in the lives and affairs of humankind. The punishment for their disobedience is the loss of their immortality. They become nephilim, the Fallen, living as humans among the humans they once protected, hunted in gleeful retribution by the children of fire.

If the balance of power shifts again, the repercussions will be felt in Heaven and on earth . . .

1

THE MAN ON THE BOAT STRIPPED HALF NAKED, exposing a lean golden chest and muscled arms.

In the parking lot across the street from the dock, Lara Rho sucked in her breath. Held it as he dropped his shirt to the deck and began to climb.

The top of the mast swayed, stark against the bold blue sky. Her stomach fluttered. Nerves? she wondered. Recognition? Or simple female appreciation?

The sun beat down, forging the water of the bay to a sheet of hammered gold. The air inside the car heated like an oven.

Beside her in the driver's seat, Gideon stirred, chafing in the heat. His corn silk hair was pulled into a ponytail, his blue eyes narrowed against the glare. "Is he the one?"

Lara leaned forward to peer through the windshield of their nondescript gray car, testing the pull of the internal compass that had woken her at dawn. They'd driven all morning from the rolling hills of Pennsylvania through the flat Virginia tidewater, wasting precious minutes in the traffic around Norfolk before they found this place. This man.

Are you the one?

She exhaled slowly, willing herself to focus on the climber. He certainly looked like an angel, hanging in the rigging against the bold blue sky, his bronze hair tipped with gold like a halo.

"I think so." She bit her lip. She should *know.* "Yes."

"He's too old," Gideon said.

Lara swallowed her own misgivings. She was the designated Seeker on this mission. Gideon was along merely to support and defend. She wanted her instincts to be right, wanted to justify their masters' faith in her. "Late twenties," she said. "Not much older than you."

"He should have been found before this."

"Maybe he wasn't meant to be found before." Her heartbeat quickened. Maybe she was the one meant to find him.

"Then he should be dead," Gideon said.

The brutal truth made her shiver despite the heat. Survival depended on banding together under the Rule. She was only nine when they brought her to Rockhaven, but she remembered being alone. Hunted. If Simon Axton had not found her . . .

She pushed the memories away to study her subject. He must be forty feet above the gleaming white deck. Snagging a rope at the top of the mast, he fed it to the two men waiting below, one old, one young, both wearing faded navy polo shirts. Some kind of uniform?

"He's been at sea," she murmured. "The water could have protected him."

It could do that, couldn't it? Protect against fire. Even if the water wasn't blessed.

"I don't like it," Gideon said bluntly. "You're sure he's one of us?"

She had felt him more with every mile, a tug on her attention, a prickle in her fingertips. Now that she could actually see him, the hum in her blood had become a buzz. But it was all vibration, like listening to a vacuum cleaner in the dark, without shape or color. Not only human, not wholly elemental . . .

"What else could he be?" she asked.

"He could be possessed."

"No."

She would know, she would feel that. She was attracted, not repelled, by his energy. And yet . . . Uncertainty ate at her. She had not been a Seeker very long. The gift was rough and raw inside her, despite Miriam's careful teaching. What if she was wrong? What if he wasn't one of them? At best she and Gideon would have a wasted trip and she'd look like a fool. At worst, she could betray them to their enemy.

She watched the man begin his descent, his long limbs fluid in the sun, sheened with sweat and sunlight.

And if she was right, his life depended on her.

She shook her head in frustration. "We're too far away. If I could touch him . . ."

"What are you going to do?" Gideon asked dryly. "Walk up and ask to feel his muscles?"

There was an idea. She gave a small, decisive nod. "If I have to."

She opened her door. Gideon opened his.

"No," she said again. She needed to assert herself.

Gideon was five years older, in the cohort ahead of hers, but she was technically in charge. "I can get closer if you're not standing next to me."

A frown formed between his straight blond brows. "It could be dangerous."

She had chosen their watch post. They both had scanned the area. It was safe. For now. "There's no taint."

"That's not the kind of danger I'm talking about," Gideon muttered.

She disregarded him. For thirteen years, she had trained to handle herself. She could handle this.

She swung out of the car, lowering her sunglasses onto her nose like a knight adjusting his helm, considering her strategy. Her usual approach was unlikely to work here. This subject was no confused and frightened child or even a dazed, distrustful adolescent.

After a moment's thought, she undid another button on her blouse. Ignoring Gideon's scowl—after all, *he* was not the one responsible for the success of their mission—she crossed the street to the marina.

It was a long, uneven walk along sun-bleached boards to the end of the dock.

The man descending the mast had stopped halfway down, balanced on some sort of narrow crossbeam, staring out at the open sea on the other side of the boat.

She tipped back her head. Her nerves jittered. Surely he wasn't going to . . .

He jumped. Dived, rather, a blinding arc of grace and danger, sending up a plume of white water and a shout from the younger man on deck.

She must have cried out, too. The two men on the boat turned to look at her, the young one with a nudge and the old one with a nod.

The one in the water surfaced with an explosion of breath, tossing his wet hair back from his face.

Cooling off? Or showing off? It didn't matter.

He stroked cleanly through the water, making for the swimming platform at the back of the boat.

Show time, she thought.

Pasting a smile on her face, she walked to the edge of the dock. "Eight point six."

He angled his head, meeting her gaze. She felt the jolt clear to her stomach, threatening her detachment. His eyes were the same hammered gold as the water, with shadows beneath the surface.

"Ten."

She pushed her sunglasses up on her head. "I deducted a point for recklessness. You shouldn't dive this close to the dock."

He grinned and grabbed the ladder. "I wasn't talking about my dive."

Heat rose in her cheeks. No one under the Rule would speak to her that way. But that was what she wanted, wasn't it? For him to respond to her while she figured out what to do with him.

"I'm flattered." This close, she could feel his energy pulsing inside him like a second heart. She tried again to identify it, but her probing thought slid off him like a finger on wet glass. He was remarkably well shielded. Well, he would have to be, to survive this long on his own.

She cast about for a subject. "Nice boat."

He shot her a measuring glance, hauled himself out of the sea, water streaming from his arms and chest. "Yeah, she is."

She tried not to goggle at the way his wet shorts drooped on his hips, clung to his thighs. "How long have you had her?"

"She's not mine. Four of us crewed her up from the Caribbean for her owners."

"So you're staying here? In town."

He shook his head. "As soon as she's serviced, I'm on to the next one."

Apprehension gripped her. She arched her brows. "You're still referring to the boat, I hope."

He flashed another grin, quick and crooked as lightning. "Just making it clear. Once I line up another berth, another job, I'm gone."

"Then we don't have much time," she said with more truth than he knew.

He stood there, shirtless, dripping, regarding her with glinting golden eyes. "How much time do you need?"

Her heart beat in her throat. Her mouth was dry. He thought her interest was sexual. Of course he did. That's what she had led him to think.

"Why don't we start with coffee," she suggested, "and see what happens."

He glanced at his companions, bundling sails on deck. "Drinks, and you've got yourself a date."

Lara swallowed. She had hoped to be back in Rockhaven by nightfall. But a few hours wouldn't make that much difference to their safety. She wanted desperately to succeed in their mission, to prove herself to the school council. She rubbed her tingling fingertips together. If only she could touch him . . . But they were separated by more than four feet of water. "Five o'clock?"

"Seven. Where?"

She scrambled to cull a name from their frustrating foray along the waterfront earlier in the day. Someplace close, she thought. Someplace dark. "The Galaxy?"

His eyes narrowed before he nodded. "I'll be there."

Relief rushed through her. "I'll be waiting."

* * *

Justin watched her walk away, slim legs, trim waist, snug skirt, nice ass, a shining fall of dark hair to the middle of her back. Definitely a ten.

"Hot." Rick Scott, the captain, offered his opinion.

"Very," Justin agreed.

Her face was as glossy and perfect as a picture in a magazine, her eyes large and gray beneath dark winged brows, her nose straight, her mouth full-lipped. Unsmiling.

Why a woman like that would choose a dive like the Galaxy was beyond him. Unless she was slumming. He picked his way through the collapsed sails and coiled ropes on deck. Which explained her interest in him even after she'd learned he wasn't a rich yacht owner.

The stink of mineral spirits competed with the scent of brine and the smells of the bay, fish and fuel and mudflats.

"The hot chicks always go for Justin," Ted said. "Lucky bastard."

Rick spat with precision over the side. He was tidy that way, an ex–military man with close-cropped graying hair and squinting blue eyes. "Next time you send the halyard up the mast, you can climb after it. Maybe some girl will hit on you."

A red stain crept under the younger crewman's tan. "It was an accident."

Justin felt a flash of sympathy. He remembered—didn't he?—when he was that young. That dumb. That eager to please. "Could have happened to anybody."

He'd made enough mistakes himself his first few months

and years at sea. Worse mistakes than tugging on an unsecured line.

He wondered if the girl would be another one.

Dredging the disassembled winch out of the bucket of mineral spirits, he laid out the gears to dry. He was working his way north again like a migrating seabird, following the coast and an instinct he did not try to understand. The last thing he needed was to get tangled up on shore.

"I'll be waiting," she'd said in that smooth, low voice.

He reached for the can of marine grease. Maybe she could slake the ache inside him, provide a few hours of distraction, a few minutes of release.

Mistake or not, he would be there.

* * *

This bar was a mistake, Lara thought.

The Galaxy was four blocks from the waterfront, off the tourist path, in a rundown neighborhood of shaded windows, sagging porches, and chain fences.

She perched in one of the dingy booths, trying to watch the room without making eye contact with the sailors and construction types straddling the stools at the bar.

Or maybe not.

At least in these seedy surroundings, no one would question if she and Gideon helped one slurring, stumbling patron out to their car later that night.

Over the bottles, a TV flickered, competing with the glow of the neon signs. MILLER. BUD. PABST BLUE RIBBON. The air stank of bodies and beer, a trace of heavy cologne, a whiff from the men's room down the hall. She folded her hands in her lap, her untouched Diet Coke leaving another ring on the cloudy table.

"Is it hot in here, or is it you?"

She looked up to find two sailors flanking her table. “Excuse me?”

The larger sailor shifted closer, trapping her into the booth. “You’re too pretty to be sitting here alone. Mind if we join you?”

She wasn’t alone. Gideon watched from an ill-lit corner, his attention divided between her and the door.

She straightened on the sticky vinyl seat. “I’m waiting for someone.”

“I don’t see anybody.” The sailor—hovering drunkenly between cheerful and offensive—nudged his companion. “You see anybody, T.J.?”

T.J.’s blurred gaze remained focused on Lara’s breasts. “Nope.”

“Let me buy you a drink,” the first guy said.

“No, thanks,” Lara said firmly.

“There you are.” A male voice, deep and smooth, broke through the noise of the bar and the wail of the jukebox. Somehow the sailors shifted, and there *he* was, tall and lean and attractively unshaven, looking perfectly at ease among the Galaxy’s rough clientele.

It was him. Her quarry from the boat.

Her heart, her breath, her whole body reacted. Her fingertips tingled. Well, they would. She was attuned to him, to his energy.

He grinned at her. “Miss me?”

“You’re late,” she said.

Twelve minutes. Not enough to abandon her mission, but enough to pinch her ego.

“Come on, baby, don’t be mad. You know I had to work.” The newcomer’s eyes danced, and she realized abruptly he was acting, playing a part for the sailors who still hemmed her into the booth. He lowered his voice confidingly.

"Thanks for keeping an eye on her. She gets . . . restless if I leave her alone too long. If you know what I mean."

Lara kept her mouth shut with an effort. The shorter sailor guffawed. His companion shifted his weight like a bull, hunching his shoulders.

"I should pay you back," the newcomer continued easily. Man-to-man, she thought, making them like him, make them side with him, diffusing the tension. He moved again, angling his body so smoothly she almost didn't see him slide his wallet from his front pocket.

Feet shuffled. Something passed hands. The sailors nodded to her and then ambled back to the bar.

Lara narrowed her eyes. "Did you just give them money?"

"I bought them a round." His grin flashed. "Why not?"

"You *paid* them to go away," she said, torn between outrage and admiration. She couldn't imagine Gideon—or Zayin or any of the Guardians—dispatching an opponent by buying him a drink.

"Think of it as supporting our troops." He met her gaze, his own wickedly amused. "Unless you'd rather we pound each other for the privilege of plying you with alcohol."

"Of course not. Anyway, I already have a drink, thank you."

He eyed her glass and shook his head. "Place like this, you order beer. In a bottle. Unless you want to wake up with something a hell of a lot worse than a headache."

He turned to signal the waitress.

Lara appreciated his concern. But his caution would make her task more difficult. Her fingers curled around the handle of her bag on the seat beside her. Maybe it wouldn't be necessary to drug his drink, she thought. Explanations were out of the question. He wouldn't believe her, and they might be overheard. But surely she could rouse something in him, a response, a spark, a memory.

Assuming he was one of them.

Perhaps she should offer to feel his muscles after all.

The thought made her flush. "I don't even know your name."

"Justin." No last name.

"Lara. Lara Rho."

She started to extend her hand, but at that moment he caught the waitress's eye and the opportunity to touch him was lost.

Lara swallowed her disappointment.

The waitress, a hard-edged, hard-eyed blonde who looked like she'd rather be somewhere else, left the knot of locals absorbed by the game on TV. "What can I get you?"

"Two Buds," Justin said.

The waitress looked at Lara. "ID?"

"Of course," she said, reaching for her purse.

Axton insisted they do their best to abide by human laws, to blend in with their human neighbors. She pulled out her perfectly valid Pennsylvania driver's license, hoping Justin would do the same, eager for any hint to his identity, any clue why he hadn't been found before now.

He smiled at the waitress. "Thanks."

The blonde cocked her hip, pulled a pen from her stack of hair. "Anything else?"

His grin was quick and charming. "I'll let you know."

Oh, he was smooth, Lara thought as the waitress sashayed away.

"So, Lara Rho." He stretched his arms along the back of the booth, his knees almost-not-quite brushing Lara's under the table. "What brings you to Norfolk?"

You.

Bad answer.

"Um." She inched her foot closer to his across the sticky

floor, hoping that small, surreptitious contact would give her the answers she needed. "Just visiting."

"For work? Or pleasure?"

Her toe nudged his. A buzz radiated up her leg, as if her foot had fallen asleep.

Deliberately, she met his gaze. "That depends on you."

His tawny eyes locked with hers. The tingling spread to her thighs and the pit of her stomach.

"I'm done with work," he said.

Her mouth dried at the lazy intent in his eyes. "Won't they be expecting you? Back at the boat?"

"Boat's been delivered and I got paid. Nobody will care if I jump ship." He smiled at her winningly. "I'm a free man."

She moistened her lips. "Isn't that convenient."

No one would miss him if he disappeared tonight.

Her heart thudded in her chest. All she had to do was identify him as one of her own kind, the nephilim, the Fallen children of air.

From his corner, Gideon glowered, no doubt wondering what was taking her so long.

If only she were more experienced . . .

The waitress returned with their beer, two bottles, no glasses.

Lara gripped the slick surface and gulped, drinking to ease the constriction of her throat.

"Let's get out of here," Justin invited suddenly.

"What?"

He reached across the table and took her hand, wet from the bottle. An almost visible spark arced between them, a snap of connection, a burst of power. Shock ripped through her.

His eyes flickered. "You pack quite a punch."

So he felt it, too. Felt something. Hope and confusion churned inside her. She dampened her own reaction, feeling as though her circuits had all been scrambled. The air between them crackled, too charged to breathe.

"I . . . You, too."

Her heart thudded. *He was not human.*

Or only partly human. His elemental energy beat inside his mortal flesh.

But he was not nephilim either. She didn't know what he was.

His energy was not light, but movement, swirling, thick, turbulent as a storm. It swamped her. Flooded her. She clung to his hand like a lifeline, focusing with difficulty on his face.

". . . find someplace quiet," he was saying. "Let me take you out to dinner. Or for a walk along the waterfront."

"What are you doing?" Gideon demanded.

Lara flinched.

"Who the hell are you?" Justin asked.

Gideon ignored him. "Are you *trying* to call attention to yourself?" he asked Lara.

Lara tugged her hand from Justin's, her mind still stunned, her senses reeling from the force of their connection. "You felt that?"

"They could feel you in Philadelphia," Gideon said grimly. "Shield, before you get us both killed."

Justin's eyes narrowed. "Look, buddy, I don't know who the fuck you think you are, but—"

Gideon gripped Lara's elbow. "We're getting out of here."

Justin rose from the booth. "Take your hands off her."

"It's all right," Lara said quickly. She struggled to pull herself together. "I know him."

Justin's mouth tightened. "That doesn't mean you have to go with him."

"Try and stop her," Gideon invited.

Lara shook her arm from his grasp. "That's enough," she said, her voice sharp as a slap.

Gideon met her gaze. "Your little energy flare just gave away our location. This place will be crawling in an hour. We need to leave before they get here."

Lara's throat constricted. "What about him?"

"Is he one of us?"

Not fully human. Not nephilim either.

"No," she admitted.

"Then lose him. He's not our responsibility."

He was right. She was still new to her duties as Seeker, but the Rule of the community, codified over centuries, was clear about their obligations to keep and preserve their own kind. And the dangers of getting involved with those who were not their kind.

Yet . . .

"Give us a minute," she said.

Gideon's face set, cold and rigid as marble. "Five minutes," he acceded. "I'll wait for you outside."

Where he could guard the entrance and scan for danger. She nodded.

With another glare at Justin, he left.

"Are you okay?" Justin asked.

"Fine," she said firmly, whether it was true or not. Why had she felt the pull of his presence if she wasn't meant to find him?

"Listen, it's none of my business," he said. "But if this guy is giving you a hard time . . ."

His willingness to look out for a stranger shamed her. Especially since she was about to abandon him to his fate.

"Nothing like that. We work together," she explained.

He looked unconvinced.

"What about you?" she asked.

He frowned. "What about me?"

Who are you?

What are you?

"Will you be all right?" she asked.

"I think my ego will survive being ditched for another guy." The glint in his eye almost wrung a smile from her.

She bit her lip. Their enemies would be circling, drawn by that unexpected snap of energy. She already had to account for one mistake. She couldn't afford another.

Besides, he was not one of them.

He would be safe. He had to be.

"Right. Well." She slipped her purse strap onto her shoulder. At least now she didn't have to drug his beer. "Take care of yourself."

As she slid out of the booth, he stepped back, lean and bronzed and just beyond her reach. "You, too."

She walked away, reluctance dogging her steps and dragging at her heart.

* * *

Justin watched his plans for the evening walk out the door with more regret than he had a right to. Her tight butt in that slim skirt attracted more than a few glances. Her fall of dark brown hair swung between her shoulders. The woman sure knew how to move.

He shook his head. He'd known she was slumming when she came on to him that afternoon. Presumably she was going back where she belonged, with Mr. Tall, Blond, and Uptight.

He hadn't lost anything more than half an hour of his time. So why was there this ache in the center of his chest, this sense of missed opportunity?

He took a long, cold pull at his bottle, his gaze drifting

over the bar. He'd been in worse watering holes over the past seven years, before he got his bearings and some control over his life. Worse situations, in Puerto Parangua and Montevideo, in Newark and Miami. He drank more beer. He fit in with the surly locals and tattooed sea rats better than pretty Lara Rho and her upscale boyfriend ever could. But he didn't belong here. He belonged . . . The beer tasted suddenly flat in his mouth. He didn't know where he belonged.

He set down his bottle. He didn't want to drink alone tonight. And he didn't want to drink with the company the Galaxy had to offer.

Careful not to flash his roll, he dropped a couple of bills on the table and walked out.

Nobody followed.

Outside, the sky was stained with sunset and a chemical haze, orange, purple, gray. The day's heat lingered, radiating from the crumbling asphalt, sparking off the broken glass. He headed instinctively for the water, free as a bird thanks to the coworker boyfriend with the ponytail, trying to figure out what to do with the rest of his evening.

Or maybe his life.

Beyond the jumbled rooftops at the end of the street, he could see the flat shimmer of the sea. He passed a homeless guy huddled in a doorway, clutching a bottle, watching the street with flat, dead eyes. Something wrong there. He kept his arms loose and at his sides as the pawn shops and tattoo parlors gave way to warehouses and razed lots.

His neck crawled. Alley ahead. Empty. Good.

He lengthened his stride, taking note of blank windows and deserted doorways. Good place to get jumped, he thought, and angled to avoid the dirty white van blocking a side street.

He heard a thump. A grunt.

Not his problem, he reminded himself. None of his business.

A woman's cry, sharp with anger and alarm.

Shit.

He circled the van, shot a quick look down the street.

And saw Lara Rho backed against the brick wall of an empty lot with a couple of rough guys circling her like dogs.

2

FOUR OF THEM, JUSTIN COUNTED. TWO ON LARA, one big guy keeping the boyfriend occupied—*Tie him up while they took her down, good strategy*—one on the ground. Even odds, almost.

Unless they were armed, in which case things were going to get messy.

Justin didn't know what he'd stumbled into. Robbery? Rape? Drug deal gone wrong?

But nobody was waving a blade around. Yet. Or a gun. He left his own knife in the sheath on his leg.

The big guy stopped dancing and bulled under the boyfriend's guard, catching him hard around the ribs, wrapping him in his arms. Goldilocks swallowed by the bear.

One of the thugs lunged at Lara. She grabbed his arm, using his weight against him, but the second one jumped in, grabbing her long hair, snapping back her head.

Justin surged forward, quick, controlled, two short jabs

to the kidneys that should have dropped him. He jerked, releasing Lara, but he didn't go down.

Justin checked, caught by a sense, a smell, fetid and somehow familiar. Like burning garbage.

Slowly, the thug turned, eyes flat in his dead face.

Fuck.

Justin hit him, palm of the heel up the nose, *crunch*, blood spraying everywhere. The smelly bastard stayed on his feet, pummeled Justin's ribs, one, two, hard. Justin blocked the third blow, slammed the side of his foot on the bastard's instep. Their legs tangled. They fell. Pain burst in Justin's elbow, radiating up his arm. They scrambled, fighting for position. Stinky clawed at Justin's face, gouging for his eyes. Justin slammed both forearms down to break his hold, bucked him up and over. Grabbing hair, he rapped the guy's skull on the ground, hard enough to stun.

The thug, blood streaming from his broken nose, looked up into his eyes and smiled.

It creeped him out. Enough he didn't follow through, and paid for it when the guy curled up. Head butt. The alley exploded in pain and stars. They rolled again, Justin on the bottom. He heard grunts, thumps, around them. *Lara?*

Stinky reared over him, bloody, smiling. Justin chopped up, striking his throat with the edge of his hand, crushing the windpipe. The guy gurgled, blank eyes bulging in his bloody mask of a face.

Drop, asshole.

He dropped.

Breathing hard, Justin shoved his body aside and staggered to his knees.

His gaze swept the scene for Lara, found her by the wall, bending over her attacker's motionless body. Safe. The air around them wavered like heat rising from a jet engine.

Justin blinked. The shimmer didn't go away. *Shit.* He must have hit his head harder than he thought.

He glanced over at the boyfriend, crawling out from under the big guy. Another one down. Okay. He breathed again, this time in relief, and bent down to press his fingers to the pulse under Stinky's jaw. Still beating. Good.

A hot breeze skittered down the alley, swirling dust, raising another whiff from the man on the ground. Justin coughed. Shuddered.

Rolling the thug to his side so he wouldn't drown in the blood from his windpipe, Justin rose shakily to his feet.

Lara leaned over her attacker, wiping his face. Not wiping, Justin amended. She had this little bottle in her hand and was making some kind of sign on his forehead. Her lips moved. Like she was giving him last rites or something.

The hair rose on the back of Justin's neck. Shaking his head, he walked over.

"You okay?"

She moistened her lips. "Yes, I . . ." Her eyes widened. "Watch out!"

A scrape behind him.

He turned, too late.

The blow clipped the side of his skull and dropped him like a stone.

* * *

Horrified, Lara watched the bottle crack against Justin's head. He collapsed in the grit of the alley. The homeless man stepped over the body, a demon staring out of his eyes.

He licked his lips. "You're next, bitch."

She was spent. Done. Drained of strength and magic.

"Go to Hell," she said and flung her vial of holy water at its head.

The demon shrieked.

A splash of holy water wouldn't stop the children of fire. But it slowed this one down.

Gideon rushed over and flung himself on the thing's back. The possessed man staggered, clawing at Gideon's hands around his throat.

Lara crawled to Justin, her arms and legs shaking, a silly little prayer whistling under her breath. *Oh no, oh please, oh God . . .*

The demon crashed to its knees in the alley, Gideon still clinging grimly to its neck.

She tilted Justin's head to open his airway, pressed her ear to his lips. A faint, warm vibration stirred her hair. Relief leapt inside her.

Gideon lumbered to his feet. "Is he alive?"

"Yes." She laid her hand along his jaw, reaching out with all her senses. Her power flickered. Sputtered. "Justin? *Justin.*"

Blearily, he opened his eyes. She peered anxiously at his pupils. In the shadow of the warehouse, she couldn't tell if they were the same size or not.

"Can you hear me?" she asked.

His gaze fastened on her face with painful intensity. His cracked lips parted. His face was a mask of dirt and blood. Her heart tripped. So much blood. The split in his scalp gaped like another mouth, red and open.

She scrambled on her hands and knees for her purse, lying in the weeds and litter.

"What are you doing?" Gideon demanded.

"He's hurt. We need to apply pressure," she explained, rummaging inside. "To stop the bleeding."

"Unless his skull is fractured," Gideon said. "Come on. We don't have time for first aid."

"What about . . ." Her gaze darted to the other figure on the ground. Their attacker.

For answer, Gideon turned the man over with his foot. The one who had been possessed sprawled motionless, staring with empty eyes at the darkening sky.

She felt sick inside. The lost souls who had attacked them were victims, too.

Demons did not usually hunt humankind. Heaven and Hell were bound by the same restrictions. The children of air and fire could not take human life or violate humans' free will without pissing off the Most High. But the demons, lacking bodies of their own, sometimes risked the wrath of Heaven by borrowing mortal bodies.

And now one of those mortals was dead. Killed. She and Gideon had killed him.

Gideon stooped briefly, tracing the *taw* on the fallen man's brow: the hilted sword, the four quarters of the wind, the sign of the children of air.

"We need to get out of here," he said.

"Right." She collected her legs and her wits. Sliding an arm behind Justin's back, she propped him to a sitting position.

He stared at her, his eyes dark and dazed.

"Justin? Can you stand up?"

He nodded. Or maybe he was simply having trouble holding his head upright.

"He can't come with us," Gideon objected.

Lara slung her purse over her shoulder and wrapped her arms around Justin's waist. "I'm not leaving him."

Not again.

Gideon shifted, irresolute. "You don't even know if it's safe to move him."

"I know it's dangerous for him to stay."

The demons might not hunt humans, but they preyed in gleeful retribution on the Fallen children of air. Human or not, shielded or not, Justin had made himself a target simply by coming to her rescue.

She thrust her shoulder under his armpit, braced her legs, and pushed them both to their feet. He lurched against her to save himself from falling. Tucked under his arm, she was acutely conscious of his height. His weight. His warm, animal scent. His body was lean, but big boned and packed with muscle.

"Get his other side," she ordered.

Gideon moved automatically to obey. Under the Rule governing their community, they were vowed to obedience. *Scire, servare, obtemperare.* "To know, to save, to obey."

She winced. So far she was failing at all three. But at least Gideon was prepared to follow her lead for now.

They shuffled toward the car parked at the other end of the lot. Justin hung between them, his bloody head lolling against his chest, his feet dragging. Dead weight.

Lara's palms sweat. She shifted her grip.

Not dead, she thought fiercely. *Not dead yet.*

The last daylight faded from the sky. Shadows collected on the ground, tripping them up. As they reached the car, Justin stumbled. Lara struggled to keep them both upright.

"Careful." Gideon unlocked the car and opened the rear passenger door.

Justin's muscles trembled. She could feel his effort to cooperate as they loaded him awkwardly into the backseat, as they folded and stuffed his long body into the car. By the time he collapsed beside her, they were both damp and panting. Her heart pounded with worry and exertion. She clasped her arms around him to keep him on the seat. He groaned and tried to raise his head.

The driver's side door slammed as Gideon got in. "You owe me another shirt."

They both were streaked with blood. She grabbed a wad of paper napkins left over from their lunch in Maryland and attempted to staunch Justin's wound. "We owe him our lives. He wouldn't be hurt if he hadn't helped us."

Gideon met her gaze in the rearview mirror. "Where to?" he asked, making it clear that whatever happened next was her choice. Her responsibility.

Her fault.

She swallowed her resentment and her doubts. "The hospital."

The engine rumbled to life.

Justin muttered against her shoulder, his speech deep and slurred.

She stroked his tawny hair, streaked with sweat and blood. "What did you say?"

His breathing rasped. "No . . . hospital."

"Sorry, pal," she said. "You need a doctor. Stitches."

A CAT scan.

"No."

She gentled her voice. "If you can't afford it—"

"No doctor," he repeated, raising his head. "No . . . police."

"He probably has a warrant out for his arrest," Gideon said.

"But he needs help," Lara said.

"So we take him back to his ship."

"It's not his ship." What had Justin said? Now that the boat was delivered, he was a free man.

His eyes had drifted shut again. His head bobbed on her shoulder. An unfamiliar tenderness wrung her heart. All that life, all that vitality, bleeding out of him . . .

"He's alone," she said. "Just like we were before we were found."

"He's not like us. You said so yourself."

For all their training and power, the nephilim were still human, with human weaknesses. Human imperfections.

She licked dry lips. "What if I was wrong?"

Gideon spared a glance from the road, his straight brows twitching together. "Do you feel something?"

"No," she admitted.

Her power had been exhausted by the skirmish with the demons. She had only a normal physical awareness of Justin's presence.

Okay, not exactly normal. The whiff of demon still clung to them. Justin's blood was on her hands. His warm, hard weight squashed her against the car door. But the powerful charge she'd experienced in the bar had faded to a faint static along her skin, as if she'd never been driven from her bed to seek him. As if . . .

Her breath caught.

As if her compulsion was satisfied now that he was found. Now that he was with her.

"Maybe we're meant to bring him with us," she said.

Gideon's shoulders stiffened. "To Rockhaven."

Recklessness seized her. *Why not?* "Yes."

"We can't bring an outsider into the community. He's a threat."

"Hardly a threat now," she pointed out. "He can't even hold his head up."

* * *

Their voices rolled like a fretful tide, rushing, retreating, never still. Justin tried to focus on the words, but pain sank red talons into his skull, gripping his brain.

Just a bump on the head. He'd survived worse.

Floating in a cold green sea, limbs leaden, lost . . .

He shook his head to clear it.

Bad idea.

Agony seared his temples, speared his neck. His gorge rose as his stomach lurched in protest. He gritted his teeth, swallowing beer and bile, fighting not to vomit in the back of the moving car.

"Easy." *Her* voice, clear and soothing, as she petted him.

Gratefully, he inhaled her scent, absorbed her touch, letting himself fall into the comfort of her body against his, sweaty, soft, female.

The white lane markers flashed and faded in the beam of their headlights.

Breathe, he told himself. *In, out, in . . .*

Jesus, he was dozing off. Or passing out. He clung to consciousness, fighting to snatch meaning from the conversation taking place over his head.

"Treat him at the infirmary," Lara was saying.

"Assuming he survives the trip." From the boyfriend.

Thanks, dipshit.

"Wow. I am so touched by your concern," Lara said.

"You know what concerns me? Trying to explain to Axton what we're doing with a dead body in the backseat."

Justin felt Lara stiffen. "Would you rather explain why we left him behind to die?" she asked.

He wasn't dying, he wanted to tell her. He was remarkably hard to kill.

"More lives than a fucking cat," the freighter captain had said when they pulled him from the sea.

But her fierce concern made him feel good. For the first time in years, a woman had his back.

Thankfully, he turned his face into her neck and slipped into the dark.

* * *

"Behind me," he ordered, his mouth dry, his voice strained. "They attack from behind."

The girl stumbled to obey, filling her hands with stones from the path.

He admired her courage. But it was his duty to protect her. His responsibility.

He turned to face the wolf—*Not a wolf, not a wolf,* pounded his heart—blocking their way. It snarled, taunting. Testing.

Tightening his grip on his knife, he braced to take its charge.

It sprang. The world exploded in a blur of heat, claws, teeth, eyes. He staggered, thrusting, thrusting, felt the blade sink in and the sickening *thunk* of iron on bone.

Pain ripped his arm. His vision blurred.

A hoarse cry. His? Hers? A flash. The air stank of scorched meat and burning hair and blood.

He struggled to tug his knife free, fought to breathe. He couldn't move. Buggering hell, he couldn't move his arm.

He groaned.

"It's all right," she said.

He struggled to warn her, but his cry was an incoherent croak.

Demons.

"Ssh," she soothed. Her hair fell thick and pale as straw around her quiet face. "It's just a dream."

Justin opened his eyes to find Lara bending over him. Shock momentarily robbed him of speech. His head throbbed. His arm tingled with the pain of returning circulation.

He blinked at her, disoriented. “Not blond.”

Her lips curved. “Only in your dreams. Disappointed?”

“No.” He struggled to lift his arm, to touch the ends of her hair. “Pretty.”

“Thanks. How are you feeling?”

“No hospital,” he mumbled. Hospitals meant bureaucracy and forms and questions. The last thing he needed was Homeland Security inspecting his passport, demanding a copy of his birth certificate.

“Shh. We’re not going to the hospital. Try to get some rest, okay?”

He sighed and obeyed, weary and relieved. *Pretty dark-haired Lara. Safe.*

But a question niggled at the back of his brain and pursued him down into the dark.

Who was the woman in his dream?

3

THE HIGH BEAM OF THEIR HEADLIGHTS SCRAPED the drive, throwing into sharp relief the marble eagles at the gate and the precepts of the Rule inscribed in stone: SCIRE, SERVARE, OBTEMPERARE. "To know, to save, to obey."

ROCKHAVEN SCHOOL, announced a discreet sign to the left of the entrance. EST. 1749.

Lara's heartbeat quickened.

The tires whispered to a stop in a pool of floodlight within range of the cameras: one mounted on the gate, two artfully hidden in the landscaping. The governors didn't let respect for tradition interfere with the need for security.

Lara rolled down her window, careful not to disturb Justin's head on her lap.

A red light blinked. The mechanized iron gate swung silently open. Gideon drove through.

She let out a breath she hadn't been aware of holding and settled back in her seat. Almost there. Almost home.

The first time she'd approached Rockhaven in the back of a car, she'd been a victim, a child, sick, sweaty, and scared half to death, with almost no memory of who she was or where she came from.

Her kind might live as humans, but they were not born as human infants. That status was reserved for the Most High. Created as children of the air, the nephilim were sentenced to earth for overstepping the role dictated by Heaven. For intervening, always with the best of intentions, in human affairs. For violating humans' free will. The most powerful in Heaven—with the most to lose, the most to forget—became the youngest on earth.

Lara was nine when she Fell.

She had always felt special—favored—because Simon Axton himself had found her. Not that she'd trusted him at the time, she recalled ruefully. Her short, brutal, bewildering experience on earth had taught her to be wary of strangers, particularly men.

But something in her had recognized and responded to the tall, terrifying headmaster. And she had fallen in love with the school at first sight. To her child's eyes, the four-story fieldstone building, with its gabled roof and uncompromising lines, had the appearance of a fortress. Rockhaven represented order. Permanence.

Safety.

The school became the only home she remembered. The only family she knew.

Moonlight gleamed on the rows of dark windows. The sky overhead pulsed with stars. Cool night air flowed through the open window.

Lara inhaled in relief. Her responsibility was almost over. The consequences of her decision, good or bad, would be determined by the schoolmasters.

She smoothed the hair from Justin's forehead, combing the matted strands with her fingers. His long body was crammed on the seat beside her, his neck and legs at awkward angles, one arm across his chest. Blood blackened the napkins stuck to his wound. She was afraid to disturb him, worried the bleeding would start again. Terrified that this time when she tried to rouse him, he wouldn't regain consciousness.

Yellow light spilled from the west portico. Not everyone at the school was sleeping. Somebody was waiting up for them.

She clasped Justin's unresponsive hand. All arriving nephilim were screened and welcomed by at least one of the governors. Often the rescued children needed medical attention. Most required a period of education and adjustment as they eased into their new bodies and community life.

She tightened her hold on Justin's hand. His skin was warm. Feverish? He definitely needed a doctor. But he was not a child.

Lara swallowed against the constriction of her throat.

He wasn't nephilim either.

She had overstepped—again—by bringing him here.

What would the consequences be this time?

* * *

Justin swayed as Lara and the Boyfriend supported him out of the car. Nothing wrong with his legs. It was his head that hurt. But the ground pitched under him like a ship's deck in a squall. His stomach rolled like a rookie sailor's. He needed to pee. Preferably without help.

Gritting his teeth, he dragged his feet up the shallow stone steps.

"One more," Lara said. "You're doing fine."

He appreciated her concern. And the lie.

They maneuvered through a doorway with stained glass insets. He kept his head down, taking stock of his surroundings from beneath his lashes. Carved wood panel walls, old, dark, muted paintings, a curving staircase fit for a hotel. A chandelier, an explosion of light and color sparkling with crystals and candles, threw patterns on the hardwood floor.

The place didn't look like a hospital, he noted with relief. But there was a vaguely institutional smell in the air, a patina of many bodies over time, a whiff of dust and floor polish.

"Where . . . are we?" he croaked.

"Home," Lara said.

Justin tried to get his mush-for-brains to work. He had no home. *"The place where, when you have to go there, they have to take you in,"* Rick liked to say.

So, okay, this was Lara's home. Would they take him in because she brought him here? Did he want them to?

He looked at the two people waiting under the light, a man and a woman, both tall and arrestingly beautiful, not old, not young. The woman's skin was the color of coffee, the man's face austere and pale. Something about the guy, his cool blue eyes or his chiseled profile or his stick-up-the-butt attitude, reminded Justin of . . . somebody.

"Who's he?" His speech slurred like a drunk's. "Your father?"

Lara sucked in her breath.

"Simon Axton." The tall blond man introduced himself, offering a lean, well-manicured hand.

Or two. Justin's vision wavered. He was afraid if he let go of Lara, he'd fall.

He shifted his weight, stuck out his hand, gave them the name on his passport. "Justin Miller."

Axton's hand was cool like his eyes, his grip firm. *Nothing to prove*, Justin thought.

Until the man's grip inexplicably tightened. His dark blond eyebrows rose. "What is this?" he asked Lara.

Justin's head buzzed. As if his skull had been invaded by a rush of wind, a swarm of bees.

Lara cleared her throat. "He . . . I . . . This is the one I was sent to seek."

Sent?

Justin pulled his hand free. He needed to sit down.

Axton glanced at the woman standing under the light of the chandelier. "Miriam?"

The handsome black woman came forward and took Justin's arm. The Boyfriend had already moved away toward the long curving staircase.

Distancing himself, Justin thought. Smart move. The ritzy entrance hall had all the tension of a bar before a fight broke out.

"Let me help you to a chair," the woman said.

He leaned on her, grateful for the support. But he wasn't about to leave Lara's side. Not until he'd figured out what the hell was going on.

"What is he?" Axton asked.

Justin frowned in concentration. Or maybe he'd asked, *"How is he?"* The buzzing in his skull drowned out everything else.

The woman—Miriam—continued to hold his arm, like a doctor taking his pulse.

Like a guard with a recalcitrant prisoner.

The pounding in his head intensified. His wound throbbed in time with his heart. He focused on Lara, warm and solid and real beside him, on her pink polished toes, on the clean, sweet scent of her hair. He breathed in, out, the rhythm of his breath like the sigh of the surf or the beat of the tide. *In*, filling his lungs, swirling in his head. *Out.*

The room stopped reeling.

A crease appeared between Miriam's brows. "He is not of air."

Heir of what? he thought, confused.

"He needs our help," Lara said.

Axton's cool blue gaze rested on her without expression. "His needs are not our concern."

"I should examine him," Miriam said. *What was she, a doctor?* "He has something. An energy. I felt it."

Amusement bubbled inside him. Some energy. He could barely stand.

Axton said something that sounded like "*she*," and Miriam shrugged. "Perhaps," she said.

"He's a threat," a different voice announced. "Let me get rid of him."

Lara's slim body tensed. *Trouble.* Justin raised his head, squinting into the shadows.

The speaker prowled from the foot of the stairs, wearing black and a sneer. Big hard dude, like those stone gods on Easter Island, large nose, strong chin, maybe six four, two hundred forty pounds, easy. Which meant he could kick Justin's ass even before the bump on his head.

"Some welcoming committee you got here, honey," he muttered.

Lara squeezed his hand. Reassurance? Or warning? "Justin was hurt protecting me," she said.

"A ruse," Stone Face said. "To get you to trust him."

Justin had heard enough. "Okay, I'm out of here."

As soon as he found his balance. His strength. A cab.

"Don't be ridiculous," Lara said. "We're hours from Norfolk."

"You should have left him there," Stone Face said.

"He needed a doctor."

Axton arched dark blond eyebrows. "There are no emergency rooms in Virginia?"

"He didn't want . . ." Lara's voice shook slightly. "He was my responsibility. I had to make a decision—"

"When you go into the field, I expect you to be guided by your training and your partner. Not indulge in misplaced compassion."

She winced.

Pain hammered Justin's skull. "So dump me back where she found me, asshole, and we'll call it even."

"Please," Lara said. To which one of them? "He wouldn't be here if it wasn't for me. We were attacked."

"You are trained in self-defense. Was it your preparation that was lacking? Or your skill?"

"There's nothing wrong with their training," Stone Face said.

"Gideon?" Axton's gaze pinned the Boyfriend like a bug. "You were Guardian on this mission."

The younger man flushed to the roots of his blond hair. "We were outnumbered. There were four of them. Five."

"Which?" asked Stone Face.

"So many?" Miriam said at the same time.

"Four and a lookout," Lara said.

"Which compels me to inquire what you did to attract their attention," Axton said.

The quick exchange made Justin dizzy. They'd been jumped in an alley. Had they been set up? Had he?

He was in over his head, the undercurrents in the room sucking his strength. He felt the walls closing in, the room whirling around him.

"Justin?" Lara's voice, sharp and worried. *"Justin."*

I'm okay, he wanted to tell her.

Except his brain was on fire and his mouth wouldn't form the words.

His eyes rolled back in his head, and the floor tilted up to receive him.

* * *

Miriam Kioni stripped off her latex gloves and dropped them on the procedure tray. "He'll have a scar, of course," she said to Simon, standing with Lara at the side of Justin's bed. Jude Zayin, the dark-browed master of the Guardians, watched silently from his post at the infirmary room door. "But the edges of the wound aligned nicely."

The hot, bright medical lamp switched off.

In the sudden dimness, Lara blinked down at the shaved patch above Justin's ear. Twenty-two stitches marched ant-like across his scalp, disappearing into the gold stubble of his hair.

Something fluttered in her chest like wings. One of his eyes had swollen shut. His tanned skin had the waxy sheen of a melted candle.

She curled her nails into her palms. "Should he still be unconscious?"

"It was easier to suture his wound while he was sleeping," Miriam said with the calm authority of her hundred years.

The nephilim were not immortal. But the wisest and most powerful of them could enjoy the span of several human lifetimes. Miriam had been master of the Seekers and the school's physician longer than Lara had been alive. Lara would have to be an idiot to challenge her.

She moistened her lips. Apparently she was an idiot. "But . . . His skull fracture . . ."

"A simple concussion," Simon said.

Water hissed in the sink. "Probably not the first one either," Miriam said.

Lara's throat worked. "What are you talking about?"

"You can't see it on the imaging equipment, but I found an old scar from a previous injury. Maybe he played football in high school."

"Or got beaten up," Zayin said.

Miriam scrubbed her hands at the sink. "Either way, it would make him more susceptible to another concussion."

"But he'll be all right?" Lara asked.

"The CAT scan didn't reveal any internal bleeding or elevated pressure in the brain," Miriam said. "He should be fine with a little rest."

"He can rest someplace else," Zayin said. "I don't want him here."

Miriam turned from the sink. "He needs at least forty-eight hours to recover."

"I don't give a damn what he needs," Zayin growled. "He's a risk."

Lara gripped the metal guard rail on the side of Justin's bed. "He's a target."

They all turned to look at her with varying degrees of surprise and impatience.

She swallowed hard and stood her ground, her heart beating like a rabbit's. "The demons will know he helped me. Us," she explained. "We can't abandon him."

"Maybe that's what they're counting on," Zayin said.

Simon pursed his lips. "You think he's one of them."

"I know he's not one of us," Zayin said flatly. "I can't read him. I don't like it."

"Miriam? You were in his head."

"Only to control his pain and monitor autonomic

function. I doubt I would have gotten that far if he weren't unconscious already." The doctor shrugged her slim shoulders. "An interesting case. His shields are very strong."

"Yes. Interesting, as you say." Simon's perfect brow creased in thought. "Very well. He may stay as long as . . . required."

Lara exhaled in relief. "*Thank* you."

Zayin's gaze met the headmaster's, flat black colliding with blue. "As long as we take the necessary precautions."

Simon inclined his head.

Justin's hand, lean and brown, twitched against the white sheet. He stank of blood and Lidocaine and something else, a male, warm, animal scent, uniquely his. Lara had a sudden image of him standing golden, free, and fearless on the mast, and her heart squeezed in pity and regret.

"I could stay with him," she volunteered. "To watch him. Wake him up."

The way she had on the car ride north.

Miriam shook her head. "It's been a long day for all of us. You need your rest, too."

"I don't mind," Lara said. "I'm not tired."

It wasn't strictly a lie. She was beyond tired, in that floaty state of awareness that was usually the product of training too hard or studying too long.

She saw the governors exchange glances.

She understood their concern. She was only a novice Seeker. Her small authority ended the moment their car rolled through the gates. She'd already screwed up. It was better, wiser, *safer* to leave Justin in their more capable hands.

Yet part of her rebelled at the thought of leaving him alone, unconscious and defenseless.

Why he needed to be defended here at Rockhaven, in

the care of three nephilim masters, was something she wasn't going to think about yet.

"I think you've done enough already," Simon said.

Her throat constricted at the implied rebuke, choking off whatever protest she might have made.

Zayin stalked forward, pulling a leather cord from his pocket, a square black bead knotted in the middle. The fine hair rose on Lara's arms as power hummed in the room.

A heth. Not a ward for protection, but a spell to bind and restrain.

Zayin slid the cord around Justin's neck, tying it so that the black bead rested smooth and shining in the hollow of his throat.

Lara swallowed in comprehension. The heth would choke any demon that broke its limits, effectively extinguishing—killing—it.

Of course, it would kill an ordinary human, too.

"Is that really necessary?" she appealed to Simon.

After a pause, Miriam answered. "The patient shouldn't exert himself. The best things for him now are quiet, dark, and limited physical activity."

A binding spell would limit his activity all right.

Taking a second, shorter cord, Zayin slipped it under Justin's ankle and then rolled back the cuff of his jeans.

Lara stiffened, staring at the black leather sheath strapped to Justin's leg.

"Dive knife." Zayin shot her a brief, hard look. "Still think he's harmless?"

She didn't say anything. They would not expect her to.

But Justin didn't draw the knife, she remembered as Zayin unbuckled the sheath and laid it on the counter. In the bar, he'd bought a round for two sailors rather than pick a fight. He'd stuck up for her with Gideon. Saved her from the demon.

She didn't know what he was, but she knew what he wasn't.

He wasn't a threat. Not to her. At least, not in the way they all believed.

Lara looked down at Justin's gaunt face, the angry lump, the line of black stitches, the purple bruise around one eye.

After all he had done for her, he was being treated like the enemy. Tied like a prisoner. Like a dog. The unfairness of it made her knuckles turn white on the rail.

Simon regarded her with cool, blue, assessing eyes. "If you're quite satisfied, I believe we're done here."

The others did not move.

Lara met his gaze, her heart banging in her chest. *She* was done here, he meant.

She was dismissed. Freed of responsibility, of blame, of consequences.

All she had to do was walk away.

"Good night, Lara," Simon said gently.

She dropped her head, relieved and disappointed. "Good night, Headmaster."

The door closed behind her with a small, defeated click.

* * *

Justin dreamed he was floating, up and down, moving with the rhythm of the waves, tied to the remains of . . . a boat? A mast, splintered and heavy. Thick wet rope constricted his chest and chafed his armpits. Cold ate his flesh, seeped into his bones. He could not feel himself, his swollen hands on the mast, his frozen legs in the water, anymore. Only cold and a throbbing in his head like fire.

He was not afraid of dying. The very concept of drowning was ludicrous, unacceptable, to his dream self.

But his body would not respond the way he wanted—expected—it to. He had a memory (*or was it another dream?*) of scything through the clear cold dark, his nostrils sealed, his eyes wide open, fluid and free, sleek and solid beneath the wave. In his element . . .

Voices drifted to him in the dark.

"Watch his head."

"Get the door."

"We need a light."

He was lifted up and carried along, swiftly, smoothly. He heard gravel crunch and insects chirr, felt the air roll under him like the sea, bearing him up on its billows. The night embraced him, alive with the scents of tilled earth and worked stone, cut wood and cultivated flowers. Land smells. Human smells. Confused, he stirred, opening his eyes.

A pattern of leaves overhead. The outline of a rooftop, silhouetted against a sky full of stars.

He floated down a path like a river, dizzy and without apparent support, flanked by tall, moving figures. A silver globe like a tiny moon hovered almost within reach. He licked cracked lips, staring at the light dancing above his head. *Impossible.*

A shadow swooped between him and the moon.

The rope tightened around him, dragging him back into the dream.

The pulse of the surge was his pulse, the rush of the ocean filled his empty heart, his aching head. *We flow as the sea flows.*

He shuddered with loss and cold, clawing the mast, clinging to consciousness. The horizon moved up and down, gray and empty as far as the eye could see. As long as he hugged the spar, he could keep his head above water. But after long . . . *Hours? Days?* . . . his concentration and his arms kept slipping. His head hurt. Every time a wave rolled the mast, he went under. Every time, he had to fight harder to get on top again.

They would search for him, he was sure. She would come for him. He was almost certain.

But when he tried to picture the nameless They, their faces wavered like reflections in a pool, scattered, lost.

"Mind the step."

The air around him changed again, became dank and still as the refrigeration of a tomb. He smelled dust and mold and old, growing things.

All motion stopped.

"Are you sure . . ." A woman's voice. Not hers.

A rush of disappointment swallowed what came next.

When he focused again, a man was speaking. *"Old storm cellar . . ."*

Their voices tumbled over each other, hard and meaningless as pebbles rattling at the water's edge.

"No idea what he is . . . what he's capable of."

"—risk—"

"Can't keep him down here like some kind of lab rat."

"—expose our children—"

"More than a matter of academic interest . . . Matter of survival."

His hips, his shoulders pressed something solid. A bed, hard and narrow as a ship's bunk. A pillow, flat and musty.

The voices cut off. He heard a scrape, a thump, before the silvery light behind his eyelids faded away.

He lay on his back under the earth, alone in the dark, in the silence. His head throbbed.

For the first time, it occurred to him he might die after all.

* * *

She crouched alone in the filth, in the dark, her heart pounding so hard her body shook with it.

He was coming back.

She pressed her fingers to her mouth so she wouldn't whimper, so he wouldn't hear and find her.

He was coming back with a present for her, he said. The thought made her curl herself tighter in her corner. "*My little angel*," he called her, which made her want to throw up. If only she'd be quiet, if only she'd be good, if only she were *nice* to him, he wouldn't have to hurt her, he said.

She heard a scrape, a thump from the top of the stairs.

And woke gasping, her skin clammy with sweat.

Just a dream.

Lara lay dry-mouthed and wide-eyed, staring into the darkness, willing her stomach to settle and her heartbeat to return to normal. Throwing off the tangled covers, she staggered across the room and jerked open the window.

She drew a deep, slow breath. Held it, while the clean night air blew away the sticky remnants of her dream.

The quad was empty, the students in their beds. No one was up but Lara and the moon. Even the infirmary was dark.

Lara frowned. Miriam had said Justin needed rest. But whoever was with him ought to have a light. Did the sleep spell still hold? Or was he lying awake, alone in the dark?

From experience, she knew better than to go straight back to sleep after a nightmare. Maybe she would just go check on him. No one had told her she couldn't visit the infirmary.

Because it never occurred to them that she would try, her conscience pointed out.

She ignored her conscience and reached for her clothes.

Minutes later, she was creeping down the staircase of the sleeping dormitory. A tread creaked under her bare feet. She froze, her heart revving about a million miles a minute. Which was ridiculous; she was a proctor now with her own apartment, and she had every right to leave her rooms if she wanted.

She stole through the silent common room, avoiding the clustered study tables, the couches crouched like beasts around the dark TV. Moonlight poured through the casements, forming silver tiles on the floor.

She fumbled with the deadbolt on the door. She had always been the good girl in her cohort. Her roommate Bria had been the one who nudged and pushed and led them into trouble, who snuck out at night and slipped in at dawn, flushed, laughing, and defiant. Lara was in agony for her friend every time Bria was called to the headmaster's office.

Bria had only grinned, shaking her wild mane of blond hair. Naturally curly. Naturally blond. It wasn't always easy, having a best friend who looked the part, like a painting of an angel from the Italian Renaissance. "What's Axton going to do, throw me out?" Bria's smile invited Lara in on the joke. "Come on, Lara, God Almighty cast us out of Heaven. You think I care if a bunch of teachers expel me from their stupid school?"

They'd been opposites in so many ways: Bria, outgoing, outspoken, and outrageous; Lara, careful, committed, and responsible.

But as the only two girls in their cohort, they were inevitably paired. For eight years, they'd shared notes and secrets, skipped gym and meals together, whispered about everything and nothing across the space between their beds after lights out. Bria was Lara's other self, her other side, secret and daring. Lara missed her more than she could ever admit, even to herself.

The school never expelled Bria. She'd been right about that. But the summer before their senior year, Bria ran away. Lara never saw her friend again.

Flyers.

The masters refused to acknowledge them. The students spoke of them in whispers. The ones who deserted the security of their own kind, the nephilim who left Rockhaven.

Lara shivered as she pulled the door shut behind her and turned her key in the lock.

She could never do that. She owed Simon everything: her home, her education, her identity.

Her life.

Wards made of glass rods chimed from the trees as she hurried along the edges of the upper quad. The night was alive with the rustle of leaves and insects, the flutter of breeze and bats. She ducked her head past the dining hall, lengthened her stride toward the infirmary.

She tested the handle. Locked. Of course.

It took only seconds to open the door with her proctor's key. The waiting room was empty and dark.

"Hello?"

No answer. No nurse behind the desk, no guard at the door.

She took a few steps forward, her blood pounding in her ears, her senses humming. They would not have left him alone.

She had a sudden, jarring image of Justin's white face, the heth gleaming in the hollow of his throat, and doubt coiled like a worm at her heart. Would they?

"Miriam?" she called softly into the dark.

Silence.

She reached out with her mind, straining for the whisper

of his presence, trying to pick out his scent, his heartbeat. The effort made her tired brain throb.

Or was that an echo of his pain?

"Justin? Dr. Kioni?"

Nothing.

Her feet followed her thoughts down the deserted corridor. She threw open doors as she passed, caution melting into anxiety. *"Justin."*

His room.

Empty.

She stood in the doorway, her gaze scraping the rumpled hospital bed. He was gone, the only signs he'd ever been there the wrinkled sheets and the black sheath on the table.

He was gone. A sudden chill chased over her skin. Escaped.

She picked up the knife left lying on the table.

Zayin's words mocked her. *"Still think he's harmless?"*

4

THE SKY WAS PEWTER AND PALE GOLD, THE SUN just breaking through the clouds to shimmer on the surface of the western sea.

Lucy Hunter sat alone in the inner bailey of Caer Subai, listening to the splash of the fountain and the restless murmur of the ocean outside the walls. After seven years, the work of rebuilding the selkie stronghold of Sanctuary was nearly complete. The towers rose tall and strong, wreathed in mists and magic. The scent of apple blossoms blew from the hills, mingling with the wild brine of the sea and the rich perfume of her garden.

Roses rioted everywhere, cascading pinks and bold reds, bright yellows and starry whites gleaming like constellations against the thick, dark foliage.

Her hands clenched in her lap. Not everything on the island was barren.

"You are up early." A deep voice disturbed her reverie.

She turned her head.

A man stood in the shadow of the castle wall, watching her with eyes the color of rain. Tall, broad, and handsome, his hair blue-black like a mussel shell. Conn ap Llyr, prince of the merfolk, lord of the sea. Even now, the sight of him had the power to steal her breath and stir her heart.

"Or couldn't you sleep?" he asked.

She turned away, unwilling to burden him with her growing sense of failure. "I had a dream."

His deerhound, Madagh, left his side to thrust a cold nose against her colder fingers. She stroked the dog's gray, bearded muzzle. It was easy to take comfort from the dog.

"You could have woken me." Conn's voice was too measured for reproach.

She stiffened anyway. "I didn't want to bother you."

In recent months—since the Thing She Didn't Think About had happened—he had withdrawn further and further into his duties, burying his own grief in the demands of rulership.

Once he would have taken her in his arms, this selkie male who did not touch except as a prelude to sex or a fight. Now he stood cool and immovable as a statue, separated by his natural reserve and her unspoken resentment.

"You are my consort." His tone was patient, controlled. "My mate. What concerns you concerns me. Tell me."

She gripped her hands together in her lap. "I dreamed I heard a child crying."

Something moved in his eyes, like water surging under the ice. "Lucy . . ."

"Not a baby," she said hastily. "A boy. A lost boy."

The wind sighed through the garden, releasing the scent of the roses. The bush he had given her threw petals like drops of blood upon the grass.

"You are upset," Conn said carefully. "Such dreams are natural."

"It's not that," she said impatiently. She couldn't stand to think about *that*. She could not bear any more of his well-meant reassurances. "This boy was *lost*, Conn. Like Iestyn."

"Iestyn is not a boy any longer. He's been gone for seven years. They all are gone."

"I feel responsible."

Conn's face set in familiar, formidable lines. "It was my decision to send them away. My failure to keep them safe."

"You sent them away because of me. Because I didn't stay and protect Sanctuary."

"You saved your brothers and their wives and children. You made the better choice for the future of our people."

She was grasping desperately at straws. At hope. At control. "But suppose they're still out there somewhere? Iestyn and the others."

"They would have found their way home by now."

"Unless they can't. Maybe my dream was a . . . a message. A sending."

Conn was silent.

"Is it possible you are focusing on one loss to the exclusion of another?" he asked at last.

"You think I'm making things up," she said bitterly.

"Lucy." His voice was no less urgent for being gentle. "You are still the *targair inghean*."

Her heart burned. Her throat ached. Locked in her grief, she did not, could not, answer.

He waited long moments while the fountain played and the wind mourned through the battlements.

And then he went away.

Lucy sat with her hands in her lap, staring sightlessly at the sparkling water. She was the *targair inghean*, the promised daughter of the children of the sea. Long ago, before she had loved him, before he loved her, Conn had stolen her from her human home so she would bear his children.

"I need you," he had told her then. *"Your children. Ours. Your blood and my seed to save my people."*

She put her head down among the roses and wept.

5

He was out there somewhere. She could feel him, just like this morning.

Lara skimmed along the tree-lined walk, her flat shoes crunching the pea gravel. She imagined Justin blundering in the dark, dazed and bleeding, hurt and resentful, a danger to himself . . . or to others.

She needed to find him. For his sake. For hers.

She had to tell somebody. Tell Simon.

Her stomach churned. The thought of facing the governors, of Zayin's scorn and Simon's disappointment, made her sick inside.

But she had no choice. A trickle of sweat rolled down her spine. *Hurry, hurry, hurry.*

The distinctive pitched roof line of the headmaster's residence poked over the trees—six chimneys and a weathervane shaped like an eagle.

Simon Axton lived alone in the original Colonial

farmhouse, set apart from the other school buildings behind the main hall. Lara had been invited inside exactly eight times. To the sunroom to take tea with her cohort on graduation day. To the book-lined library for cocktails with the schoolmasters and other proctors over the holidays. Once or twice to bring Simon a file he'd left at the office.

Lara approached the front porch, her steps slowing, anticipation burning a hole in her gut. Too late, she realized she should have called. But what would she say?

What could she say? She was supposed to be in her room.

Simon's cool dismissal pounded in her head. *"If you're quite satisfied, I believe we're done here."*

The thought of his displeasure dried her mouth. She stared up at the darkened windows, listening to the whisperings and rustlings and cracklings of the overgrown garden. A soft thump sounded from the back of the house, some small, nocturnal animal hunting in the night.

Her heart thudded.

Suck it up, she ordered herself. *Get it over with.*

Straightening her shoulders, she marched toward the steps.

That noise again, like a prowling cat or a raccoon testing the garbage cans or . . .

She caught her breath. Or like an escaped patient, skulking in the bushes.

Goose bumps rose along her arms. She stood frozen, her mind racing, her breath whooshing in and out of her lungs. He couldn't be . . .

Here?

Maybe. Why not? How far could he get, with a skull fracture and the heth around his throat?

She thrust her hand into her skirt pocket, wrapping her fingers around the knife—his knife, Justin's—and was instantly electrified as if she'd grabbed a live plug. Her nerves sizzled. Like a bug flying into a bug zapper.

She strained her senses.

There? Almost. Almost . . . *There.*

A whisper of warmth, male, animal, alive. A swirl of wild energy, around the corner, behind the house. Intangible. Unmistakable.

Justin was here, somewhere nearby.

Clutching the knife like a divining rod, she plunged into the darkness at the side of the house, stepping over beds of hostas and lilies of the valley, creeping under the black and staring windows. It was like her Seeking—was it only this morning?—or the game she'd played as a child. Warm. Cold. Warmer. Hot.

She shivered. A dangerous game, with high stakes and an unpredictable playmate.

Warm, warmer . . .

A thick oak raised its arms over the backyard, obscuring the star-strewn sky. She stepped into the mottled light, her gaze scanning the dappled ground, the silvered plants, the velvet shadows. Against the foundation, the door to the storm cellar yawned open, a gaping black hole.

HOT.

The knife burned in her pocket. The air left her lungs.

There. Sprawled across the stone threshold, one arm reaching for the wooden door as if to shut it behind him. His hair was bleached, his skin pale in the moonlight. The bandage on his forehead was dark with blood.

Justin lifted his head and met her gaze, his eyes nearly black in the shadows, burning with intensity. "Help . . . me."

She inhaled through her teeth. "You shouldn't be here."

Like a fox, bloodied and desperate, run to earth under the farmer's house.

Incredibly, he smiled. Or was that a distortion of the moonlight? "No," he whispered agreement.

She took a cautious step forward, keeping her ankles out of reach. "You need to go back to the infirmary."

"Can't . . . breathe."

"It's the heth."

He stared at her dumbly.

"Cutting off your air." He must be very strong—or stubborn—to have overcome both Zayin's binding and Miriam's sleep spell.

It was clear, however, that he'd reached the end of his rope. Literally. His breath wheezed alarmingly. His head sank back to the ground. His body was cut in two by the shadow of the cellar, his legs disappearing down the stairs. He turned his face to watch her, eyes open, unmoving, like a wounded animal.

She bit her lip. There was no way she could undo the Master Guardian's heth. She didn't have the power. Or the nerve.

But she couldn't stand idly by and watch him choke. Not if she could help him.

"Here." She knelt in the long grass beside his head, feeling his thin breath warm and moist against her bare knee.

Cautiously, she touched his throat, tested the leather thong. It didn't *feel* tight. The bead, black and smooth as onyx, was almost invisible in the dark. She gave an experimental tug, and her fingers stung as if she'd grabbed a thistle in the garden. *Ouch.* She jerked her hand away.

She drew a slow breath. *Now what?*

In her mind, she could hear Simon's calm, lecturing voice as he addressed the fundamental powers class. *"Magic is a matter of discernment, will, and grace. Before you attempt to use your gift, you must understand what should be; what can be; what must be."*

What should be . . .

She was already on her knees. Ignoring the bead, she gripped the cord between two fingers and her thumb. Closing her eyes, she bowed her head and focused on the knot. Imagined it loosening, softening, sliding . . .

She felt a faint vibration in her fingertips, a lurch in her stomach. Opening her eyes, she peered hopefully at Justin.

His widened gaze met hers. His mouth opened soundlessly, like a fish gasping for air. Like a man dying.

Oh, skies. She had to *do* something.

What can be . . .

Air, she thought frantically. That was her element, wasn't it? If she couldn't break the heth's power, she would at least give him air.

She flung herself on him, rolled him to his back. With one hand, she tilted his head, pinched his nose. The other she slapped to his chest. His throat arched. His mouth gaped. Drawing a deep breath, she leaned forward and opened her mouth over his.

His lips were warm, moist, firm. She blew her breath into him, poured herself into him. The world spun.

In you. Me, in you. My breath, my life, in you.

She was the air filling his mouth, dilating his throat, swelling his lungs. He tasted like salt and sweat and freedom, dark, rich, forbidden flavors.

What must be . . .

Inside her, something fluttered and erupted, a thousand beating wings fighting the sky. Roaring filled her head, a rush like wind or the sea. Power thrummed and thundered along her veins, welled and spilled from her eyes, her mouth, her hands. It lifted her up, she was rising, falling, flying . . .

No, that was his chest, she realized, dazed.

Justin's chest, rising, his lungs expanding with air.

His arms closed around her. She gasped and released him. They both shuddered.

She pushed herself up, one hand on his hard, lean torso, one hand on the cold ground. Dizzy, she looked down at him. "Are you all right?"

His eyes met hers, black as night with a thin edge of gold like the sickle moon. "What . . . was that?"

She rocked back on her heels, pressing her lips together, holding the taste of him inside. What was she doing? What had she done?

"First aid," she said.

Wicked laughter lit his eyes.

It was more than first aid, and they both knew it.

More than a kiss. Did he realize?

She was no magic handler. All nephilim were taught what they were and what they once could do. Most learned to shield and make a little light, to bend air and set wards. But most gifts remained latent. This went beyond anything Lara had done—or felt—before.

She rubbed her arms, holding herself together. "We have to get you back."

The animation drained from his face. He was still very pale, she noted with a thrum of anxiety. "Can't."

She felt another flutter. Panic, this time. "I can't hide an attempted escape. But if I return you—if you return of your own volition—the governors will be more lenient on us both."

"Can't . . ." Another slow, rasping breath. "Walk."

"Oh."

His eyes drifted shut again as if the effort of speaking had exhausted his strength. His lashes looked very long and dark against the sharp white angles of his face.

Her angel's breath had revived him. But for how long?

Lara hugged her elbows as she considered her options. She couldn't move him. She couldn't walk away.

She glanced up at the dark windows of the house, fighting the hollow in the pit of her stomach, knowing what she had to do.

Her hand trailed from his chest. She climbed to her feet. "I'll be right back."

His lean hand curled, warm and possessive, around her ankle. "Don't leave."

Her heart lurched. "I'll be right back," she repeated and ran.

* * *

Lara peered through the leaded glass insets at the side of the door. Even through the swirled and textured glass, she could see the hall was empty. The doorbell's echo faded away.

Simon didn't come.

Her heart hammered. Why didn't he come?

She tried knocking and heard—finally!—the headmaster's deliberate tread descending the stairs. The foyer light switched on, making the colors in the window bloom.

Simon opened the door. Just for a moment, something flashed in his eyes. She felt hot and awkward, as if she'd been caught running in the hall. Or kissing a bleeding stranger in his back garden . . .

She fought the temptation to smooth her skirt, to check her buttons. *Stupid.* Simon had more important things to worry about than what she did or with whom. And so did she.

She must have roused him from bed. He was still wearing the long, loose pants and shirt most nephilim favored for training and sleeping. The wide-sleeved shirt hung open over his naked chest. His long, narrow feet were bare.

"Lara. This is unexpected." His usually smooth voice was roughened with sleep.

She averted her gaze, uncomfortable with this unfamiliar, intimate view of the headmaster. She really should have called first. "Yeah. Um, sorry. I need your help."

"What is it? What can I do for you?"

"Me?" Surprise made her squeak. "Nothing. I . . . It's Justin."

Simon went very still. "Justin."

"Out back. Please. Hurry."

"Lara . . ."

"He must have . . ." *Escaped* was too strong a word. "Walked out. I found him trying to get into your storm cellar."

Did she imagine it, or did some of the tension leave Simon's shoulders? "And you came to tell me."

She nodded.

"Very good."

His approval made her flush.

"He is there now?" Simon asked, already moving, gliding down the steps, silent as the air.

She hurried after him. "Yes, he can't walk, he can barely talk . . ."

"He spoke to you?"

The sudden sharpness of his tone made her blink. "Well, not really. The heth . . . And his head . . ."

Simon rounded the corner of the house and stopped. Lara watched him take in the scene with one glance, the gaping cellar door, Justin's body on the stairs. His eyes were still closed, his chest moving. Thank God. The residue of magic drifted over the ground like the smell of gunpowder on the Fourth of July.

Lara rubbed her arms, feeling the charge like static against her skin.

"You may go," Simon said. "I will deal with this."

At the sound of his voice, Justin turned his head. His gaze slipped past Simon and stabbed her, his eyes dark with accusation.

For no reason at all, she began to tremble.

"It's all right," she said quickly. "Everything's going to be all right now."

"Stay there," Simon ordered. "He may be dangerous."

"He's not, he . . ."

Simon stooped, his back to her. She felt a change like a drop in temperature or a shift in the atmosphere, and Justin slumped.

Simon cradled his head before it hit the ground.

Her heart rolled over in her chest. "What did you do?" she whispered.

Simon glanced over his shoulder, brows raised.

Oh, right, like she wouldn't recognize his magic whammy.

But maybe she wouldn't have a day ago. Or even an hour ago. Maybe the spell she had worked on Justin had made her more sensitive. Or maybe it was his kiss . . .

"I relieved his pain," Simon said.

"You knocked him out."

Simon shrugged. "He will be easier to move this way."

He was the headmaster. She trusted him. She did.

She watched as he brought his cupped hands to his mouth and blew softly. Mage fire kindled in his palms, a globe of silver light, cool and unconsuming. He released it to float above his head, tethering the light with a word.

Simple magic. She could do it herself, most of the time.

But Simon Axton had other magic, other powers, painstakingly accumulated or recalled over the years of his very long life.

He raised his arms in command and Justin's body levitated, hovering over the cellar threshold.

In silence, Simon waded into the shadow of the stairwell, nudging Justin ahead of him like a man on a raft. The mage fire followed. Lara watched, anxious and uneasy, as the stone walls swallowed the descending light.

"Where are you . . . Aren't you taking him back to the infirmary?"

"He'll be safe here." Simon's reply was muffled by the ground. "Quiet."

Quiet, yeah. Like a grave is quiet.

She scrambled through the canted door, ducking her head to avoid the rough-timbered ceiling. There was a nasty moment going down the steps when she thought about snakes and spiders and things that lived in holes underground. But then the passage opened into a small room, cool and musty, with shelves along one wall and a couple of bunks on the other.

Simon was already lowering Justin's body onto the bottom bunk. But she had time to notice—just before his head hit the pillow—that it was already dented. His shoes were under the bed.

She sucked in her breath.

Simon turned at the sound.

Their eyes met.

He must have seen her working things out. The bed. The shoes. The heth. The knife. And Justin, sprawled across the threshold to the cellar, half in, half out.

She wet her lips. "He didn't walk out of the infirmary."

Not on his own. They'd brought him here, Zayin or Simon. She saw that now. He must have woken alone, in pain, in the dark. No wonder he'd tried to escape.

And she'd dragged him back like a barn cat with a bloody mouse and deposited him at the headmaster's feet.

"How," Simon asked softly, "did you discover he was gone?"

Her mind stuttered. She raised her chin, forcing herself to hold his gaze. "I couldn't sleep." He would know why, he'd found her, he knew everything about her. "So I decided to check on him."

"Your sympathy does you credit." A pause, while they both looked down at the man on the bed. "Unfortunately, the same cannot be said of your judgment."

Pain squeezed her head. She could not think. She could not breathe. "He shouldn't have been left by himself."

Simon's lips thinned. "Apparently not."

"I found him," she said. "I can stay with him. Let me help, we have a connection, I—"

"Your *connection* is your problem. You are too close to this matter to see clearly where your responsibility and your loyalty should lie. Perhaps you need to take some time for reflection."

"I know you're disappointed in my performance as Seeker," she said through stiff lips. "But please, I have the calling. If you give me another chance . . ."

"Seeking is a gift," Simon said. "Even if I wanted to, I could not deprive you of your vocation."

She exhaled in relief. "Then—"

"However, I can and will determine your other duties at Rockhaven."

Her *other* duties?

She worked for him. In his office.

Adult nephilim remained in the community, under the Rule that governed every aspect of their lives, that brought them closer to their un-Fallen perfection, that unified and defined them. The younger ones lived in the dorms as proctors. A few qualified as teachers at the school. Most graduates, however, went to work in the settlement's glassworks factory. Rockhaven Glass had been in operation for a hundred and thirty years, providing exquisite stained and textured art glass for designers all over the world and a steady income for the nephilim.

Lacking any other skills, Lara had expected to put her business education to work in the distribution center. But Simon had found a place for her in his own office. She'd always liked to imagine that the headmaster took a special interest in her, in her future.

"I can look after him and still do my job."

"You are mistaken," Simon said with icy calm. "From now on, you cannot see him, cannot speak to him, cannot visit him, is that clear?"

A direct order this time, Lara thought dully. He was taking no chances on her disobeying him again.

"Until I can trust your judgment, you cannot work for me," Simon continued. "Tomorrow morning, report to the raptor house. For the time being, you may assist Keeper Moon."

Crazy Moon, the mews mistress, who preferred her injured birds to people.

Lara's hands shook. Her throat constricted. "You're banishing me to the birdcages?"

"By your own actions, you have endangered the community we are sworn to preserve. You leave me no choice."

"But I'm wasted in the mews. At least . . ." She floundered for a compromise that would leave her pride intact. "Send me to the glassworks."

"You are not an artist."

"No," Lara admitted. Maybe once she'd dreamed . . . But

she wasn't Gifted like the rest of her kind with an artist's creativity. She couldn't sing or play, spin or weave, paint or draw. She had a head for figures and a knack for organization. That was all.

"Your chemistry marks were never high enough to consider you for the lab side," Simon continued with dispassionate brutality. "You have neither the strength nor the training that might qualify you for the furnace."

His assessment was no more than she expected. Maybe what she deserved. But she winced, all the same.

"I can still answer phones. Track orders. I've got computer skills . . ."

"I think . . . Something quieter. More contemplative," Simon said. "The Rule calls us to self-knowledge and obedience. You have proven yourself sadly lacking in both. This is an opportunity for you to reflect on your true place in the community."

Her true place? she wondered bitterly. *Reporting to Misfit Moon? Cleaning up bird shit?*

Her eyes stung. Her heart burned. All the reflection in the world wouldn't make her see this as an opportunity.

This was punishment.

She blinked, her gaze flitting to the bed. The worst part was, she wasn't the only one suffering for her insubordination. Justin was being punished, too.

The chill, small room pressed in on them. She and Simon stood face-to-face, toe-to-toe, like fighters, like lovers. She raised her chin again, a gesture of defiance. She had never defied him before.

Another first, she thought, trembling with exhaustion and daring. It was a night for them.

"Can I at least say good-bye?"

Simon's eyes flickered. "He won't hear you."

"Then it shouldn't matter to you. But it does to me."

His face was cool and impervious as marble. "As you wish."

A tiny victory. She would make the most of it.

She approached the bunk. Even spellbound and unconscious, Justin looked messy and attractive and vibrantly, painfully alive. She knelt beside his bed like a girl at prayer, hands in front, resting on the rough wool of his blanket.

Awareness traced down her spine like a bead of perspiration. She looked over her shoulder. Simon stood in the center of the room, his eyes gleaming silver in the mage fire.

"Do you mind?" she asked pointedly.

His jaw set. "Not at all," he said politely and turned his back.

Taking a deep breath, she leaned over Justin's pillow and pressed her lips to his. Her hands fumbled in her skirt. Her heart drummed wildly in her chest, in her ears. She held the kiss as long as she dared, willing her breath into him. Her right hand slid from her pocket and thrust under his mattress. He never moved.

She sighed. "All right. I'm ready."

She pushed to her feet. Simon was waiting. Head bowed, eyes lowered, she walked past him, leaving her small defiance behind.

Along with Justin's dive knife, a lump under his mattress.

6

HE WAS SHAKEN. CHANGED. SHE HAD CHANGED him. Lara's kiss—*soft lips, warm breath, her life, her strength, in him*—had ripped through him with the force of a tornado, churning him to the depths. He floundered in a sea of memory and desire, at the mercy of his dreams, a plaything of the waves, a prisoner of his own mind.

He wanted . . .

He needed . . .

His world was ended, everything lost, drowned, submerged beneath the waves. He had to find . . .

"Find what?" A man's voice, deep and penetrating, dragged him back to his body, to his splitting head and the flat, hard cot. "What are you looking for?"

He disliked the voice instinctively. An impression surfaced, too fleeting to be called a memory, of a large hard man wearing black and a sneer. No name.

"Who are you?" the voice asked.

The question pried at his brain like an oyster knife, slipping through his weakened defenses, threatening to rip him open, to plunder the soft gray flesh inside. Pain speared his head. His throat burned. He recoiled in self-defense, retreating deeper, down, down, through levels of pain.

But the voice pursued him. "Where are you from?"

The sea.

All his memories began with the sea, warm and sunlit, gray and storm cast, the clear cold salt dark.

A sense of loss swept over him, leaving him parched and alone with his pain. Too much pain. He couldn't find his way through it, he could not think, he could not *remember* . . . Why couldn't he remember?

God, he was thirsty.

"Would you like some water?" A woman.

For a moment his heart leaped, buoyed by her memory. *Her arm around his shoulders. Her breath, mingling with his. Her mouth, warm, moist, sweet . . .*

But she wasn't the one. He knew it before she touched him, before he surfaced to see the dark, worried face bending over him. She smelled wrong, like rubbing alcohol instead of like dawn, fresh and full of possibilities.

"I'll be back," she had promised.

But she did not come again.

"Where . . ." he croaked.

Is she?

"Ssh. Drink this." A straw poked his lips.

He closed his mouth gratefully on the plastic, holding the water carefully in his mouth before letting it trickle down to soothe his throat. Only as the flat taste lingered on his tongue did he realize it was drugged.

Time stretched, passed, hours—days?—measured by

the rasp of his breathing and the sound of footsteps and the coming and going of the silver light.

And the questions, always the questions, pursuing him into the dark.

"Who are you?"

"What do you want?"

"Where do you come from?"

He closed his mind, closed his mouth stubbornly on the answers, but in the dark between times, visions leaked and flooded his brain. A tumbled shore of sand and shale. Green hills cradling the water like a cup. A broken castle on the cliffs, its ancient towers glazed with light.

Danger.

His heart hammered. His head pounded with impending doom. The wave was coming. He had to save them. He had to save . . .

"Who?"

A man with eyes like rain, a girl with hair like straw, a dog . . .

Their images spun away, snatched by the rising and falling sea. He couldn't save them. He could no longer save himself. His strength was gone, everything was gone, smashed, drowned, vanished beneath the waves.

He did not answer.

"Of course he doesn't answer. I'd be surprised if he can even hear you."

That voice. He recognized that voice. Fucking Axton. His lips drew back in a snarl, but he did not speak. Didn't open his eyes. Let them think he was asleep or drugged or dead.

"It's his shields."

"It's the drugs."

"—danger with concussion," the woman was saying. The doctor, he remembered. Marian? Miriam.

"Appropriate dosage for a human."

"Well, he's not human, is he?" snapped the first speaker.

He was listening now, but the words had no more meaning than the tolling of a buoy.

Not human.

Not *human*?

"Tell me something I don't know."

"Well," the doctor said slowly, "his toes are webbed."

For an instant, he couldn't breathe. Something flashed in his brain, stronger than recognition, more elusive than memory.

And then the footsteps faded. The light behind his closed lids ebbed away.

He lay with the sound of the sea's long retreat echoing in his head, his thoughts raucous and meaningless as the cries of seabirds over something that has died.

He wasn't dead yet.

But he might as well be. He felt like a diver plunged unexpectedly into the water, unable to distinguish up from down, past from present, dreams from reality.

He needed answers. Help. A weapon. They'd taken his knife.

Something hard—a loose slat, a broken coil—poked his shoulder blades.

If they were going to lock him up, he thought with a sudden flash of clarity, they might at least have provided a comfortable mattress.

The lump at his back gave him a focus. He could fashion a tool from wood or wire. A shank. It took several tries, but eventually he managed to roll onto his side. Panting, he jammed his hand between the frame and the mattress and touched . . .

Not a slat. A knife. His knife, shaped to his palm.

Lara. He felt her presence as keenly as the blade. Her touch, lingering on the handle. Her energy, vibrating through his fingertips. Her breath, in him. He saw her, her eyes large and gray beneath dark winged brows.

He clung to her image like hope, like the spar, fighting to keep his head above water. He had his weapon. Now all he needed was answers.

And a way out.

* * *

The whispers of her disgrace were up before she was.

Lara heard the stutter of conversation when she entered the vaulted dining hall the next morning, a sudden drop in noise level followed by a rustle like wind through corn. She stood with her breakfast tray at the end of the serving line while the younger students craned to get a look at her and the other proctors carefully avoided her eyes.

Her stomach sank.

The teachers took the first two meals of the day in the faculty dining room, leaving the proctors to monitor the students. A few proctors patrolled the tables or ate with favorites from their floors, but most grabbed this chance to sit together. Lara carried her tray to join them at the round tables at the end of the hall. One or two people collected their trays and left without a word.

Heat rushed to her cheeks.

It didn't mean anything, she told herself. Breakfast service was nearly over. She was late, that was all.

She saw Gideon sitting with his girlfriend Ariel. The

young Guardian looked heavy-eyed and grim, as if he hadn't slept any better than she had.

She offered him a quick, sympathetic smile. "Hi, Gideon."

He barely nodded in reply, his attention fixed on his plate. Ariel glared at her and whispered something to the girl on her other side.

Lara's smile faltered before she looked away.

She found two members of her cohort, David and Jacob, sitting together at an otherwise empty table. They were deep in a discussion about restoration glass, but as she approached, Jacob thrust a booted foot under the table, pushing out a chair for her. Gratefully, she sat. David speared a piece of pineapple from her plate, waving it around on the end of his fork as he argued about ways to duplicate the color effects of arsenic.

"Fluorspar doesn't produce the same fire," he insisted.

"But it's more consistent," Jacob said. "Not to mention legal."

Buffered by their undemanding company, she began to relax. The buzz of conversation, the clatter of plates and glassware, mingled with the swirl of steam from the serving line, rising in the vaulted, sunlit room. This was her reality. This was her life. Last night was like a wonderful, terrible, moonlit dream.

Memory unfurled inside her like a bird beating to get out. The long lines of Justin's body on the cellar steps. His mouth, salty and warm. The surge of power and freedom and lust she'd felt when she was with him. In him.

Taking a deep breath, she reached for her orange juice. She'd done everything she could to help Justin. Maybe it would be enough.

A shadow fell over her fruit plate.

"Leave him alone." Ariel stood flanked by her friend

beside their table, her pretty face contorted. "Haven't you done enough already?"

Lara lowered her juice glass. "Excuse me?"

"I can't believe you have the guts to even speak to him after what you did."

Speak to . . . Gideon, Lara realized. Ariel was talking about Gideon.

"I didn't do anything."

"You got him in trouble with Zayin because you failed as Seeker."

Lara glanced at Gideon, already walking with his tray toward the bus line, his back stiff, his face turned away. "Is that what he told you?"

"He didn't have to. All the lower cohorts are saying you didn't come back with a new student last night."

Ariel's friend nodded. David hunched his shoulders, apparently fascinated by the congealing eggs on his plate.

"They're kids." Lara kept her voice even with effort. "They don't know what they're talking about. And neither do you."

"Really?" Ariel set her hands on her hips. "Then why did Master Zayin pull Gideon off lampwork?"

Lampwork—crafting beads with a torch from colored glass rods—was a coveted apprenticeship. The beads were imbued with power as well as color, used not only for jewelry but for charms.

Lara bit her lip. If Gideon had been dismissed from spell work, no wonder he was upset. "I don't know. I'm sorry. It's probably only temporary."

"You two better watch out," Ariel said to David and Jacob. "If Zayin finds out you're hanging around with her, you could be reassigned, too."

Jacob pushed back his chair. "That's crap. Zayin's not

going to stop us from taming fire because your boyfriend screwed up."

Ariel's eyes glittered with moisture. "He didn't. Take it back."

"What is this, high school?"

"Gideon did his job," Lara said quickly. "I'm the one responsible for . . . for the mission."

An uncomfortable pause.

"That's all right then," David said. "I mean, you work for the headmaster."

"Not anymore," Ariel said with satisfaction.

Lara's throat tightened.

"Lara? What's she talking about?" Jacob asked.

"I hear your friend is in really deep shit." The girl with Ariel tittered. "Literally."

"She's working in the bird house," Ariel said with gleeful vindictiveness. "With Crazy Moon and the other cuckoos."

"Oh, hey." David's good-natured face creased in sympathy. "That sucks."

Lara swallowed. "It's only temporary," she said again.

And heard Simon saying, *"Until I can trust your judgment, you cannot work for me."*

Her hands shredded her napkin in her lap. He would forgive her, eventually. Everything could go back to normal.

If only she'd be quiet, if only she'd be good . . .

"From now on, you cannot see him, cannot speak to him, cannot visit him, is that clear?"

She stared down at the bright pattern of fruit on her plate, all appetite gone.

* * *

Dust motes danced in the diffused brightness of the raptor enclosure. Lara's rake rattled over the gravel subfloor, turning up broken bones and hardened pellets, the remains of small dead rodents, digested and undigested.

The big bird perched in the corner turned its wicked head, surveying her with a bright, suspicious eye.

Lara froze like a rabbit. Moon *said* the bird wouldn't attack. But Moon was crazy. Everyone knew that.

As if summoned by the thought, the mews keeper appeared in the door of the cage. She was tall, like most of their kind, and striking, like all of them. But her wavy hippie hair was tied back with a leather jess, her strong, angular body swallowed by a shapeless brown tunic. Her blue eyes were cloudy and vague.

"When you've finished sweeping, you can scrub out his bath." Moon flapped her hand at the metal pan weighted by an old tire in the middle of the cage.

Lara eyed the scummy water without enthusiasm.

Self-knowledge and obedience, she reminded herself. She didn't know what Simon expected her to learn in this dirty, shadowed hole. But she knew what she had to do.

"Okay."

The keeper padded across the enclosure, her slippered feet silent on the newly raked floor. "There's my lovely boy, then," she crooned to the bird. "You're one of Simon's girls, aren't you?"

It took Lara a moment to realize Moon was speaking to her. She flushed. "I work for him, if that's what you mean."

"I don't care if you dance for him naked," the keeper said. "But he found you."

"Yes."

"Thought so. I'm good with faces," Moon said with satisfaction. "Better with birds, but still, I remember. You came in here with your class, a dozen years ago."

Lara's heart beat faster at the memory. Bria had made

her stay behind in the shadowed mews when the rest of their cohort had escaped to sunlight and safety. Her friend had been fascinated by the birds, their daggered feet, their cruel, curved beaks, their caged grace.

She shrugged to hide her discomfort. "Everyone comes once. It's part of the life science unit."

"But I remember you," Moon said. "You were friends with that little blond girl. The flyer."

Lara's mouth jarred open. No one talked about the flyers. Ever. After Bria ran away, it was as if the other girl had never been. Lara had grieved for her friend in silence and alone. "She was my roommate."

Moon cocked her head. "Never came back."

"No," Lara whispered.

"I meant you."

"Oh." Lara fought an absurd urge to apologize. "No, I . . ."

"Most of them don't," Moon said frankly. "Unless they want to use the birds in the flight cages to practice spirit casting."

Lara shivered. Under the Rule, only Masters had the authority to project their spirits into other creatures. The Gift was too close to the demonic power of possession, too much like usurping free will, to be considered quite safe. Even Masters were restricted to using it on birds, fellow children of the air.

She glanced at the large golden-eyed raptor in the corner. "They do that . . . here?"

"Not so much. All of the Masters at least try it. Most don't have the knack. And even fewer have the inclination."

Raising her arm, the keeper pressed against the bird's haunches until it either had to step back or be pushed from its perch. Lara held her breath as, with a disgruntled flap, the bird hopped onto Moon's glove.

Moon stroked its breast. "A lot of our birds come to us because they've been injured—trapped, maybe, or shot. That's why they leave us alone, the Masters. They want to fly, but they can't stand to be reminded they're no different than my birds."

"Hunted?" Lara ventured.

The keeper met her gaze, her vague blue eyes suddenly sharp and clear. "Caged."

Lara stared, speechless. She had a mental flash of Justin, lean and golden, balancing against the bright blue sky, plunging into the sea in a flourish of foam and daring. Free.

Until now.

She moistened her dry lips. "But . . . the birds are all freed eventually. When they're well enough to survive on their own."

"That's what they teach in your life science unit, is it?"

Lara nodded slowly. She had never questioned the school masters' expertise.

"It's true for some. The ones that aren't hurt too badly to be rehabilitated and released." Another sharp glance, bright with pity or derision. "Or so used to being locked up and hand fed they can't adjust to life outside."

Lara's heart thumped. The tawny raptor on Moon's arm watched her with wicked, golden eyes.

"What about him?" she asked. "What will happen to him?"

"Tuari?" The keeper stroked the bird's bronze plumage. He opened his beak softly against her fingers. "He won't have an easy time of it. He doesn't belong here. He's not like the others."

"He's not one of us," Zayin had said last night about Justin.

Not human. Not nephilim either.

"What difference does it make?" Lara asked fiercely. "If he needs care."

"Oh, we can care for him. But he doesn't have a place here. Or out there. The others are all native species, hawks and owls. Tuari's a golden eagle. God knows what brought him to us, but he's totally out of his range, poor boy." The keeper's eyes clouded again. "Even if I set him free, he'd be lost."

* * *

Moon's words hung in the air like the smell of newts, pungent and impossible to ignore. They haunted Lara as she raked flight pens and scrubbed birdcages, breaking her nails and her heart.

"He doesn't have a place here. Or out there."

She rubbed her forehead, but the words kept circling, picking, attacking. They kept her company at dinner when no one else would. They whispered in the carrels during evening study and followed her up the stairs after lights out.

She held on to the banister as she climbed. The darkness of the stairwell suited her mood. After her so-called period of reflection, she was dirty and exhausted and more confused than ever. What she needed was a hot shower and an uninterrupted night's sleep. Everything would look better in the morning.

Including Justin?

She stopped, a tight, fluttery feeling in her chest, trying to remember what Miriam had said. Forty-eight hours to recover from the concussion. And then what?

"Even if I set him free, he'd be lost."

She dragged herself the rest of the way to her room. She closed and locked the door. Stripping her filthy T-shirt over her head, she dropped it with a sigh to the floor.

As a proctor, she had her own closet-sized bathroom.

She turned the shower as hot as she could stand, letting the pulse pound her tight muscles, the water sluice over her head, desperate to rinse away the stink of the mews and her lingering sense of guilt. Steam billowed in the air, slicked the tiles, condensed on the mirror. She breathed in the moist, shampoo-scented air. Released it, expelling tension on a sigh.

Wrapped in a towel, she opened the door to her room.

The window was open. Night whispered against her bare skin. Her body hummed with awareness.

A sound, a breath, a disturbance in the air . . .

Her mind blanked in terror. It was her nightmare, a man in her room, in the dark.

She sucked in her breath.

"Don't scream," Justin said from the direction of her bed.

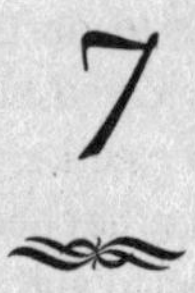

HE COULD SEE IN THE DARK. *"CAT'S EYES,"* CAPtain Rick had said the first time he'd watched Justin climb the rigging at night.

He could see her now, Lara, silhouetted against the slanting light from the bathroom, the quick rise of her breasts above the knotted towel, her small hands curled into fists at her sides.

He could smell her, soap and fear, and under that her skin, her scent, female, sweet. Arousing.

"Don't be scared," he said hoarsely, which was a crock—she should be scared, she barely knew him. And what she could probably make out was hardly reassuring.

His head hurt. His throat burned. For seven years, his past had been a blank to him. Now his brain seethed with unfamiliar images. With questions. Something had changed within him, and the one person he trusted for answers was braced in front of him, watching him with wide, wary gray eyes as if he were about to jump her.

"I'm not going to hurt you," he said.

Her body remained tensed, slim taut lines and the gleam of her breasts against the darkness of the room. "You shouldn't be here."

"I won't go back to the cellar."

"This is the first place they'll look for you."

"I've got nowhere else to go."

"Don't say that," she snapped.

It was true. So he said nothing, watching her.

She wet her lips. "How did you get in?"

He nodded toward her open window. "Climbed."

"But the heth . . . you couldn't get past the threshold before."

His memories were all mixed up, but he remembered sprawling half out of the cellar door, a weight on one leg like a cement cast, a noose around his neck.

He remembered that bastard, Axton.

He remembered her lips, her scent, her hair falling down to brush his face. Her breath filling his lungs.

"Yeah, I figured that out." Slowly, so he wouldn't spook her, he straightened his leg, stuck out his ankle. "I got rid of one. Cut it off."

Her eyes widened. "What about your throat?"

He shrugged. "I can breathe." Her kiss had done that much for him.

"You removed Zayin's spell?"

Her talk of spells made his skin crawl. He didn't believe in magic. But he had a sailor's healthy respect for luck. Not to mention some kind of voodoo charm hanging around his neck like a fucking albatross. Under the circumstances, he was prepared to be open-minded.

"I don't know about spells," he said. "But I'm still wearing the necklace. Every time I tried to get the blade under, I damn near slit my throat."

She switched on the lamp that stood on her desk. He squinted in the sudden yellow light. Christ, she was lovely, all that milky skin rising above the towel, her slim, bare legs, the curve of her hip under the terrycloth.

"Show me," she said.

Show me yours and I'll show you mine.

Wordlessly, he tugged on the neck of his T-shirt.

She made a soft, distressed sound.

He didn't know what it looked like, but he could feel the cord, a line of fire around his neck, the bead a burning coal in the hollow of his throat. His skin felt hot and swollen.

He smiled crookedly. "I don't suppose you want to try that kiss of life thing again?"

He thought she'd refuse. Hell, he thought she'd run.

She took a hesitant step toward him. "When I opened your airway, it must have turned the magic outward. Do they know? Did they see you like this?"

He wanted to say yes, to play on her sympathies, to buy her loyalty by any lie at his disposal. He had to get out of here. But faced with her anger and concern, he went with honesty.

"It didn't start to feel this way until I got outside." He angled his head to give her a better view. "Is it bad?"

"It looks painful. How does it feel?"

He shrugged again, pulling the tender skin. "About the way it looks."

Still wearing the towel, she approached him and the bed. "I'm not a healer."

"Your healer Miriam's been keeping me drugged and locked up in a basement. I trust you."

She sat beside him, the mattress dipping beneath her

slight weight. She leaned away to avoid rolling against him, but his gaze was drawn to the knot of her towel, the shallow indentation between her breasts, the pulse beating just there beneath her jaw. Her hair smelled damp and clean.

He had to close his eyes, dizzied, distracted by her nearness.

She laid cool fingers on the raw skin of his throat. Her touch drew away the heat and the pain.

More magic? He didn't care. He wanted to rub himself all over her for comfort like an animal. Catching her wrist, he pressed his face into her palm. Her hand trembled against his cheek. He inhaled her, smelling her fear and the faint notes of her skin, fresh as lilies in the rain.

"What do you want?" she whispered.

You.

"Help. Answers."

She eased back from him, her hand slipping from his grasp. "I'll tell you what I can."

He couldn't think of any acceptable reason to grab her again, so he said, "Just tell me the truth. What is this place?"

"A school. A private boarding school."

"For what? Wayward girls and boys? The criminally insane?"

"Nephilim."

He forced his gaze from the pale swell of her breasts. "Neff . . ."

"Neh-fill-eem," she pronounced carefully.

He tested the word against the echoes of his dreams like a man dropping a stone into a well to test for depth. But there was no ripple, no memory, nothing.

"What's that, like a cult?"

"The Fallen children of air." She searched his eyes. "You really don't remember? Anything?"

When she looked at him like that, with those clear, dark-lashed eyes, he wanted to say yes. To a drink in a bar, to a ride in her car, to sex on her narrow white bed . . .

"Justin?"

"I remember the sea," he said.

The sea and a sense of loss.

"That's it?"

"A dog." A flash of memory, tall as a wolf, graceful as a deer, with a thin whip of a tail and a narrow, bearded muzzle. Justin smiled. "I remember a dog."

Lara frowned, apparently not amused. Or satisfied. "What about your life before you went to sea? Your family? Your childhood?"

Fatigue and pain and the echo of Zayin's voice, prying, sliding into his dreams, needled his temper. But Lara was his only ally. His only hope.

"I don't have a family." Or want one. He didn't want to be tied down. *Tied up, drifting in the cold green sea, everything gone, lost . . .* "I don't remember my childhood. I don't remember much of anything before seven years ago."

Except in his dreams . . .

"What happened seven years ago?"

"Shipwreck." Beneath the towel, she was naked. He forced his gaze up to meet her eyes. "I was the only survivor. Norwegian freighter captain found me tied to a mast and fished me out of the North Sea."

"And since then?"

He grinned. "Sweetheart, I'd be happy to tell you the story of my life some other time. Right now, I just want to get the hell out of here."

"You can't leave."

He looked her up and down. "You going to try and stop me?"

"N-no," she said slowly.

"Good. I need your help."

"I can't—"

"A car." He interrupted before she had the chance to say no. "I figure you owe me a lift."

"Where are you going?"

An island, its green hills forming a jagged cup around the shining sea, its ancient stones imbued with power . . .

"Anywhere there's water," he said firmly. "A shipyard, a marina. I've got contacts, I can get a berth."

He needed to be at sea. Assuming he could find a boat captain willing to hire a crew member with a broken skull and a hex burning around his throat.

She shook her head, her damp hair sliding like water over her bare shoulders. "It's too dangerous."

"I'll be okay. I've had practice flying under the radar."

"You have very good shields."

He had no idea what she was talking about. "I have very good papers."

"Papers?"

He shot her a grin. "The best money can buy. No memory, remember? No birth certificate, no social security number."

Her gray eyes were clear and solemn. "It can't have been easy creating an identity on your own."

"You do what you need to do to survive." He wasn't proud of it. When he jumped ship on the New Jersey docks, he'd been a kid, exact age unknown, without money, education, or prospects. For a couple of years, he'd done any work that was offered, legal or not. "Anyway, as long as the police aren't searching for me, I'm good to go."

"Not police. But there could be . . . people looking for you."

He didn't like that ominous little pause.

"Why?"

"Because of who you are." She moistened her lips. "What you are. What you did during that fight."

Fuck. "Did I kill somebody?"

He couldn't go to jail. Being locked up again would kill him.

She shook her head, her gaze dropping to her lap.

He got a bad feeling in the pit of his stomach. "So, these guys who are after me . . . What do they want? Turf? Revenge?"

"They believe you are one of us."

"Why would they think that?"

"Because they felt your power. They will guess that I was searching for you."

Searching for . . . Shit.

His head hurt. Her scent swam in his senses. He couldn't think.

"You picked me up."

She nodded.

"I thought you were slumming," he said.

"I was Called to find you."

"You left me." He remembered that much. "For the ponytail."

She winced. "I'm sorry. You were not what I expected."

His mind scrambled back to their first meeting. "You knew I wasn't some rich guy with a boat. I told you that up front."

"It's not that. I thought you would be like us. But you're different."

"Not . . . nephilim."

"Not nephilim," she agreed. She waited a beat and added, "And not human."

Not *human*?

Another flash of memory, voices talking over his head. *"His toes are webbed."*

The room wobbled. He took a breath—soap and Lara—and held it until everything steadied inside. So his feet weren't exactly like everybody else's. Big fucking deal.

"Bullshit," he said.

For seven years, he'd lived hand to mouth and moment to moment. He survived by not thinking any further than his next meal, his next job. *We flow as the sea flows.* The whisper surfaced from another life.

He wrenched his thoughts away. He didn't dwell on the past. Or his dreams.

Or his damn feet.

"You have power," Lara said. "Enough for Simon to consider you a threat."

He shot her a look. "I wasn't a threat until he locked me in his basement. Now I'm pissed off."

"I'm sorry." She frowned at her hands in her lap. Her towel had parted above her knee, along her thigh. Her cheeks flushed with earnestness. "You have to believe me. I didn't think . . . I thought they would help you. I wanted to help."

He wanted to believe her. *Her hand on his chest, her mouth on his mouth, her breath in his lungs . . .*

"Prove it," he said. "Help me now."

Her fingers twisted together. "I can't. I've been forbidden to see you. To speak with you. To have any contact with you at all."

"What are they going to do, give you detention?"

"You don't understand. I am sworn to obedience."

She sounded like a cop. Or a nun.

"Shut up and do as you're told?" he drawled.

Her eyes darkened. *Something there*, he thought. A shadow of hurt, a flicker of doubt. "Not always," she said.

"Then come with me," he said, surprising himself.

Until the words came out of his mouth, he had no idea he was going to say them. He wasn't looking to get tangled up in a relationship. No ties, no strings. But there was something between them. A connection. He didn't understand it, but there it was. He didn't like the thought of leaving her here with psycho Axton and his hex-happy henchman.

"I can't," she said. "I can't leave Rockhaven."

He should be relieved. He couldn't rescue her if she didn't want rescue. But . . . "They're not keeping you here, are they? Against your will?"

She shook her head. "This is my home. I am bound here by the Rule."

"Rules are made to be broken."

"Not this Rule." Her voice was earnest. "It's our way of thinking. Our way of life. It's what sets us apart from the rest of the world and binds us together as a community. Without it, we cannot attain perfection."

Some perfection. It sounded like a cult to him.

"You don't belong here," he said. "You're not like the rest of them."

"I am," she insisted. "I'm with my own kind here. My family."

He didn't know enough about families to argue with her.

"All I need is a ride," he said. "I'd call a cab, but I don't know where the hell we are."

Or where he was going. North, maybe.

"Pennsylvania. Bucks County," she said.

He didn't know Bucks County, Pennsylvania, from Bumfuck, USA, but he had a working sailor's knowledge of the East Coast. "How far from the Port Authority?

Newark," he added when she just blinked those lovely eyes at him.

"I don't . . . Two hours?"

"That's good." Damn good. "I can go anywhere in the world from there."

North, he thought again. He was almost sure of it.

"You'll be home before breakfast," he said.

"Fine." She stood.

He should have been happy with his victory. He was getting the hell out of here. He watched her cross to the dresser and open a drawer. Unease tickled his spine. "You can come back, right? They won't kick you out for giving me a ride?"

"Oh, yes." He tried not to be distracted by the tumble of her hair, the curve of her butt. "They'll take me back." Her tone was flat.

"But . . ."

She glanced at him over her shoulder. "There are always consequences for disobedience."

"Right." His mind weighed, calculated, decided. "Then you can't come with me."

"But you just said . . ." She turned, scowling, her clothes clutched to her chest. "You need me."

"I should have said, you can't come with me willingly. You can't help me without getting into trouble."

"So?"

He grinned, suddenly cheerful despite his splitting head. "So I'll have to kidnap you."

* * *

Lara's breath huffed out. "Be serious."

"I'm dead serious," Justin said, and despite his smile, she almost believed him. "I don't want to see you hurt. Tell Axton I forced you. He can't blame you then."

Memory uncoiled inside her, dark and insidious as smoke. No, Simon would not blame her if she were forced.

She shuddered, her hands closing convulsively on her clothes. "What if he calls the police?"

"You really think your buddy Axton wants the cops on his turf?"

"Probably not," she admitted. Rockhaven was its own community under the Rule, school and glassworks forming an isolated enclave in the rolling countryside. Simon would not seek help or accept interference from their neighbors. "But if he thinks I've been abducted . . ."

"You'll be home before he has time to file a report."

"He'll still have questions."

"So tell him the truth. I broke into your room. I had a knife." Justin's lips curved upward, teasing, daring. "You couldn't resist me."

She stuck out her chin, uncomfortably aware of her nakedness under the towel. "I'm not a victim."

She would not be a victim ever again.

"You think you should struggle?" He cocked his head, as if considering. "Right now, you could probably take me. But if you want it to look good, we could knock over the lamp or something. Rumple the sheets."

She flushed. Her awareness of him lay on her like a second skin, twitching with his very pulse, his every breath. She was exquisitely conscious of the effort it cost him simply to sit upright and smile. The echoes of his pain throbbed in her temples, the bite of the heth gnawed at her own throat. She could feel the sweat at the small of his back, the faint tremor in his legs of drugs or exhaustion. He must be half dead with pain and fatigue.

And yet he felt more alive to her than anyone she had ever known.

"We want them to think I was coerced," she said coolly. "Not seduced."

"Too bad." Another glint from those golden eyes. "I was prepared to be convincing."

Her pulse fluttered. He was weakened and desperate. How could he flirt with her now? "You convinced me to drive. That will have to be enough for you."

For me.

He grinned, undiscouraged and approving. "That puts me in my place."

It took all her will not to smile back.

"I have to get dressed," she said and escaped into the tiny bathroom with her clothes.

He stood when she came out. He filled her room, as tall as Simon and leanly muscled. "Where's your car?"

His size, his sudden shift, took her aback. "I don't own a car. But I know the code to the garage."

"Keys?"

"Hanging up inside."

"Convenient."

"It's meant to be."

There were no thieves among the nephilim. Their vehicles, gray sedans and blue school vans, were held in common.

He nodded once. "Ready, then?"

Be serious, she'd said. But this Justin, with his quick, hard questions and cool, hard eyes, filled her with doubt.

A chill chased up her arms. Simon had accused her of endangering the community, of lacking self-knowledge and obedience. What made her think she knew better than the headmaster? Than Zayin?

Justin watched her. Waiting. The black bead gleamed against the burned skin of his throat.

"I'm not sure I can even get you through the gates," she blurted out.

His gaze remained steady on hers. "I guess we'll find out."

Her chest hollowed. She poised on the edge of a decision, about to jump.

When she Fell, the moment of choice had passed without effort or reflection. Her act of disobedience had been sheer reflex, a burst of compassion, an impulse born of love.

Why that child, unloved even by the mother who gave her birth? Why that moment, when the girl was almost free of her short, miserable existence? Of all the children Lara had watched and guided over the centuries, what made this one's pain so intolerable, her life so precious?

Lara didn't know.

The choice then—her immortality or the child's soul—had been no choice at all. But by stopping the girl from taking her own life, Lara had doomed herself to Fall.

She was not that pure anymore. That fearless. She knew now that she could make mistakes. She had learned, in her soul and her fragile flesh, that she could hurt and be hurt. She had paid for her disobedience by becoming human. What would the price of disobedience be this time?

And what, she wondered, would it cost her to obey?

She looked at Justin, his lean, stubbled face, his long, amber eyes. The bandage on his head. The lines of pain around his mouth.

"You don't belong here. You're not like the rest of them."

She was. Oh, she was. Something other, something more than human. Or maybe something less.

Caged.

She had the right to embrace the security of her own

bars. But she could not make that choice for him. There were worse sins than disobedience.

She took a breath. Released it slowly. "I'll take you as far as Newark. There are things you need to know." Even if telling him violated the precepts of safety and the rule of silence. "But you have to promise to listen."

8

CLOUDS SCUDDED ACROSS THE PINPRICKED SKY. The trees rippled and sighed. Lara gathered moonlight in her palms, bending the rising air around them, murmuring a quick glamour under her breath. Any student glancing out the dormitory windows would only see two shadows gliding over the lawn.

Beside her, Justin stalked as silent as the night, dimmed to black and silver by the uncertain light.

"Here," she whispered.

The garage loomed out of the landscape, built two levels down into the side of a hill roofed with trees and sod. She tapped the door code into the keypad.

The double doors hummed. Light slanted across the drive.

"Kill the lights," Justin snapped.

"They're automatic."

He grabbed her elbow. She felt the jolt of his touch before he dragged her under the opening door. Releasing her arm, he mashed his palm on the controls. The mechanism checked. *Clunked.* The doors lowered slowly.

Heart pounding, Lara scanned the pegboard hung with keys. A row of six blue school vans occupied the numbered spaces closest to the doors. The other cars—a fleet of gray Ford Taurus sedans—were parked in the row behind and on the lower level.

"Give me the keys to a van," Justin said.

"What? No." Didn't he see the Rockhaven logo painted on the sides? "They're too identifiable. We'll take a Taurus."

"You can drive whatever you want. But give me the keys."

She was still reeling from the effects of his touch. Automatically, she obeyed his tone of command.

He glanced from the numbered key in his hand to the row of painted parking spaces. "Thanks."

She watched, mystified, as he climbed into the number three van. The engine roared to life. The van backed across the cement lane and stopped. Justin got out, slamming the driver's side door, and stooped by the front tire. His arm jerked. She heard a pop, a hiss, before he straightened, still holding his dive knife.

"Get us a car," he said.

Her brain sparked back to life. "What are you doing?"

He moved to the next tire. "Making sure nobody comes after us."

Slash. Pop. Hiss.

She winced. "But—"

"Park by the doors. I need to block the other lane."

She ran for a car at the end of a row, close to the ramp that led to the lower level. Through the windshield, she watched Justin make quick work of the remaining tires before raising the van's hood. Metal banged metal.

Oh, *skies*.

Her mouth dried. Simon would be furious.

She rolled down her window. "You didn't say anything about destroying school property."

"You got a better idea?"

"No, but—"

He raised his head and looked at her, his face hard. Determined. Dangerous. "If I block the exit with a couple of these vans, I won't have to touch the other vehicles. Now move the car."

She released the brake, feeling vaguely betrayed, as if she'd befriended a stray that turned into a tiger. She maneuvered her car into the narrow space by the garage doors. In her rearview mirror, she saw Justin help himself to another key from the pegboard.

He drove the second van into place behind her, across the lane. *Slash, slash* on the tires. *Bang, bang* under the hood.

She gritted her teeth.

The passenger door opened and he slid in beside her, hot and male and overwhelming. The heth gleamed in the hollow of his throat. "Let's roll."

Setting her jaw, she shifted gear.

* * *

Pain sank its talons into his skull. His eyeballs ached. His throat throbbed.

Justin glanced at Lara's rigid profile. She was pissed, but she hadn't panicked on him. Or bailed.

The red haze over his vision faded. He was pushing her, he knew. Playing the connection that sparked between them. Trusting her innate decency and compassion to overcome her loyalty to Axton.

She deserved better than that arrogant, ruthless prick and his stone-faced henchman.

Too bad he didn't have anything better to offer.

Justin released his breath. At least they were free. He was free. For now.

The hot kernel of anger inside him eased.

She drove without headlights, knuckles white on the wheel, leaning forward to peer at the dark, winding road. He could feel the moisture in the air, the rising wind of a gathering storm.

Something flickered through the trees. A fence. The black gleam of metal pickets following the dip of the ground, the curve of the road. Ahead of them, a small, square gatehouse rose out of the gloom.

Lara braked before they reached the metal barrier.

Justin tensed. "Guards?"

She shook her head, the shadows sliding over her face. "Not at night. The exit gate is automatic."

"Then why are we stopping?"

She turned to him, eyes wide in the dark. "Are you sure you want to go through with this? Once we're outside the gates, I can't guarantee your safety."

She was worried about him, which was both convenient and oddly unsettling. Or maybe she was still fretting over Axton's probable reaction to his escape. Not to mention eight slashed tires and two busted timing belts. "I like my chances out there better than in here."

"You don't even know where you're going."

The bead at his throat pulsed in time with his heart. They'd been down this road before. "You're wasting your breath." *And my time.*

She blinked once. "Probably," she agreed coolly.

What did that mean?

"Rockhaven is warded," she continued. "The wards will not stop us. But Zayin's binding might. Crossing the barrier will probably trigger the heth."

"Trigger?"

She drew a finger across her throat.

He swallowed reflexively, feeling the raw skin pull at his neck. "I thought you fixed that."

"I couldn't remove it. I don't think the heth will kill you, but you'll need to stay in contact with me as we go through the gate."

"You want to hold hands?"

That earned him a glance, brief and unsmiling. "I'm driving. You'll have to hold on to my leg. I think . . . I hope that will be enough."

Enough to get them clear?

Enough that the damn cord or hex or whatever it was wouldn't strangle him?

He didn't ask. He could either trust her or they could turn back.

"Best damn offer I've had all day," he said and laid his hand on her thigh.

She sucked in her breath. So did he. Even through the denim of her jeans, he got some crazy contact high from touching her. Not like the jolt in the bar this time—more a low-level hum, like the vibration of a ship's motor through the soles of his feet or the tug of the wind in the lines.

Her eyes widened. Her lips parted—*pink, soft, moist, mine*—before she pressed them together.

"Here we go." She lifted her foot from the brake.

Maybe it was his imagination. Maybe it was those tall iron pickets clustered like spears on either side of the road. But as they approached, Justin could feel the barrier rushing up on them, closing in on him, tightening his throat.

The gate quivered and retracted. Lara's leg flexed under his hand. She stomped on the gas and the wheels spun, spitting up gravel. The car lurched forward. The cord around his neck burned like a whiplash.

"Hold on," she shouted.

Energy seared his palm and charged his arm. Inside him, something swelled and surged. The engine roared. The car shook like a jet plane, and with a pop, a rush, a snap like the crack of a whip, they were free, speeding through the gate and into the night.

* * *

Zayin raised his head from Miriam's smooth, scented shoulder, uneasy even in the act of coitus.

"Jude?" His lover raised her hand to his cheek, her inner muscles clenching around him as if to prevent his withdrawal. "What is it?"

He did not answer her. He was hot and hard, deep inside her, poised on the brink of completion, in the grip of her wet heat. His blood pounded in his head, in his loins, drowning the faint warning tingle of his brain. He thrust once, twice, plunging like a runner at the end of his race, hard, fast, now.

Now.

She cried out, her fingers digging into his shoulders. He shuddered and flew, free of earth and the limitations of his human body.

For long seconds he lay on her while his heartbeat slowed. His respiration evened. Rolling off her, he reached for his pants.

"What is it?" she asked again from behind him. "A flyer?"

He shook his head. He had tagged three of the nephilim as primed to take off in the next few months or years. A quick mental check placed all three still within the compound. Which left . . .

"Lara," he said.

Miriam inhaled sharply, a sound of distress. "Does Simon know?"

Zayin stood to pull his pants over his hips. "He will soon." He glanced at Miriam over his shoulder. "He wants her, you know."

She exhaled on a sigh. "I know." She sat, the sheet falling from her breasts. "She was so wounded when she came to us. So young. He was waiting for her to heal. And to grow up."

"He's a fool," Zayin said.

"But not a predator," Miriam answered quietly.

Their eyes met. Held.

Zayin was the first to look away. "It's the boy who concerns me. We still don't know what in creation he is."

"He's with her?"

"I'm sure of it."

"Then you'll find them."

"I'll kill him."

They both knew what was at stake. The nephilim no longer possessed their full angelic powers. Hunted by their ancient Adversary, they banded together for survival.

Every student learned that the gates, the walls, the wards were there for their protection, forged to keep the demons at bay. Their continued existence depended on the strength of the community. Even those who chafed under the discipline of the Rule acknowledged the value of its precepts. *Scire, servare, obtemperare.* How could the Fallen regain even the shadow of their former perfection except through the pursuit of knowledge, the preservation of their kind, and the practice of obedience?

Yet every now and then—once or twice a year and then

not again for three years or five—Zayin would wake in the night to a feeling like a feather drawn across his neck. *Flyer.*

He couldn't save them all.

But he always went after them.

* * *

Ozone charged the air. Moisture spangled the windshield, gleaming like fish scales against the dark night.

Justin lowered his window to feel the damp air against his face, his heart pumping with relief and adrenaline. "You did it."

"Not really." Lara flipped on the headlights.

He glanced across the seat, caught by her tone. In the blue glow of the dashboard, her face appeared tense and unhappy. "You got us out. You saved my neck back there. Literally."

"It wasn't me. Not only me. You got us through the barrier."

Thunder cracked and rolled. He could feel the swirling energy of the approaching storm cell. *That moment when the engine roared, when something inside him surged, powerful and fluid, to meet her need.*

He shook his head. "I didn't do anything."

"You have power."

He had nothing.

Better for both of them to remember that. To believe it. As soon as they reached the coast, he'd be gone, and she'd be going back to . . .

Axton.

The thought stuck in his gut.

"If you say so."

"Don't you care?"

He hunched his shoulders to relieve the knot forming between his shoulder blades. "That crap matters to you, not to me."

She gripped the steering wheel tighter to negotiate the unlit, narrow road. Or maybe she was imagining her hands around his neck. "Aren't you even curious to know what you can do? Where you come from?"

"I can't go back," he said. "That's all I care about."

"How do you know?"

His mind blanked. How *did* he know?

Memory slammed into his skull like an iron spike, riveting his brain.

He stood on the deck of the thirty-foot boat, his knuckles white on the rail, his heart threatening to pound through his bony ribs. The earth groaned. The water trembled.

The wolfhound tied to the mast behind him shivered and barked.

"Go," Conn commanded. In the cold dawn light, the prince's face was brutally, brilliantly clear, his eyes the color of rain. "Do not come back until I summon you."

Justin's throat burned with swallowed tears. He tasted salt.

The air shook as the ground rumbled again. Or was that the sky?

"Justin?" *Lara*. Her voice was a lifeline in the storm. He grabbed it, struggling to focus on her face.

"Are you all right?" she asked anxiously.

His head throbbed.

Was he all right?

He swallowed, dragging himself back to the present. "Fine."

"You remembered something."

"It's gone now."

Everything gone, lost, vanished beneath the waves . . .

Lightning struck over the hills. The air was thick and still. Against the low backdrop of clouds, a pitched roof loomed, swallowing the road ahead. A bridge, with a wide barn mouth and rough hewn walls.

"I could help you remember," she said. "I'm not as experienced as Zayin, but I've had training."

Justin eased back in his seat. "Is Zayin the big bastard in black?"

She bit her lip. "Yes."

That dark voice, sliding like a knife into his dreams, slowly prying him apart . . .

Justin set his jaw. "No, thanks."

"You promised to listen," she reminded him.

"I don't make promises."

Not anymore. Especially not to women. But they heard what they wanted to anyway.

The car rattled onto the bridge, the sound amplified by the wooden sides. Lightning flickered like a strobe light through the timbers. Thunder boomed. The hair rose on the back of Justin's neck.

Lara moistened her lips. "That was close."

He eyed her white, strained face. "You want to pull over while it passes?"

She shook her head. "It's not really raining yet. We should put as much distance as—"

FLASH. CRACK.

BOOM.

The air sizzled. The car lurched as Lara slammed on the brake. Justin squinted, half-blinded by the blaze searing the back of his eyeballs, struggling to see through the darkness and the . . . *smoke*?

He smelled it, curling down from the roof. Saw the first red tongues of flame crackle and curl, licking through the charred hole and along the beams.

The bridge was on fire.

"Drive," he shouted.

They had to get off the bridge before the flames caught hold. Before the roof collapsed.

But it was already too late.

The fire leaped with the force of an explosion, reaching for the timbers in the walls, the wooden rail along the sides, the hood of the car. A blazing curtain swept down, sealing the exit.

"Back," Justin yelled.

Lara had already thrown the gear into reverse. The tires squealed and spun. The Taurus careened trunk first over the bridge, aiming for the black hole at the entrance. A taillight scraped and shattered along the wall as Lara fought the wheel.

BOOM. Hiss. The night went white, then black.

She screamed and stomped the brake again. The jolt smacked the back of his skull against the headrest.

Buggering hell.

Justin stared in disbelief as another gout of flame sprang up behind them. *Lightning never strikes twice, my ass.*

Black heat, red flames, billowed to engulf the car. Lara flung open her door.

He grabbed her arm. "What the fuck are you doing?"

She ripped free of his grasp, her eyes shining in the flickering orange light. He lurched for her. Checked, swearing, and fumbled with his seat belt. She stumbled from the car, feeling her way along the hood. Smoke spewed from the hole in the roof. Sweat poured down his face as the flames roared with greed, reaching for her with hungry fingers.

He yelled in warning, in fury, in fear, as she stood in the middle of the narrow bridge, her slender body outlined by the inferno. She flung her arms and spread her fingers wide.

Was she out of her frigging mind?

Her hair streamed and swirled in an invisible updraft.

He stared through the windshield, transfixed, as misty gusts shot from her fingers and tore at the smoke. Wind blew from her open mouth, forming a column, a funnel of clean air with her at its center, pushing out, pushing back, forcing the fire away from the car.

At the end of the bridge, a chink opened in the wall of flame, a doorway to the sweet dark night.

A way out.

His heart leaped and pounded in a primitive beat of survival. *Go, go, go . . .*

Through the crackling heat, the rush of wind and beating fire, he heard her gasp. "Hurry. Can't hold . . . them long."

Them?

That smell. It whispered along the edge of his memory like flame across paper, leaving a smoldering gap. He bared his teeth in response and crawled over the stick shift into the driver's seat.

Smoke coiled and dropped from the ceiling, covering Lara in a heavy black blanket, scratchy, smothering. She flapped her hands, fighting the fire for air.

The shaft of clear air shrank. The fire was winning. The wind whipped, funneling the fire. Feeding it.

She coughed, her arms trembling over her head. "Go!"

Go. Leave her?

Screw that, he thought and got out of the car.

* * *

The fire was a beast, breathing, beating, hungry. It clawed at Lara's throat, lapped at her strength, sucked at her air. Her arms shook. Her legs felt weighted, her heart leaden.

She could hold off the fire. Barely. She could not extinguish it.

Somehow the demons had found them, tracked them, trapped them. And now she would pay for her pride and disobedience with her life. Justin would pay. Unless he seized the moment her magic had won for them and ran.

Go, she thought. *Please go.*

A figure burst out of the smoke, black against the flames, like a demon through the gates of Hell. Hard arms seized her around the waist.

Her heart stopped.

Justin. She smelled his sweat, warm and healthy against the acrid scent of fear and burning. She felt his energy, strong and bracing, surge around her like a wave.

Her body sagged in recognition and relief.

Damn him. He should be gone, he had to get away. She struggled to free herself, but he was already moving, dragging her toward the exit.

She dug in her heels. "Take the car."

"Shut up."

Wood groaned and twisted. The bridge shook like a subway train. Even if she convinced him to get in the car and drive, the bridge might collapse anyway.

She sucked in her breath and felt his strength sweep into her. She threw everything she had, everything she was, ahead of them at the flames.

What must be . . .

Grabbing his forearm, she ran with him into the tunnel of fire.

9

THEY RAN. HEAT SCORCHED JUSTIN'S FACE, SINGED his hair, seared his lungs.

A burning beam crashed behind them. The road pitched like the deck of a sinking ship, and Lara stumbled to her knees. Sparks swarmed them like a cloud of glowing insects, lighting, biting, burning. Her hair smoldered.

Justin hauled her up and into his arms, staggered with her to a hole in the wall. The supports swayed. A flaming chunk of debris dropped into the river, flowing fifteen feet below.

"I can walk," Lara croaked.

"I can swim," he said, and jumped with her over the side.

For one moment, he flew. Like a skiff in a storm, like a kite on the wind, he sailed through the air, through the clouds, where the currents tumbled and swirled like river water. He felt the rain, flashing like a school of bright fish above the earth. High. So high.

And free.

Lara shrieked and clutched his neck. He heard a crack of wood or lightning before the skies opened and the rain came down.

He held her tight, and the water closed over their heads.

Water singing in his blood, rushing in his ears. They plunged down, down, into the shock of cold, the relief of wet, the welcome of the river. A thousand silver bubbles burst with them into the dark. Pain gone. Heat gone. Only water, all around.

Water was his element.

The realization burst in his brain. He was a child of the sea, a creature of the water, elemental, immortal.

Or he had been, once.

His mind churned. He floundered. He *remembered. A broken castle on the cliffs. A man with eyes like rain, a girl with hair like straw, a dog . . .*

Sanctuary.

A profound sense of loss speared his chest. The river roared in his head.

They had sent him away, he remembered. To save him, they said. And then . . . And then . . .

Against him, Lara struggled, and he realized abruptly she couldn't breathe.

He kicked to the surface.

The night exploded around them as they broke into the air. The fire beat at his back. Rain pelted his head. Smoke billowed black against the flames, gray against the night sky. Lara coughed and clung to him, the one solid thing in his universe. He hauled her toward the bank, swimming strongly against the current.

River and sky blended together in the slashing, splashing rain. His feet touched bottom, silt and stone and weed.

He waded toward the dark shore, water sloshing around his thighs.

Lara staggered hard against him. He lugged her with him up a bank slick with mud and grass. They collapsed together on the slope like a couple of shipwreck victims.

He turned his head.

She lay beside him, her dark hair plastered in rivulets against her skull, rain streaking her delicate, determined face.

Here. Real. Alive.

A smear of mud decorated her cheekbone. She watched him without moving, her gray eyes the color of smoke, reflecting the light of the fire. Behind them, another section of bridge crashed into the river.

"Well." He grinned to hide the churning of his gut. "That's one way to make sure they can't follow us."

A laugh escaped her, a small, surprised chuckle like a bird's.

He inhaled sharply and cupped her face. The laughter faded from her lips and eyes, leaving only that faint, arousing surprise. With his thumb, he traced the angle of her cheek, the fullness of her lower lip. Her skin was cool from the river. Her mouth was warm. He rose on one elbow to kiss her—softly, but a real kiss this time, with tongue and intent. She tensed and then melted under him like sugar in the rain, sweet and wet and warm. Her kiss anchored him. Calmed him. He shifted, hooking one leg over hers to pull her closer, moving his hand down to palm her slight breast, to feel her breath catch, her heart beat, her nipple push against his palm.

He needed this, needed her, solid and real against him, wet and open and under him.

Lara.

He rolled with her on the muddy bank, his body heavy, hot, on fire for hers. He nuzzled her throat, inhaling her scent, clean rain and wet woman. Her hand rested on the back of his neck, the brush of her little finger like a trickle of rain at the edge of his collar.

She murmured, acquiescence or protest. "Justin . . ."

He raised his head to look her in the eyes. He wanted to give her something. A piece of himself. "Iestyn," he told her. "My name is Iestyn."

* * *

She didn't think, didn't want to think. No time to consider, no opportunity to be afraid. Only *this*, his mouth, his touch, his broad shoulders over her like wings. Only *now*, lying on a riverbank in the rain, free from the Rule and its consequences.

She was submerged in sensation, her senses brimming with him, his tang in her nostrils, his taste on her tongue. His leg was heavy over her thighs. His erection pressed hard and urgent against her hip.

This. Here and now.

He said something—his name?—and she raised her hand to trace the shape of his lips in the dark.

She didn't want to talk. She wanted to feel. To feel him.

He said it again, softening the J, swallowing the vowels. *Yess-ten.* "My name is Iestyn. I am . . . I was a child of the sea."

She struggled to surface. "You . . . What?"

His calloused fingers feathered her hair. She couldn't see his expression, only the outline of his head against a backdrop of flame, and the shape of his shoulders, shielding her from the rain. "I was an elemental. Like you."

An elemental. Like . . .

She blinked. Not like her. Not really.

His lips were warm against her neck. She shivered and closed her eyes, her mind slowly returning to her body. "Are you sure?"

He smiled against her throat, making the nerve endings there jump in delight. "It's not the kind of thing I'd make up."

She lay still, thinking hard. Thinking back. Had he been lying before, then? To her? To Simon?

She opened her eyes. "How long have you known?"

He shrugged, apparently unfazed by her questions. "I just remembered. When we went into the water."

That moment. That one wild moment of terror and glory, when they'd plunged from the bridge and she'd felt like she was flying.

Not flying. She willed her thoughts back to earth. She didn't have that power anymore. But he . . .

If he were a water elemental, a child of the sea, that would explain everything: his unfamiliar energy, his impressive shields, his resistance to Miriam's drugs and Zayin's magic.

"So I was right," she said slowly.

He kissed her collarbone. "Right about what?"

Her mind whirred. What if there was nothing wrong with her judgment, her discernment, after all? What if . . .

A trickle of excitement slid down her spine. "I *was* Called to find you."

He raised his head. "I don't think so. I'm no angel."

"But you defeated the demon in the alley. You saved my life on the bridge."

"By jumping over the side."

"It was more than that," she insisted. "Something happens when we touch."

"Was happening." His tone was wry. She felt him, warm and hard against her hip. "Until you got distracted."

She ignored him, resisting the humor in his voice, the tug of temptation in her blood. She had to think.

She'd always been taught that the children of the sea were neutral in Hell's war on Heaven and humankind. Simon had dismissed the merfolk as untrustworthy, irrelevant to the nephilim's struggle for survival.

But suppose that together, they could be more? The possibility quivered inside her. She could be more. What if her Seeking was in response to a greater purpose, a higher calling? Simon would have to acknowledge her value to him. She would be pardoned.

Vindicated.

"Don't you see? This changes things. Now that we know what you are . . ."

"What I *was*," Iestyn corrected harshly. "I'm nothing now."

She frowned, reluctant to relinquish her brief fantasy of being welcomed back to Rockhaven, problem solved. Sins forgiven. "Don't say that."

"Lara, when we jumped . . ." He rolled off her and sat staring at the burning river. "Nothing happened."

She struggled to sit up, recalling the shock of his touch, the burst of rain and power as they shot from her element into his. "How can you say that?"

"Because nothing happened to me." Emptiness echoed in his voice. Her heart squeezed in instinctive sympathy. "The children of the sea are shape-shifters. But in the water, I did not Change."

The fine hair along her arms rose. Shape-shifters.

Well.

She hugged her knees for warmth, regarding Iestyn's profile in the sullen light of the fire—strong nose, firm lips, hair flattened to his head by rain and the river. Too beautiful to be merely mortal.

She'd known he was different. She hadn't considered how different. "Change into what?" she asked cautiously.

"I am selkie. A man on the land, a seal in the water," he explained. "But I need my sealskin to Change form."

Her throat thickened. The nephilim could spirit cast into birds. But nothing in her training had prepared her for an elemental who turned into a seal. Or who, um, didn't.

She swallowed. "Where is it? Your sealskin."

"I don't remember." He turned his head to meet her gaze. In the orange light of the fire, his eyes were like the eagle's, fierce and bright. "Without a pelt, I am trapped in human form. If I were finfolk . . . But I am not. Not elemental. Not immortal. I'll grow old and die."

She sucked in her breath. Some of the nephilim lived two or three hundred years—more than twice as long as humans. But eventually they, too, aged and died. "You mean, like me?"

He didn't answer.

She rubbed her arms. Not quite like her, she realized. She was Fallen. He was merely . . . lost.

She licked her lips. "I want to help you."

"You've done enough already."

The echo of Simon's rebuke made her wince. "That's cold."

"I didn't mean it like that." His warmth, his regret, sounded sincere. "You got me out of there. And at least now I've got my mind and a piece of my memory back."

"I can do better. I want to help you go home." The rightness of her decision settled in her stomach.

"I have no home."

"Back where you belong," she clarified. "With your own kind."

He went very still, his head lifting, like a dog on the scent or a man hearing his favorite song come on the radio. And then he shook his head.

"Look, I appreciate the thought. But Sanctuary is gone. Destroyed. If any of my kind survived, I don't know where they are. I don't belong with them anyway."

Her heart thrummed. "I'm a Seeker. I could help you find them."

"Why?" he asked bluntly.

"You saved my life. Isn't that reason enough?"

"For you to risk your life?" He shook his head.

"I'll be safe with you." She hoped. *And you will be much safer with me.*

"You'll be safe if you go back."

But not trusted. Not valued. Disgraced. Dismissed. Demoted.

"If I go back now, I'll be cleaning birdcages the rest of my life."

"Better me than bird shit?"

Amusement. She stuck out her chin, determined to convince him. "For the moment. Or would you rather hear I can't live without you?"

"Don't say that." His voice was suddenly serious. "If we find them, I'll be gone. Even if we don't find them, I won't stay."

His earlier warning echoed in her head. *"Once I line up another berth, another job, I'm gone."*

It was more than a sailor's excuse this time, she thought. Simon warned that the children of the sea were changeable as the tides, fickle and unsteady.

She bit her lip. "I don't need you to stay. I just need . . ." *What?* "A chance to prove myself," she said.

"To Axton?"

"To Simon, yes." *And to myself.* She shrugged and slid him a sideways glance. "Of course, if you insist that I go back to him . . ."

Iestyn made a sound very like a growl. "Fine. We better get moving, then." He stood, looking down at her. "Unless you plan on waiting for the fire truck."

It wasn't an invitation. It was a dare.

She scrambled to her feet, her heart pounding in her chest. She'd won. For now. She was leaving Rockhaven—not for a brief mission in the company of a Guardian, but truly *leaving*—for the first time in thirteen years. The thought was liberating. Terrifying.

She trudged after him, her shoes squelching and slipping in the mud and grass. At the top of the bank, he waited and offered his hand.

She didn't need his help to get up the slope. She must not depend on him. They were as different as . . . as air and water.

But they were allies now. She would help him find his people. And maybe in the process she would find herself.

She grasped his lean, strong hand, a flutter in her chest like hope.

* * *

"Where are we going?" Lara asked.

Good question. Iestyn took her elbow to help her over the ditch at the side of the road.

Right up there with *"What happened to your sealskin?"* And *What the hell was I thinking bringing her along?*

He glanced up the long, curving driveway flanked by stone columns—the kind of driveway that promised a big house at the end. No gate. But this close to Rockhaven, he was taking no chances. "You know who lives here?"

She shook her head.

"Then that's where we're going," he said.

He could tell from the look on her face that she had more questions, but she kept them to herself. Maybe she realized he didn't have any answers. Or maybe she was out of breath.

She pulled her arm free. "I'm okay."

His jaw tightened. "You look beat."

She was soaked and shivering, the angles of her face too sharp, her lips too pale. But for the past three miles, she'd put one foot in front of the other without complaint like the angel she was.

He'd heard sirens tearing up the night ten minutes ago. He should have left her on the riverbank to be rescued by some gung ho fireman. Some smitten volunteer who'd wrap her in blankets and take her back to Rockhaven. Back to that cold, controlling son-of-a-bitch Axton and a lifetime of cleaning out birdcages.

He felt his lips pull back in a snarl and adjusted his expression.

Not his problem, he recited silently. Not his responsibility. She was a grown woman. Barely. She could make her own choices.

And she'd chosen him. He just wished he didn't feel so damn good about that.

She pointed to a circular sweep of brick and concrete, where skinny trees in black pots were placed at intervals like sentinels around a castle wall. "Don't we want to go that way?"

"Nope." He steered her down a gravel path off the main drive. "Big house in the country, probably has a security system. What we want is . . ."

The smell of mulch and gasoline. A low roof-line against the trees.

"There," he said in satisfaction.

An open-sided shed sheltering tools and a wheelbarrow, a riding mower, and a rusting ragtop Jeep. He leaned in the open side, searching for keys. In the glove box, under the floor mat, over the visor . . .

The keys jangled as they fell onto the driver's seat.

He held them up to Lara. "Magic."

Her eyes widened before she caught herself. "Guesswork." And then, "How did you know they were there? That any of this was here?"

He shrugged. "Owners usually like to hire somebody else to do their dirty work. This is probably the caretaker's Jeep."

"And we're just going to take it?"

He slanted her a look. "Unless you want to drive the lawn mower."

The engine chugged to life. He checked the gas. Half a tank. Good enough.

Lara's teeth chattered as she climbed in beside him. "Are you okay to drive?"

He had the mother of all headaches, his magic choker burned like a son of a bitch, and if he didn't lie down soon, he was going to fall down.

"I'm good," he said, trying to sound confident and cheerful instead of insane. "You?"

Her eyes were bruised with exhaustion, her pretty lips blue with cold. She squared her slim shoulders. "I'm fine."

"You're amazing," he said honestly.

She smiled and ducked her head.

The Jeep bumped onto the road, picking up speed as they hit the asphalt. He fiddled with the controls, swearing as a blast of cold air shot from the dashboard.

"Heater's broken," Lara observed.

Figured.

The long dark road was going nowhere. At the next

intersection, he turned right, relieved when a gas station appeared and then a route sign. The Jeep leaned around a ramp and rattled onto a highway. Rolling hills and country estates were broken up and swallowed by train tracks and subdivisions, strip malls, and overpasses sprayed with graffiti.

The white mile markers flashed by. Lara huddled in her seat, hugging her arms. At this speed, the Jeep's rag top and open sides didn't offer much protection.

"Pull that tarp over you," he ordered. "It'll cut the wind some."

She twisted around in her seat to drag the tarp from the back. The heavy canvas released the sharp scent of bark, which mingled with the lingering smells of smoke and river mud. Lara wrinkled her nose as she adjusted the tarp around her. Mulch trickled from her shoulders to the floor.

She plucked a fold from her knee. "There's enough here for us both."

He shook his head. "I don't get cold."

She looked at him sideways. "Is that a guy thing?"

"A selkie thing. Warm blood," he explained.

Webbed feet. No pelt.

His smile faded.

"At least it stopped raining," she offered.

"We didn't need it anymore," he answered absently. "All it takes is one good downdraft to cut off the moisture flow."

Lara left off fussing with the tarp. "Weather control? Is that a selkie thing, too?"

His skull pounded. His head split like a tearing curtain, revealing . . .

Mist. Gray stone walls with the damp running down, and a fountain playing in the center.

"Weather working is the simplest gift and the most

common," the castle warden lectured in his deep, burred voice. "The first to come and often the easiest to master."

The boys sprawled on the bench and on the courtyard grass, watching the clouds, bored with a lesson they'd heard too many times before.

"It is the water you cannot see that creates the rain and clouds," Griff droned on, "that cools and warms the earth and sustains all life. This is the water you must know and control if you want to work the weather."

The fog swirled. White lights pierced the gloom.

Yellow lights, coming toward them.

A blare of sound. A horn.

The wheel jerked in his hands as Lara grabbed it and the Jeep shuddered and straightened. The oncoming truck roared by in the opposite lane.

Shit. His hands shook. He eased his foot from the accelerator, sweat breaking out on his forehead.

"Pull over," Lara ordered.

"What happened?"

"You blacked out."

"No, I . . ." He inhaled, willing his hands and his stomach to settle. "Maybe."

"What else could it be?"

The Jeep's tires rumbled onto the shoulder and coasted to a stop. He clicked on the blinking hazard lights: *warning, warning, warning.*

"Flashback. I thought I remembered . . ." But the vision was gone, lost in the mists of his brain. "It's nothing. One too many knocks on the head."

"Miriam said you'd had a concussion before."

"From the shipwreck." He struggled to pull himself together. "At least, that's what the freighter captain thought."

"So maybe the second injury shook things up." Her voice soothed, talking him down. Her hand touched his knee, giving comfort. "Maybe that's the reason you're starting to remember."

"Could be." He blew out his breath and faced the truth.

Every spark of memory, every jolt of power, had followed some contact with her. The touch in the bar. The kiss on the cellar stairs. The embrace on the riverbank. Maybe she had been sent to find him. Maybe she was meant to save him.

He recalled the oncoming semi.

And maybe his returning memories would get them both killed.

"Iestyn?" Her fingers tightened. "What is it?"

"It's you," he said. "You . . . affect me."

"You think I'm helping you to remember?"

He met her eyes. "Not only that."

Whether he wanted it or not, whether he left her or not, he was tangled up in her, snared by the way she made him feel. When they touched and when they didn't. When she moved. When she breathed.

Christ.

He put his head down on the steering wheel, feeling like he'd slammed into the semi after all.

After a moment's silence, she got out of the Jeep.

Good. He listened to the sound of her footsteps as she rounded the hood. He needed a moment. He needed . . .

She nudged his shoulder through the opening on the driver's side. "Move over. I'm driving."

"Pushy, aren't you."

"I never have been before. It's you." He raised his head to look at her. Her clear eyes were dark, uncertain. A smile trembled on her mouth. "Apparently you affect me, too."

She took his breath away. "Lara." He stopped, unsure what came next.

"Over," she said.

He dragged his sorry ass into the passenger seat and watched her fumble with the seat, the mirror, the ignition. Careful, controlled, the kind of woman he usually had nothing to do with. When everything was adjusted to her satisfaction, she pulled back onto the freeway.

And almost immediately put on her turn signal.

"What are you doing?" he asked as they rumbled into the exit lane.

"Finding a place to spend the night."

"You're wasting our lead. We could be miles away by morning."

"You need to rest and I'm freezing. We need a hotel."

He wanted to argue with her. But the truth was, they both needed sleep. If Axton's crew caught up with them, they were in no shape either to fight or to run.

"Not a hotel. A motel. The cheapest, sleaziest motel you can find."

"Don't we have money?"

"I have my pay from my last job. But we need someplace that takes cash and doesn't ask questions."

She turned off the exit ramp into a warren of suburban sprawl, dirty brick and broken concrete and signs with the letters falling off. OIL CH G. W C ME. S RVED HOT.

Eventually she found what he was looking for, a long, two-story building with peeling brown paint and sagging white railings and broken glass glittering in the parking lot. She pulled up under the blinking sign, HEART OF JERSEY MOTEL. The pink light of the neon heart flickered over her face. Iestyn grinned. "Very romantic."

She didn't smile. "I'll check us in."

"I'll do it."

She engaged the emergency brake. "You can't go up to the desk like that. You look like you've been in a bar fight."

"Which means I'll fit right in with their regular clientele. You don't."

"I'm just as scruffy as you are."

"You still don't look like the kind of girl who rents rooms by the hour. You've never been in a place like this."

She winced. "You have no idea what kind of girl I am or where I've been."

He sure as hell didn't know what he'd just said to hurt her. To piss her off. He was no good at relationships that lasted longer than a night or two. He didn't do touchy-feely. He didn't hold hands.

But he reached for hers, covering her fingers on the steering wheel. "What's the matter?"

"Don't touch me."

No good at relationships at all.

So he let her go, keeping his eyes on her face. "All I meant was that you're too beautiful for some bored night clerk to forget." For him to ever forget. "We can't afford to attract attention."

"I know." She let go of the wheel, folding her hands together tightly in her lap. "Sorry for overreacting."

"Not overreacting. You've had a rough night."

She flashed him a grateful glance. "Something like that."

Woman calmed. Crisis averted. But he couldn't shake the feeling that this wasn't over, that there was something more.

He did a quick scan of the dark parking lot: empty cars, broken bottles, weeds pushing through pavement. Damn. He couldn't even tell her to lock the car doors.

"Anybody comes up to the Jeep while I'm in the office, you lay on the horn."

She arched her eyebrows. "I thought we didn't want to attract attention."

Her flicker of spirit reassured him.

"Just do it," he said and went to get them a room.

Not a nice room, he thought after they were inside.

He secured the double locks on the door and stood with his hands in his pockets, trying to see it through her eyes: the mirrored wall, the nasty carpet, the broken lamp shade. The ancient TV was bolted to the dresser. The three porn channels were free, the desk clerk had informed him with a smirk as he handed over the key.

Lara's arms were folded across her body, like she didn't want to touch anything. Probably afraid of catching an STD from the bedspread. Or maybe she was just cold.

Iestyn cleared his throat. "Not exactly what you're used to."

"You either."

"I've slept in some pretty rough places."

"It's better than the storm cellar."

"But not as clean."

She smiled at that, but her back remained rigid. He could feel her discomfort from across the room.

"You can shower first," he offered, trying not to remember how great she looked in a towel, slim bare legs, pale bare arms, her dark hair damp on her shoulders.

She nodded, but she did not move, her attention apparently riveted by the two double beds that took up most of the floor space.

Reluctant suspicion took hold in his mind. She was, what? Twenty-two? Twenty-three? She couldn't possibly be . . . "You ever stay in a room with a man before?"

She met his gaze, her eyebrows lifting. "Are you asking if I'm a virgin?"

Damn it, he was embarrassed. "Yes."

"No."

He leaned one shoulder against the door frame. The boyfriend, he thought. The one with the ponytail. "So angels have sex?"

"The nephilim have human bodies," she said with dignity. "We use them in the usual human way."

"To have sex."

"And to eat and to sleep. All normal bodily functions. Sex is not that big a deal with us."

He grinned, feeling better about the boyfriend. "It is if you do it right."

"I meant, human sex is not a true union. We do not mingle spirits."

"Just bodies."

Her brow puckered in annoyance, but he noticed her rigid posture had relaxed. "Why are you making such an issue of this?"

Wasn't it obvious?

"Because I want to have sex with you," he said.

10

LUCY DRIFTED UP THE CIRCULAR STAIR OF THE prince's tower. Chinks in the thick walls admitted narrow bands of moonlight, striping the stone.

She shivered in a sharp wind from the sea. She had waited too long to make this climb. Confessing the difficulty she was having coping to Conn felt uncomfortably like another failure. But the longer she kept her feelings to herself, the more the distance between them grew.

She had lost their child.

She would not lose his love.

Blinking, she emerged into the prince's study at the top of the stairs. Windows pierced the round room, north, south, east, west. The children of the sea did not make or mine, farm or spin. Caer Subai was furnished with the salvage of centuries, plucked from human shipwrecks and restored after the demons' attack seven years ago: amphorae from Greece and ivory from Africa, Viking gold and Italian silk.

As she entered, Conn looked up from his desk, walnut and iron, rescued from a Spanish galleon off the coast of Cornwall.

"Lucy." His posture relaxed, but a faint wariness remained in his eyes. She had not sought him here for months.

Time to change that, she thought. But she was at a loss how to begin.

A map spread across the surface of his desk, glowing like the night sky with pricks of multicolored light.

"What are you doing?" she asked, wandering closer.

He straightened. "Looking for your lost boy."

Her brows pulled together. Her heart quickened in her chest. "What?"

"You know how the map works. Each light represents an elemental's energy. Not the angels, of course. The children of air are forbidden from interfering in earthly affairs. But here we are." He tapped the bright blue cluster off the coast of Scotland, waved a hand at the smattering of stars across the seas. "The children of earth here and here."

He traced his finger along the glowing green ridges of the mountains. She walked around the desk to see. As she drew closer, his faint, familiar musk teased her senses.

"Demons here," Conn continued, with another poke at the map. Red pulsed along the fault lines, spattered across the continents like blood.

"But see here." He leaned forward over the desk again, making her very aware of the heat of his body, the strength of his arms. "These spots of blue inland? Here, on the Mid-Atlantic coast, and here. These could be your lost . . ."

Children.

"The ones who were lost," he said stiffly.

Tears choked her throat, swam in her eyes. "You listened."

He looked down his long nose at her with a hint of his habitual arrogance. "Of course."

She swayed toward him, more moved by his act of faith than she could say. "Conn . . ."

He moved away from her to stand in front of the window, hands clasped behind his back. "I thought I would leave in the morning," he said, staring out at the moonlit sea.

"Leave," Lucy repeated blankly.

He nodded. "It will be an opportunity to see Morgan and your brother Dylan as well. I have not conferred with either of them in weeks. They are wardens. Perhaps they picked up on this sending, too. If you are right, if there is a chance that Iestyn and the others are alive . . ." He broke off, his voice raw.

He cared.

Emotion flooded her heart. Not just for the survival of their kind. He cared for the children he had gathered and protected and finally sent away.

How had she been blind to it until now?

But he had always been good at hiding his feelings. He had learned over centuries of rule to never reveal emotion. Never admit weakness. And she had been too wrapped up in her own feelings to understand.

"I could come with you," she said.

Conn's head raised. His shoulders were rigid against the moonlit glass. "Your power would be . . . a great assistance. But are you well enough for such a trip?"

His concern touched her. He was putting her feelings before what needed to be done.

"I'm fine. I'm healed." Physically, at least.

He turned to face her. "We do not need to see your brothers, if you do not wish it."

"Why wouldn't I . . . Oh." Seeing her brothers meant

seeing their families. Their children. Caleb's wife Margred was pregnant again.

Lucy straightened her shoulders. "I want to go with you." She held out her empty hands to him. "I don't want you to be so far away."

Conn met her gaze. His silver eyes had the sheen of the sea beyond their windows, glazed by the moon. "I am never far from you, Lucy. You are always in my heart."

She stumbled toward him and he took her hands and pulled her into his arms.

11

"I WANT TO HAVE SEX WITH YOU."

Lara released her breath, oddly relieved now that they'd acknowledged the elephant in the room.

"It is important for you to be open about sex," Miriam had told her in counseling. *"To be honest about how you feel. Shame and fear breed in secrecy."*

But outside of her required therapy sessions, Lara never talked about what had been done to her thirteen years ago. Not to earnest Jacob, her one sexual partner at Rockhaven, and never, ever to Simon.

Openness was obviously not a problem for Iestyn.

Probably sex wasn't either.

She wasn't sure how she felt about that. Thankful? Resentful?

Intrigued.

She angled her chin, testing her reaction, watching his. "That's it? That's your pickup line?"

He grinned at her, all charm, easy and unthreatening. "You think it needs work?"

Her pulse quickened. "I think you can do better."

He strolled forward, all lean grace and golden eyes like a hunting cat. Her stomach fluttered. Not, she thought, with fear.

"Let's see," he murmured and bent his head.

His breath was warm, his mouth firm and persuasive. His lips rubbed and withdrew, pressed and lingered, teasing, tempting, gentle. She closed her eyes, absorbing the flavor and the tenderness of his kiss, feeling her breath go and her knees turn to water.

More warmth. More pressure. Her heart soared, beating in her chest, and yet he did not touch her with anything but his mouth and one hand, cupping the back of her head. His thumb stroked her jaw, and she opened for him, taking his scent deep in her lungs, his tongue inside her mouth.

Too much. Too fast. She was drowning in sensation. Suffocating.

But even as she stiffened, Iestyn eased away. He kissed her lightly on the tip of her nose, on the arch of her eyebrow.

"There's an all-night Walmart two blocks away," he murmured against her hair.

She opened her eyes, struggling for a light tone. "Are you asking me on a date?"

His silent laughter brushed her cheek. "If this was a date, I'd buy you flowers, not a change of clothes. What size shoe do you wear?"

His consideration shook her. "You want to buy me clothes."

"Actually, I'm good with you naked. But you might appreciate something clean after your shower."

She was dying to shower, desperate to scrub away the smell of smoke. But . . . "You're going now?"

"Or I could stay and scrub your back."

The invitation was there, the intent was there, gleaming in his golden eyes, but softened with humor, leashed by his will.

She shivered with nerves and desire, her gaze slipping from his. "No, thanks."

He frowned, misunderstanding the reason for her trembling. Or perhaps understanding too well. "You don't mind being left alone?"

Memory slammed into her. *The cheap room. The sound of footsteps stumbling down the hall. Her heart pounding as she hid under the bed. "Angel, I'm back."*

She swallowed a whimper. Straightened her spine. "Sometimes I prefer it."

"We're out of the way here," Iestyn said. "Second-floor corner unit. And the door double locks."

She nodded wordlessly.

He frowned. "Unless locks don't work against demons."

She pulled herself together. "I can set simple wards. I'm not afraid of demons." *Only ghosts.* "Anyway, it's highly unlikely they followed us here."

"They found us before."

"Because we used magic. Power attracts them."

"Like shit draws flies."

She scowled. "Don't you take anything seriously?"

"Yeah. Your safety." He rubbed his stubbled jaw. "How do you know they won't burn the place down while I'm gone?"

His protectiveness warmed her. "They don't usually attack so openly. First, because they won't risk attracting Heaven's attention. And second, because they can't assemble that much energy in so short a space of time. Most of the time they must borrow other matter—other bodies."

"Like in the alley."

She hugged her arms. "Yes."

He searched her face. Apparently what he saw satisfied him, because he gave a short nod. Stooping, he unstrapped the dive knife from his ankle and offered it to her, hilt first.

She recoiled slightly. "That's yours."

"I'm loaning it to you. You need it more than I do."

"But I just told you—"

"That you're safe from demons, yeah, I know. Hell, a knife's probably no good against demons anyway."

"Actually, fire needs oxygen to survive," she said seriously. "If you cut the body's airway, the demon must leave its host or die."

"Good to know." He offered the blade again. "Take it."

"Why?"

"For the same reason you gave it to me back in the cellar."

She stared at him, confused.

He closed his fingers over hers on the hilt. "To remind you you're not alone."

* * *

Lara grabbed the tiny bottle of shampoo, averting her eyes from the coin-operated condom dispenser on the wall above the toilet. She pushed open the mildewed shower curtain and winced. *Yuck.* Maybe she should wear her wet sneakers into the tub? But then they would never dry by morning. She wasn't that confident of Iestyn's ability to return with shoes.

He would return. She *was* sure of that. And when he did . . . She shivered and cranked on the shower.

At least the water was hot. She stood under the scalding spray, letting it pound her scalp and sink to her bones, flaying herself with the cheap washcloth as if she could scrub away her memories.

"Sex is not that big a deal with us," she'd told him. *"Why are you making such an issue of this?"*

A chill chased down her back despite the hot spray. *That's what you get for lying.* Sex was an issue for her, too. Had been an issue. She wasn't a victim anymore.

And maybe, with him, sex would be different. Easier. When she was with him, she felt different. Lying with him on the riverbank, she'd felt warm and eager and unafraid. Something unfurled inside her as she remembered. Her nipples tightened. A flush rose in her skin to match the heat of the water. Shutting off the shower, she reached for a towel.

He was gone long enough for the flush to fade, for her nipples to pucker again with cold. She checked her rudimentary wards: a taw traced in the dirt of the window, another scratched in the paint above the door, two crossed lines like a hilted sword. But until Iestyn came back, she had nothing to do. She paced the narrow space before the dresser, wrapped in a skimpy, scratchy towel, her hair in wet strands down her back, trying not to think. When the knock came, she flew to the peephole.

Iestyn stood on the landing outside, his hands full of plastic bags. She tugged open the door and then hung back, suddenly conscious of her nakedness under the towel.

His eyes darkened at the sight of her, but all he said was, "There's a comb in one of the bags. I'm going to clean up."

There was a comb, she discovered, investigating as he disappeared into the bathroom. And a brush. Canvas sneakers—size eight—jeans, a couple of tops, a zippered hoodie, and a multipack of cotton panties. But no bra. No nightshirt. She dug into another bag and found more T-shirts, men's size large.

She glanced at the closed bathroom door before dropping her towel.

Ripping open the plastic, she yanked on one of the large T-shirts, layering the hoodie over it for good measure. The mirrored wall told her she looked ridiculous, her long bare legs poking out from under the white shirt and bulky navy fleece. But at least she was warm. She pulled a face. And her nipples were covered.

The last bag held toiletries: toothbrushes, a razor, a tube of antiseptic cream. She frowned over the last, squinting to read the label.

The bathroom door opened. Iestyn emerged, lanky and golden in a cloud of steam like a seraph streaming from Heaven. The towel slung low around his hips was every bit as small as hers had been.

She jerked her gaze up. And widened her eyes in dismay. "Impressive."

He grinned. "Thank you."

She bit her lower lip. "I meant your throat." She stepped closer to get a better look.

Red stripes seared his neck just under the cord. The skin around the lampwork bead looked even worse, cracked white edges around a scarlet burn.

She reached to touch him, to heal him, and he caught her fingers. Her nerve endings sparked. Her blood hummed and quickened.

"No magic," he said. "I don't want any demons finding us tonight."

"But you're hurt," she protested. His neck looked almost abraded, raw and angry.

He shrugged. "I bought some stuff to put on it."

She remembered the tube of antibiotic ointment in her hand. "Let me."

Using their linked hands, she drew him to the bed. He sat on the edge of the mattress, and she moved between his thighs, his knees on either side of her legs, his bare feet flanking hers.

She sucked in her breath, acutely conscious of his difference, his size, his maleness, his . . . toes. His toes were webbed.

Her hand shook.

"I feel better already," he murmured close to her breasts.

Heat climbed her neck and into her face. "Hold still," she ordered, although he hadn't moved.

She smoothed ointment into the crease of his neck, feathered it around his stitches and the awful sore in the hollow of his throat. His skin was very warm. Damp hair the color of oiled oak, gold and brown and bronze, fell into his face. He smelled like shampoo and something else, something musky and masculine. She felt his coiled stillness, the rigidity of his muscles, before he turned his head and kissed the tender inside of her arm.

His jaw was rough, his lips velvet. Sensation tightened her breasts.

He made a sound, a growl, low in his throat and looked up. Her breath caught at the hungry, knowing look in his eyes. She pressed her thighs together.

Holding her gaze, he stroked her breasts with his fingertips, learning her by feel like a blind man reading Braille. Her heart pounded. When his exploring fingers found her taut peaks, he smiled and pinched gently.

"You're beautiful," he said, still watching her face.

She closed her eyes, unable to bear the heat in his eyes, the excitement of his touch, any longer. His stubble rasped against her T-shirt. She felt his warm breath on the inside curve of her breast, and then his mouth replaced his fingers as he suckled her through the cloth.

She arched, clutching at his shoulders, his hair, careful

of his head wound. The damp strands slipped like wet silk through her fingers. Pleasure flamed in the tips of her breasts, kindled like fire in her belly at the tug of his mouth, hot, wet, insistent.

His arms came around her to bring her closer, one large hand sliding from the small of her back to the swell of her bottom, down the back of her thigh and up again under the T-shirt. She sucked in her breath as his flesh met her naked flesh, as his warm, calloused hand spanned her buttocks. Her legs trembled.

He nuzzled the underside of her breast, biting softly. Her eyes opened in alarm and delight. The fire inside her grew, licking between her legs.

Yet a small, rational part of her mind floated apart like an observer in a corner of the room. She watched in the mirror as he widened his legs, drawing her in between them. His towel parted. She felt the brush of his body hair on her thighs, the nudge of his erection, hot satin over stone.

She gasped as he leaned back, lying against the bed, taking her down with him. Her legs sprawled. Her hands scrambled for support. *Motel bedspread*, her mind observed. *Not very sanitary*. Maybe she should pull back the covers . . .

He adjusted her firmly against him, cupping, stroking, his erection lodged solidly against her belly. Her brain shut off. He brought her head down for another kiss, his mouth lush and wide, rubbing, searching. She was open to him, wet and open, her knees on the towel, her thighs straddling his hot flanks, he was *there*, thick and inescapable. *He's very large*, her mind pointed out worriedly, but her body didn't care, her body wanted his, wanted all the things he was doing to her with his hands, with his mouth.

Until he rolled with her, pressing her back into the

mattress. She stiffened automatically, her brain returning to her body with a *whoosh.*

She gritted her teeth, managing not to freak out at his weight heavy between her thighs. *This is Iestyn,* she reminded herself, focusing on his face. She wanted him, or she had until a moment ago. *Just relax.*

But she couldn't relax. She couldn't breathe. She wasn't in control of him or her own body, and that scared her more than anything.

"I can't do this," she said tightly.

He kissed her neck. "Sure we can."

"No, I *can't.*" A trickle of panic traced down her spine. She shoved at his shoulder. "Let me up."

He rolled instantly to one side. She bolted upright, sitting on the side of the bed, panting and humiliated.

"Sorry." She couldn't look at him. "I guess I overreacted again."

"It's okay," he said, although she knew it wasn't. "Want to tell me what's going on?"

She snuck a look at him, lying propped on one elbow, his warm golden gaze fixed on her face. He was being nice. Somehow that made her feel even worse. "It's not you," she felt compelled to say. "It's me."

He laughed. "Kiss of death, honey. Right up there with, I hope we can still be friends."

She flushed. Smiled. "You must think I'm being stupid."

"No." His tone was thoughtful. Despite his laid-back pose, she got the impression he wasn't really relaxed at all. Maybe the fact that he was still fully erect was a clue. "I think you've been hurt. Who hurt you, Lara?"

She shook her head. *"It is important for you to be open about sex,"* Miriam's voice replayed in her mind, but the doctor wasn't the one faced with explaining to another hot, nice, sexy guy how damaged she was.

"Axton?" Iestyn's tone was grim.

She couldn't let him think that. "No. Simon *saved* me."

"When?"

She tugged her towel from under his hip and wrapped it around her. "It doesn't matter. A long time ago."

He didn't say what he must be thinking. That if it didn't matter, there was no way she would have stopped him just now. "How long ago?" When she didn't answer, he rephrased the question. "How old were you when you were . . . hurt?"

She stared at the ugly brown carpet between her naked feet, not wanting to see his expression change from warm sympathy to horror. To pity. "Nine."

He swore.

She swallowed painfully. "Of course, that was only my physical age at incarnation. As an elemental, I'd lived many centuries before that."

"Bullshit. You were a little girl."

She cleared her throat. "Technically. As I said, I was newly Fallen, so—"

"Was it a demon?"

Demons hunted the Fallen, she had told him. "No. Just a sick, bad man." That's what she'd called him in her head during the two days of her captivity. The Bad Man.

"Give me his name. I'll kill him."

Okay, not pity. Fury. Typical male response. Useless to her, but warming all the same. "You're too late," she said. "He's already dead."

Silence, while he processed this new information.

"Axton?" he said again.

She nodded. Simon had swept through the seedy apartment like the wind of God, a tornado of destruction. The nephilim did not kill except in self-defense. Simon administered the Rule, he did not break it. Only that one time. Only for her.

"So the son of a bitch did one good thing," Iestyn said. "That explains why . . ."

She stiffened defensively. There was nothing improper between her and Simon. "Why what?"

"Why you trust him," Iestyn said simply, disarming her.

She turned her head. He sprawled beside her, lanky and golden and still half-erect, his skin smooth satin over muscle.

For one moment, she allowed herself to yearn. To hope. Maybe she hadn't ruined everything. Maybe he could accept her past—accept her—and move on.

"You know, I have had sex since then," she said, trying to sound matter-of-fact, like she'd had half a dozen sexual partners instead of only one.

"With the ponytail guy."

"Who?"

"Blond guy in the car. Your boyfriend."

"Gideon? He's not my boyfriend."

"So this other guy . . ."

Jacob. *"He's perfect for you,"* her roommate Bria had claimed. *"He's steady. He's in our cohort. And,"* her friend finished triumphantly, saving his best qualification for last, *"I haven't slept with him yet."*

"Which makes him unique," Lara had said dryly.

She almost smiled, remembering. Jacob had been . . . Not perfect. But earnest and convenient and too wrapped up in his own reactions to worry much about Lara's.

"He'd be the one who convinced you sex was no big deal."

Heat crawled up her face. "Well, it wasn't. He didn't . . . And I couldn't . . ."

She'd wanted to feel whole. Jacob had wanted to get

laid. Achieving their goals had proven more awkward than painful. After the first few times, they'd improved beyond cautious acceptance on her side and a fumbling rush on his, but the sex was never great enough to inspire either of them to keep trying.

Jacob had been honest breaking up with her. *"I like you, Lara,"* he'd said, his brown eyes sincere. *"As a friend. But . . ."*

"He said I had too much baggage," she told Iestyn.

"Fuck," Iestyn said. The laughter that usually lurked at the back of his eyes and the corners of his mouth was gone. "I'm sorry."

She couldn't tell if he was expressing sympathy over Jacob's rejection or apologizing because he basically agreed with him.

He got up—*Don't leave me*, she thought—and flipped back the covers of the other bed.

Regret stung her eyes. "Me, too."

Sorry she had wimped out earlier and missed her chance with him. Sorry . . . Not that she had told him, but that it so obviously made a difference.

"Are you going to be all right?" he asked quietly.

Lara sagged. Skies, she was tired. Down-to-the-bones exhausted and sick almost to death of being defined by something that had been done to her thirteen years ago. She would not be a victim. She didn't want him to see her as that scared, damaged child in need of comfort.

So she straightened her spine and lifted her chin. "I'm fine," she said, because it was important he believed that.

That she believe it.

* * *

Iestyn lay on his back in the ratty motel room, contemplating the stains on the ceiling tiles and listening to the soft sounds of Lara in the other bed. The creak of the mattress. The rustle of sheets. The catch of her breath.

She had to be exhausted, but she was still sleepless, still restless, still making him crazy.

"I can't do this," she'd said, a thread of panic in her voice.

So they wouldn't.

But, God, he wished he could touch her.

Not for sex. Okay, yeah, partly for sex. Tough to pretend he didn't want sex with his hard-on tenting the covers.

He'd never been big on cuddling. Foreplay, fine. Non-sexual contact, not so much. He had a feeling, dimmer than memory, deeper than instinct, that his ingrained dislike of casual touch was part of who he was. What he was. But he would have liked to comfort Lara. To hold her in his arms, rub her back, stroke her hair, and tell her how amazing she was.

Except she didn't want that.

"I'm fine," she'd said, with a tilt to her chin that meant, *Hands off, asshole.*

Given time and opportunity, he could probably change her mind. But putting the moves on her now, when she'd asked him to stop, when she was alone and vulnerable . . . He couldn't do it.

She was only with him because she wanted to help. She'd stood up for him against Axton. Axton, who had saved her, who had done what Iestyn couldn't do, destroyed the sick son of a bitch who'd hurt her. Yet Lara had turned her back on her hero, on her people, her family, because she thought it was the right thing to do. She believed in Iestyn even before he believed in himself.

The least he could do was try not to screw her over.

He glanced toward the other bed. She lay on her side, one

arm tucked under her pillow, her knees drawn almost to her chest. The light creeping under the bathroom door outlined the angle of her shoulder, the curve of her hip. He studied her face. Dark, winged brows, long black lashes. Her mouth like a lily at night, cool, pale, closed. He imagined warming it with his, pictured her lips flushed and open, swollen and damp from his kisses. Recalled the mind-blowing softness of her breast in his hand, the delicate point of her nipple. Her taste.

She shifted and sighed.

He shifted, too, reaching down to adjust himself in the dark, remembering the way she'd gasped and arched when he suckled her.

Her clear gray eyes opened, staring directly at him. "Am I keeping you up?"

Busted.

He raised his knee so she couldn't see his erection standing like a mast against the sheets. Not that she meant her question the way it sounded. "I'm good. Go to sleep."

"I can't."

Did she have nightmares? Probably. The thought made his back teeth grind together. He unclenched his jaw, made his voice as gentle as possible. "You've had a stressful day."

"It's not that." She flipped onto her back, making the mattress squeak. Her breasts moved in interesting ways under the T-shirt. "My hair's wet."

He forced his gaze back to her face. He didn't know what to say. The Heart of Jersey wasn't the kind of hotel that stocked hairdryers in the guest rooms.

"And now my pillow's wet, too."

The complaining edge to her voice made him grin. He didn't dare hope she was as frustrated as he was, but at least she wasn't lying there shattered, reliving her past.

"You have two pillows," he pointed out.

She flounced back onto her side and fixed him with those big gray eyes. Hopeful. Expectant.

Frustration and desire churned inside him. What did she want from him? Whatever it was, he would find a way to give it to her. But he needed a freaking clue. "You want one of mine?"

She was silent so long he wondered if maybe she'd fallen asleep after all. Then, "All right."

He sat up, reaching behind his back for a pillow.

But he never had a chance.

Before he could toss it to her, she climbed out of bed, all smooth bare legs and bra-less breasts, and plucked the pillow from his hands.

"Thanks," she said and slid into bed beside him.

12

EVERY MUSCLE IN IESTYN'S BODY TIGHTENED. "What are you doing?"

Dickhead. Like it wasn't obvious.

Lara propped the pillow behind her and settled against the headboard, the bounce of her breasts momentarily robbing him of breath. "I thought if I slept with you, we could both get some rest."

Rest. Right.

The T-shirt was damp where he'd had his mouth on her. He forced his gaze up to meet her eyes.

"You want to sleep with me," he said. Like he needed her to draw him a diagram when his brain was already playing the movie in glorious 3D color and surround sound.

"Mm." She tilted her head, gauging his reaction. Despite her casual tone, the pulse beneath her jaw beat like a caged bird. "That's a euphemism."

"It's a mistake," he said harshly.

She blinked. "Why?"

"Because . . ." His mind blanked as his blood abandoned his head and went south. "I can't give you what you need."

She glanced at his lap, still covered by the sheet. Raised her eyebrows. "Apparently you can."

He strangled a laugh. "I mean . . . I can't be who you need."

Her brilliant gray eyes softened. "What if you're what I want?"

His mouth dried. His pulse pounded.

"Damn it, I'm trying to do the right thing here," he said.

"The right thing for you? Or for me?"

"For you. I'm probably screwing up—hell, I know I'm screwing up—but cut me some slack. I haven't had a lot of practice thinking about other people."

Her lips curved, but she didn't look happy. "You know, I'm getting pretty tired of other people deciding what's best for me."

He sucked in his breath. That's what she was running away from. Asshole Axton and his angel horde. He didn't want to be like them, didn't want control of her life or her choices. He didn't want the responsibility. But . . .

"I don't want to hurt you," he said.

This time her smile reached her beautiful eyes. "I think you underestimate yourself."

She reached out, her fingertips tracing the shape of his lips, the sensitive skin at the corner of his eyes. The tenderness of her touch clogged his throat.

"So, do you want to . . . sleep with me?" she asked. "Really sleep."

The hesitation in her voice nearly did him in. Hell, yes, he wanted to sleep with her. He wanted to peel her out of that

T-shirt and get his hands on what was under it. He wanted her on him and him inside her for whatever was left of the night. For however long they were together.

He looked into her eyes, shining with trust, and knew he couldn't do it. She might say sex wasn't that big a deal, but women often said that. In his experience, most of them felt differently in the morning.

He wasn't taking advantage of her. He owed her too much, liked her too much, for that.

"Sleep would be good," he said.

She nodded and scooted down on her pillow, making the mattress and everything under the T-shirt shift. He closed his eyes briefly. He must be out of his mind. He settled next to her, tucking her alongside him, her head under his chin, her arm across his chest, her smooth legs against his thigh.

Torture.

Her hair smelled fresh like rain and clean like soap. It was also, he discovered quickly, still damp.

Sleep was hopeless. He lay staring at the ceiling, trying not to disturb her, forcing himself to breathe slowly and steadily in and out. He could feel the faint vibration of their connection, the beat of her heart, the whisper of her breath. In and out . . .

He dreamed again. Dreamed and remembered.

* * *

Three of them boarded the ship in the gray dawn light. Four, if you counted the dog. Iestyn, his arms full of ninety pounds of wet, excited deerhound, definitely counted the dog. If not for the prince's hound Madagh, they might all have Changed into seal form instead of leaving Sanctuary by boat.

Or maybe not. Iestyn boosted the shivering dog onto the swim platform at the back of the boat before hauling himself, dripping, from the cold sea.

How did you outswim the end of the world?

The dog's claws scrabbled on the smooth deck. Roth set down the sea chest and turned to help.

At the ship's rail, Kera stood, her gaze fixed on the rocky shore where the sea lord Conn stood with Griff, the castle warden, to see them off.

Kera's face set in lines of mutinous distress. "I should stay."

"The prince commanded us to leave," Roth said.

Kera raised her chin. "I could help in Sanctuary's defense. I am Gifted."

"You're a pain in the ass."

Iestyn ignored their squabble. The three of them had been raised together since before the age of Change. The magic of the island that kept their elders from aging prevented the young selkies from reaching maturity for a very long time. Once there had been enough of them to fill a classroom. But he and Roth and Kera were the youngest.

The last.

Seabirds clamored around the southern cliff face, disturbed by the fretting wind or the tension in the air. Small waves slapped the rocks below the towers of Caer Subai. Iestyn eyed them anxiously.

Miles away, outside the wards that protected the island, demons labored under the crust of earth to turn the sea itself against the children of the sea. When the ocean floor erupted, the quake would create a tidal wave, a roaring wall of displaced water that would crest and fall on Sanctuary.

Unless the sea lord stopped it. Somehow.

A white bird, its wings sharply angled as a kite, circled the mast like a portent.

Madagh caught sight of Conn on shore and whined, pressing against Iestyn's thigh. Iestyn rubbed the dog's bearded muzzle. He knew exactly how the dog felt.

Lucy might have stopped the destruction of Sanctuary. In the brief time she had lived on the island, Lucy Hunter had channeled the flood of the wardens' power and tapped a well of feeling in the cold, proud sea lord as deep as it was unexpected.

But Lucy was gone now.

When the demons threatened, she had turned her back on the prince and her selkie heritage to protect her human family in Maine, half a world away.

No one dared speak of her desertion to the prince. But among themselves, Iestyn and his friends could talk of little else.

"Traitor," Kera denounced her.

But in the weeks Lucy had been on Sanctuary, she had been Iestyn's friend. She stood with him back to back against the demons. She had healed his wounded arm.

Iestyn tightened his fingers in the rough fur of the dog's back, his throat constricting. He would have gone with her, if she had asked. He would have followed her if he dared.

The cold wind whipped through Iestyn's clothes and tugged at the rigging. On shore, Conn's face was set like stone, his eyes like ice.

"You are our hope and our future," the prince had said that morning to the three young selkies before ordering them away.

Iestyn had wanted to argue. Lucy was the important one. He wished Prince Conn would go after her and find her before it was too late.

The earth rumbled. Iestyn's heart pounded as he bent to secure the barking dog to the rail.

Unless it was already too late.

* * *

He woke suddenly, his heart drumming in his ears and in his chest. There was somewhere he had to go, something he had to do. "*You are our hope and our future . . .*"

"Who's Lucy?"

Lara's voice. Lara's face hovering over him, revealed in the crack of light from the bathroom. Her side pressed warm and soft against him, breast, hip, thigh. His body reared awake.

He cleared his throat. "Who?"

Her gray eyes narrowed. "You were dreaming about a woman. Lucy Something."

"Lucy Hunter." Memory engulfed him like a wave. He couldn't breathe. "Lara . . ." He gripped her shoulders too hard, his fingers denting her smooth flesh. "What happened?"

She caught her full lower lip in her teeth. "I'm not sure. It's this connection thing we've got going. Like I was in your dream, but watching it, you know? I could see you—you were younger in the dream—and I could sort of hear your thoughts, but I didn't understand everything that was going on."

Neither did he.

Seven frigging *years*. Gone. The realization was as sharp as a knife, the loss as new as yesterday.

And Sanctuary . . .

He shook his head to clear it. "What happened to Sanctuary?"

"That's the island in your dream?"

He nodded.

"I don't know."

"You're telling me your lot wouldn't notice if the demons sank an island into the sea?"

"This isn't *Star Wars*," she said with a flash of spirit. "It's not like we feel a disturbance in the Force. Or maybe the masters would, but they wouldn't tell me about it. I'm only a novice Seeker."

"Well, that's just fucking great," he said.

She looked at him with those big, clear, wounded eyes, which made him feel like an even bigger piece of shit for taking out his frustration on her. "Sorry. It's not your fault. There's nothing you can do."

Nothing he could do. If Sanctuary was gone, everything was over, had been over for seven years. His skull throbbed. The only difference was that now he knew. He felt gutted, hollowed, as if everything worthwhile had been stripped from him, leaving nothing but bones and skin.

Not even skin.

His seal pelt was gone, too.

He covered his eyes with his upraised arm. Swallowed the ache in his throat. Nothing had changed, he told himself. Nothing had really changed. He was still just a yacht bum, a drifter, without ties or responsibilities.

"Why would the demons destroy Sanctuary?" Lara asked. She lay on her stomach beside him, her warm hip against his thigh, comforting. Distracting. "The merfolk have never sided with Heaven or humankind. What did the demons hope to gain?"

Reluctantly, he focused on her words. "We had something they wanted. Something our prince would never give up."

"What?"

He lowered his arm, irritated by her persistence. "Lucy Hunter."

He watched her turn over his answer in her mind. "I can understand them hating her because she's human," she said slowly. "But . . ."

"Half human, half selkie. Lucy's mother was the sea witch Atargatis. There's a prophecy that a daughter of her mother's lineage would change the balance of power among the elementals."

And if Sanctuary had fallen, the balance of power had shifted in ways Iestyn couldn't begin to imagine. Didn't want to think about.

Maybe the demons had initially attacked Lara because she was nephilim. But if they'd declared open season on his kind as well, she was in more danger than ever. He couldn't be responsible for her safety.

"I'll rent you a car in the morning," he said. "You can go back."

Lara rose to her knees, making the mattress and everything under the T-shirt bounce. "Wait a minute. I'm going with you. To help you find your people."

He looked up, into her eyes. "My people are gone. You've got nothing to prove anymore. You can't help me."

She sat back on her heels, dragging half the covers with her. He made a grab for the sheet. Nudity didn't bother his people, but he was exposed enough already.

"There must be other merfolk," she said.

"Not many. Our power and our population have been declining for years. Centuries."

"But you're immortal."

"In the sea," he said patiently. "To live on land, to live in human form without aging, we need the magic of Sanctuary."

Instead of arguing, she nodded. "So at least we know where we're going now."

Hadn't she heard a word he'd said? "I'm not dragging you halfway across the world looking for Sanctuary."

"We're not going to find Sanctuary."

"Good bet. Seeing as it probably doesn't exist anymore."

"We're going to find Lucy Hunter."

Her eyes were so fierce and bright, her voice so clear and determined, he didn't have the heart to tell her she was pinning her hopes and his future on a wild-goose chase.

Or maybe he didn't have the guts. He still felt oddly hollow inside. Empty. As if he wasn't completely inhabiting his own body.

He was conscious of hers, though. The pressure of her knee against his hip. The quick rise and fall of her breasts. Her weight beside him pinning the sheet, anchoring him to the bed. With her beside him, he wasn't drifting. Wasn't lost.

His blood began to flow and pound in his chest, his head, his groin.

She was so damn beautiful, those dark winged brows setting off her incredible eyes, her straight, delicate nose, her full, pink, soft lips.

Their eyes met and clung. She must have registered the change in his expression, the charge in the air, because her long black lashes swept down. Even in the dark, he could see her blush. She had to see his reaction, too, standing up stubbornly under the sheet. But she didn't back down or push away.

"Maine, right? Didn't you say . . . In your dream, you thought about her family in Maine."

She wouldn't leave him alone.

He really liked that about her.

But now his head hurt and he was tired of arguing. When a beautiful, nearly naked woman was in your bed, maybe it was better to go with the flow, to avoid confrontation. "Could we talk about this in the morning?"

"There's nothing to discuss. We're going to Maine."

Maine. Why not? His own personal compass needle had been swinging north for a while.

So instead of telling her right this minute that there was no way in hell he was taking her with him, he said, "If we don't get some sleep, we won't be fit to go anywhere."

She smiled, flushed and triumphant. His heart lurched. She settled beside him, sliding under the sheet. He put his arm carefully around her, and she nestled against him, her breasts squashing the side of his chest, her clean hair tickling his chin.

She felt warm. Smooth. Solid. Gradually, the empty ache in his chest eased. The noise in his head faded away.

We flow as the sea flows.

But when he was with her, the turbulence calmed. He would be content to lie with her like this, motionless, for hours. Maybe even forever.

Her fingers spread across his chest. Her warm breath teased his nipple to attention. His cock stirred.

He grimaced. Okay, not completely content. Not entirely motionless either.

She moved her leg, getting comfortable, and then froze, her thigh brushing his erection.

"Ignore it, and it will go away," he forced himself to say lightly.

"Really?"

Despite the ache deep in his balls, the disappointment in her tone made him grin. "Eventually."

She slid her smooth leg down his hair-roughened thigh and back up again, watching him through her lashes. "How long?"

His mind blanked. She wanted to know *how long* he . . . Oh.

"Minutes." Hours. Maybe for as long as she was next to him. "Unless I, uh, take matters into my own hands."

"Like this?"

Her soft, warm hand closed gently around him, zapping his brain and sending a wave of molten heat pouring through his veins. He started to sweat.

"If you pay it attention, you'll only encourage it," he warned.

She chuckled.

He loved making her laugh. Loved that she was lying with him, warm and pliant and unafraid.

"You didn't answer my question," she said.

"What question?" He wanted to talk to her, to reassure her, but her hand on his dick made conversation difficult.

She stroked him lightly. "You didn't tell me if you like this."

Okay, that was an easy one.

"Love it."

Although in truth, she was almost too gentle, her tentative touch promising more than it satisfied. But those were *her* fingers, skating over the broad head of his cock. *Her* palm briefly cupping his balls. Her sweet incompetence was searing pleasure and teeth-grinding agony.

"I've never been particularly . . . handy," she said, and even with his blood throbbing he appreciated that she'd actually attempted a joke. "Is this right?"

He grinned over her head in the dark. Angels and their fucking rules. Maybe they had rules for fucking.

"Whatever feels good to you," he said hoarsely. "Whatever you want."

Her smile flickered. She drew the covers down his body. He caught his breath as the sheet dragged over his erection.

With flattering concentration, she explored him slowly, thoroughly, tracing the ridges and indentations of his torso, the narrow trail of hair below his belly button.

She was beautiful in her absorption, her lashes fanning her pink cheeks, her lips parted. Moist. She raked her fingers up his inner thighs, combed the crisp, short hair at his groin, taking him to Heaven and to Hell. He was desperate for her, his shaft pulsing in time with his heart.

Her exploration was arousing her, too. He could see the stiffened peaks of her breasts against the soft cotton of her T-shirt. He could smell her sweet desire.

His cock jerked, demanding her attention. She fit her hand around his hot length, cupping the underside of his shaft, and he shuddered, hips arching off the mattress.

Her hand froze. "I'm sorry."

He dropped his head back on the pillow—*See? Harmless*—and forced himself to smile. "I'm not."

She bit her lip. "Did I hurt you?"

His grin came naturally this time. "You're killing me. In a good way," he said hastily when she looked at him with those big, uncertain eyes. "My junk's not fragile," he added, trying to ease the tension, to tease another smile to her beautiful face. "You can tug on it all you want."

"Even here?" Her hand squeezed delicately.

His grin spread. Never in a thousand years had he imagined giving whack lessons to an angel. "Whatever you want," he repeated. "Whatever you do feels good to me."

* * *

Lara trembled. Iestyn might claim he had no experience thinking about the needs of others, but with those words he'd given her exactly what she needed.

Safety to experiment and explore.

Freedom to indulge her curiosity and desire.

And she did desire him. Her yearning tightened her breasts, weighted her womb. Her sensory world shrank to this bed, this moment, this man. She touched him, reveling in the velvety expanse of his torso, marveling in his hard-muscled abs, his solid thighs. His erection jutted thick and tall from its nest of rough curls.

Her breathing quickened. She could do whatever she wanted with him. Whatever felt good.

Impulsively, she leaned forward and nuzzled him, enjoying the glide of hot satin over stone against her cheek. She liked his salt-and-man smell. Her tongue darted out. His taste. Greatly daring, she opened her lips over his sleek crown, taking him like a plum into her mouth.

His fingers gripped her hair. She stiffened. But he didn't try to hold her head or force her mouth. He only gathered her hair up out of the way so he could watch. Watch her with a heavy-lidded, lazy, sexy look that melted her insides.

She smiled at him, licking her lips.

His answering laugh sounded more like a groan.

An unfamiliar confidence swelled her chest. Jacob had made her feel safe. But no other man had made her feel so powerful, so sure of herself and him.

She took another swipe of him with her tongue and then crawled up his lean, hard body, seeking his kiss. Her lips bumped his chin before his hands came up to steady her shoulders. Her legs straddled his thigh. She found his mouth, warm and sweet and reassuring under hers, and licked into him, using her tongue to explore his mouth with leisurely delight. Yum. She kissed him again, longer, harder, deeper, their mouths engaging in a conversation without words. *Yes. Again. More. Now.*

His heart thudded under her palms. He was warm and

solid between her legs, hot and hard against her stomach. She molded herself closer, rubbing herself against him in a kind of fever. He felt so good. His hands found her hips and lifted her over him. She wriggled. Even better.

"Lara." He squeezed her gently, holding her still.

She raised her head.

He watched her steadily with burning golden eyes. "Are you sure you want this?"

Her heart expanded to fill her chest. He worried about her. He cared about her. Nothing could have made her feel safer or more certain.

But she wanted to lift that shadow from his eyes. From her memory.

"I want . . ." She reached between them and caressed him boldly. "This."

His choked laugh was music to her ears. "Then don't let me stop you."

* * *

Iestyn could feel how wet, how ready she was. Hot and slippery, nestled against him. Burning above him, glowing and unafraid. She lit the dim room like a star.

Her cloudy hair tumbled down around them. Her eyes were deep as the night as she rubbed herself against him, rocking above him, using him for her pleasure, beautiful in her delight.

She wiggled, working his broad head with her heat, his heavy shaft lodged between her slick folds, almost there, almost . . .

He inhaled through his teeth. "Condom."

She was in control, but it was still up to him to protect her. She was too inexperienced to know what she was doing, to understand the risks they ran.

He frowned, something about that thought niggling at the back of his mind. She lurched, reaching across the bed, smothering his last resistance. No thought could compete with the mind-blowing sensation of her wet sex grinding against him, her sweet tits practically in his face.

He captured one taut peak in his mouth as she swept one hand under her pillow. She hummed her pleasure. But before he could really get to work, she sat up, depriving him of his prize.

Not that he could object. Her new position pressed her open sex even more firmly against him. And in her hand, she brandished a little foil packet.

There was a surprise. "Where did you . . ."

She tore it open. "Bathroom."

Relief shuddered through him. She wanted this. Had planned for it. Maybe she knew what she was doing after all.

She turned the condom over in her fingers, fumbling in the dark.

And maybe not.

He took the condom from her and sheathed himself.

She barely waited until he was covered before she pushed his shoulders to the mattress, raised her hips, and . . .

His mind blanked as she sank down on him. Tight. Perfect. He was buried to the hilt, gripped by her wet heat. He gritted his teeth and thrust up, seating himself even more deeply inside her.

She didn't move.

She held herself very still above him, a stunned expression in her wide, darkened eyes.

His stomach muscles tightened. He didn't breathe. Carefully, with his thumb, he pushed a strand of dark hair out of her face, tucking it behind her ear. "Okay?"

Slowly, very slowly, her gaze focused on his. Her smile, when it came, blinded him with its brilliance. "Very okay."

She leaned forward to kiss him, her breasts brushing his chest, her kiss warm on his mouth.

The movement pulled their bodies apart. Instinctively, he arched, seeking a deeper connection. She caught her breath and pulsed around him, beginning to rock, finding her rhythm. He caught her hips to help her, each glide, each push, each pant, bringing them closer.

Sensation wracked him as their sweat-slicked bodies moved together. She held him tightly deep inside, gripping his shoulders, her short fingers digging in. Her lips parted, her eyes narrowed in fierce concentration.

"I can't," she choked out, straining against him.

"You will." He palmed her buttocks, feeling her muscles clench and squeeze inside and out, dragging him with her to the edge. "Come on, baby. Fly."

He reached for her, for the place where they were joined, and pushed her over.

Impaled on his cock, imprisoned by his arms, she cried out his name and flew.

His world spun dizzily out of control. Holding her close, he fell.

13

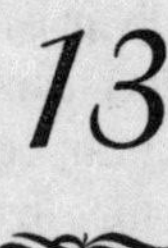

THE GRAY LIGHT OF DAWN EDGED THE SHABBY motel curtains. Iestyn turned his head on the pillow. Lara slept heavily beside him, her dark hair a tangle, her face pure and soft in the cold, uncompromising light.

He could be gone before she woke. To Maine. Now that he had a destination—he wouldn't go so far as to call it a plan—he didn't need to drag her with him. This wouldn't be the first time he'd slipped early from a woman's bed to avoid an argument in the morning.

The scent of sex lingered on the sheets, but no trace of cigarettes or booze or stale perfume. Physically, he felt better than he had in days, his body loose and relaxed, his headache a manageable throb, the burn around his neck a mere distraction. He stretched, careful not to disturb the sleeping woman at his side. It would be a shame to waste his current well-being on regrets or recriminations.

And yet . . .

Desire stirred. Again. She was so damn beautiful. Those long, dark lashes. That moist, kiss-swollen mouth. Her fingers curled protectively into her palm as if she held a kiss or a secret.

She was full of secrets. And surprises.

Who'd have thought his angel would be so hot in bed? Just thinking about the way she'd gone down on him last night was enough to flood his veins with liquid fire. Yet she was so guarded, so modest, she hadn't removed her oversized T-shirt, even when they'd made love a second time.

Of course, they'd both been half asleep. He had roused to find her still sprawled over him, soft, warm, delicious. He'd covered himself with another condom from the stash under her pillow, giving silent thanks for her tendency to plan ahead. With a contented sigh, she'd moved over him, her lashes fluttering open as he'd slipped into her welcoming heat. *Heaven.* Lips joined, fingers linked, he'd loved her with slow, deep strokes until she'd quivered and was still, until he'd shuddered and exhaled into her hair.

Sex so tender, so ardent, belonged in a dream.

Ruefully, he regarded his hard-on, jutting against the sheet.

He could be out of here before she woke. The problem was, he didn't want to go.

After last night, he could hardly slap some money on the dresser and take off. Yet he couldn't leave her without funds. Without a car. Without a word.

Without a kiss.

He leaned forward and touched his lips to hers.

* * *

Lara woke, the warmth on her lips seducing her into opening her eyes.

Iestyn.

The shock of connection caught her unprepared. Sun-streaked hair, sun-bronzed skin, sun god face. Something hot and liquid gleamed in his eyes and pooled deep inside her. The tug of need left her dizzy, dazzled, and uncertain.

Her face flushed.

"What can I do for you this morning?" he asked with easy warmth.

She had no idea how to respond.

Last night she'd talked him—talked *herself*—into having sex. She'd told him she wanted to. She'd told herself it would be enough. But his question this morning made her feel more needy than needed, unsure of her moves and his motives. *"What can I do for you?"*

What was she supposed to say? *Rock my world? Tell me you want me? Say that you love me?*

Her pulse jumped. *No.*

She drew an unsteady breath. "Not a thing," she said coolly.

His eyes narrowed. For a moment she waited, her heart beating wildly, for him to . . . What? Take her back in his arms to that safe place in the heart of the storm, that place where she could fly.

"Fine." He dropped a hard, brief kiss on her mouth. "I'll grab a shower, then."

Naked, he rolled away from her and strolled into the bathroom.

She refused to acknowledge her sinking feeling as disappointment. She'd had a lover. She'd even had an orgasm before. Sort of.

Sex was *not* that big a deal.

A memory of Iestyn's glinting eyes came back and stole her breath. *"It is if you do it right."*

Well.

Maybe.

She listened to the sound of running water from the bathroom. Last night in the dark, she'd felt safe with him, safe and solid and right. Relaxed enough to let go, grounded enough to fly.

Of course, it was possible he hadn't felt the same. In the clear light of morning, she recognized that safe sex was an oxymoron. Sex was never safe. There was always a risk of being hurt physically or emotionally, the danger of disease. Pregnancy.

Rejection.

The shower hissed. A cold finger traced down her spine.

Iestyn hadn't hurt her. He'd taken care to wear a condom both times. He'd satisfied her sexually beyond her wildest dreams. Twice.

But his consideration had only put her at greater risk. She was in real danger now of losing her perspective.

Her chest squeezed. Or her heart.

A tap creaked. Iestyn swore.

Lara got out of bed, tugging her T-shirt down her thighs. She felt better prepared to deal with an annoyed male than a playful one.

She stopped in the bathroom door, momentarily transfixed by the sight of his very bare, very fine ass as he bent over the tub. "What's the problem?"

He glanced over his shoulder. She thought his gaze lingered on her legs before he said, "Something's wrong with the water temperature."

"It's an old motel," she pointed out reasonably, trying to ignore her dry-mouthed response to that look. To all that warm male flesh a few feet away. "Maybe you need to let the water run to get hot."

His brows pulled together. "That's what I thought. But

when I turn on the tap . . ." He suited his action to his words, and a flood of scalding water burst from the faucet. Steam boiled to the ceiling.

"Skies!" She yelped and jumped back. "Turn it off!"

The flow of hot water stopped.

Lara eyed the cloud of steam curling overhead like an evil genie against the water-stained tile, her heart thumping. Something wasn't . . . right. She reached for the cold tap on the sink.

"Careful," Iestyn warned.

She turned the handle. Just a little bit.

Metal screeched. Water exploded into the sink, white-hot. She yanked on the tap, fighting the pressure from the pipe, choking the geyser to a trickle. Plumbing rattled and groaned. An ominous hiss escaped the faucet.

Iestyn moved purposefully past her. "I'll call the front desk."

"Don't bother." She forced the words past her tight throat. "We have to check out. Now."

He stopped directly in front of her, a solid male wall. "Why?"

She raised her gaze from his chest to his face. Licked her dry lips. "The demons have found us."

* * *

Iestyn squatted on his heels in front of the Jeep. He couldn't leave Lara now.

He wouldn't go back to Rockhaven.

So for the time being, they were stuck with each other.

He tightened the screws on the Jeep's new New Jersey license plate, trying hard not to feel cheerful about that.

Lara tossed the plastic Walmart bags in back. Her eyes

had widened when she saw him removing the plate from the Corolla five spaces down, but she hadn't said a word in protest.

He grinned. His angel was adapting to all kinds of new experiences. Good and bad. Once she dropped her little bomb about the demons, she'd taken five minutes, tops, to throw on her clothes and clear the room. No fuss. No wasting time. He'd crewed with guys who weren't as steady in a crisis.

He watched her climb into the passenger's side, her new jeans pulling across the slender curve of her butt.

And they for damn sure didn't have her ass.

He gave the screw head a final twist with the point of his knife and swung in beside her.

"All set?" He put the key in the ignition, released the clutch.

She nodded, her face set and white. He was no good at relationships, but even he could tell something was bugging her.

They bounced out of the parking lot and under a bridge, following the highway signs along narrow gray streets full of dry cleaners and Chinese restaurants, drugstores and tattoo parlors. The lights went on in a coffee shop.

Even this early in the morning, traffic was picking up. He didn't know this town. He just hoped the demons were as lost as he was.

Lara stirred. "Do you know where we're going?"

He slanted her a look. "North."

He hoped. He looked for another highway sign . . . and nearly swiped the mirror off a delivery truck idling in a loading zone.

His heart rate jumped. He steadied the wheel and shot another glance at Lara's pale, set face. "What?"

"I owe you an apology."

Surprise almost made him smile. "Babe, most times

I spend the night with a beautiful woman, she doesn't apologize in the morning."

She turned pink. With anger or embarrassment? He hardly cared. Pink was better than pale and miserable. "It's not that. Well, not exactly. The thing is . . ." She took a deep breath. "It's my fault you almost burned in the shower."

"Don't say that. You warded the motel room, right?"

"I used the taw to seal the door and windows. But—"

"So they heated the pipes." He had a flash of lugging buckets up a spiraling stone stair, of the demons using the hot springs under the sea lord's castle to access the heart of the selkies' Sanctuary. The brief vision made him dizzy. He shook his head to clear it. "There wasn't anything you could do to stop them."

"They shouldn't have been able to find us."

He'd wondered about that. He shrugged. "Maybe they followed me from Walmart."

"The children of fire do not hang out at Walmart."

"How do you know? There were some pretty creepy characters in the electronics aisle."

Her lips twitched before she pressed them together. "Even if there were demons in the area, your shields should have prevented them from noticing you. And if they had found you, you would have been attacked before you reached the motel."

"So if they didn't see me, how did they track us down?"

She folded her hands in her lap. "Demons' reference points are not entirely physical."

"What the hell does that mean?"

"The children of fire are the only elementals to lack matter of their own. They have no physical presence beyond what they borrow. But they are aware of energy. Attracted to it."

She'd said something like that last night, he remembered. "You mean magic? But we didn't do any. At the motel."

"No, but we . . . There's a connection between us. When we joined, I felt a definite, powerful release of energy."

"Babe, that wasn't magic. You came."

Her blush deepened. "Thank you. I'm aware of that. But we also broadcast power."

She was serious.

"You're telling me that when we have sex, it sends up some kind of flare? Like the Bat-Signal?"

"Not the Bat-Signal. But if the demons picked up on our combined energies . . . it's my fault."

He wasn't big on assuming responsibility. But he couldn't let her beat herself up because they'd made love. "Not your fault," he said firmly.

"My idea, then. *I* climbed into bed with *you*."

"Not the second time."

She flicked him a glance, measuring, uncertain.

"Of course, we could test your theory," he continued, trying to provoke her smile. "Make love again and time how long before the bastards show up."

Her sputter of laughter delighted him. But, "That's not funny," she said.

He sobered abruptly. "No," he agreed. "Because if you're right, if the demons have some way to trace the two of us together, you're safer if we split up."

"I don't want to do that."

Her soft certainty drilled a hole in his gut. He didn't either. Not because he needed her to find the merfolk, if they still survived. Not because he was using her for sex. He *liked* her, her loyalty, her tenacity, her determination to do the right thing whatever the cost. She gave him purpose and direction. In a world where everything was fluid, she was a beacon, clear and true.

None of which mattered compared to her safety. He couldn't let his craving for her company jeopardize her life. Better for them both, perhaps, if he left her now. It wasn't like he had anything to offer her beyond this moment. Besides sex.

"We don't have a choice," he said.

"There's always a choice."

He shot her another glance. Lara Rho would never go with the flow. She was a fighter. He wished he didn't admire that about her.

"Okay. Give it to me."

She met his gaze, her eyes vulnerable, and his heart tumbled at the look in her eyes. Not so certain after all. "The demons seem to respond to the connection between us."

"Yeah, so?" he asked, seeing where this was going, not liking her direction at all.

"So." She took a deep breath, released it slowly. "All we have to do to lose them is not have sex again."

* * *

The room stank of demon.

Demon and sex.

Jude Zayin stood on the landing outside the open door of Room 230, his face impassive, his neck muscles tight. Corner room, second floor, hard to access. He'd bet Miller had chosen it for that reason.

Slippery son of a bitch.

Automatically, Zayin scanned the room for unpleasant surprises.

Nothing. No threats. And no quarry.

He stepped inside.

"We can clean the room for you," said the maid—dark,

wide-hipped, hard-eyed—who had shown him upstairs. "Five minutes."

"I won't be here that long."

"But you paid for the room."

So he could search it. Two beds, one barely disturbed. The other . . . He laid his hand on the cold sheets. The other bed had been well used.

Simon would not be pleased.

"You here alone?" the maid asked.

He glanced at her, registering the invitation in her posture and her eyes. Did she expect him to pay for more than the room? "I prefer it," he said.

She shrugged. "Takes all kinds. Let me know if you change your mind."

He shut her out of the room, taking note of the rune, a taw, scratched in the paint above the door. Lara's work, he guessed. He found another written in the dirt of the window. The wards had not been tampered with. But the demons had gained entrance anyway.

The tension in his neck spread to his shoulders. Demons and angels were forbidden from directly interfering in earthly affairs or violating human freewill. But that wouldn't stop the Hellspawn if the perceived payoff outweighed the risk of Heaven's wrath. The demons were expending an unusual amount of energy on this hunt. Which meant they already had a stake in the game.

Or a player.

He moved swiftly through the room. The demon taint was strongest in the bathroom. He touched a finger to the faucet. Still hot.

His cell phone played two quick measures of the "Hallelujah Chorus." Simon's ring tone. It amused Zayin to associate Handel's lush music with the ascetic headmaster.

He picked up the call. "Zayin."

Simon didn't waste time on preliminaries. "Have you found them?"

"I found the nest. The birds have flown."

"How long ago?"

"The clerk said they checked out before seven. Say, four hours."

"So you failed to catch them."

He'd been slowed by the disabled motor fleet and the burned bridge. But he would not make excuses to Simon. "I'll find them," he said instead.

"You must. Before he hurts her."

Zayin surveyed the rumpled bed, the discarded condom wrappers, and resisted the urge to snort. "I doubt she's suffering. He may even believe he is protecting her."

"I don't give a fuck what he believes." The obscenity from the usually calm and collected headmaster made Zayin narrow his eyes. "As long as she's with him, she's in danger," Simon continued. "Is Miller still wearing the heth?"

"Whatever good that does." The failure of his charm rankled. "Obviously it hasn't stopped him."

"But it might still bind. Enough to save her."

Zayin wasn't normally slow on the uptake, but he didn't understand why Simon was fixating on the damn heth. Once Miller escaped the grounds, the charm's usefulness was through. "The heth's power is to contain, not to control. It won't affect Miller's behavior at all."

"Not *his* behavior," Simon said.

Silence.

Zayin's gut clenched as he worked that one out. He tightened his grip on the phone. "You think he's possessed."

"It was always a possibility. He was exposed when they were attacked."

"He's got strong shields."

"Which could mask the presence of another elemental."

"Then why wouldn't the demon take him over before they reached Rockhaven? It could have overpowered them on the road."

"Maybe its plan was to reach Rockhaven."

Chilling thought.

"Besides, Miller was injured," Simon continued. "Maybe Miller's unconsciousness slowed it down. And then you laid the heth on them both, and the demon was trapped inside its host."

Anger licked Zayin. "When were you planning to tell me?"

"I thought you knew. But you insisted on questioning him yourself. I saw no point in sharing suspicions that might influence your interrogation."

"And in the meantime you had a demon captive in your basement to study."

Simon's silence answered him. Knowledge was power, and Simon kept as much power to himself as he could.

"You secretive prick," Zayin said in disgust.

"Perhaps we could leave your wounded feelings aside for the moment and focus on the danger to Lara," Simon suggested.

"She wouldn't be in danger if you'd been honest with her," Zayin said. "With any of us."

"I warned her Miller couldn't be trusted. I told her to stay away from him. I forbid her to have anything to do with him."

"Which explains why she ran off with him the first chance she got."

"She did not run off," Simon said. "I believe he coerced her."

"I don't give a fuck what you believe." Zayin turned the

headmaster's words back on him with savage satisfaction. "Miller was enough of a problem when we didn't know what he was. But you had to play God, devising your little tests, not letting anyone in on your plans. Now he's a double threat."

"So you eliminate two birds with one stone," Simon said. "Miller and the demon. Just bring Lara back safely."

Miriam had said Simon was waiting for Lara to heal. To grow up.

Too late, Zayin thought.

He had never taken much interest in the girl himself. Despite her young age at her Fall, her powers had never seemed particularly impressive. He found both the headmaster's desire and his self-denial vaguely pathetic.

Zayin had no real desire to feed Simon's obsession. But if he returned Lara to Rockhaven, Simon would owe him. An indebted Simon suited Zayin's own needs very well.

So he would find the two by whatever means necessary, dispose of Miller, and fetch the girl home.

Unless the demon killed her first.

14

PITIFUL, THAT'S WHAT SHE WAS.

Lara sat upright in the bouncing passenger seat, fuming. Churning. But really, was it too much to hope for some kind of reaction from a man you'd recently had sex with when you told him you couldn't have sex anymore?

Iestyn could have offered her a little reassurance. Maybe even an argument.

Instead, she got . . . Nothing.

She clenched her hands together in her lap. Maybe he didn't care. No sex, no problem. No magic. *"You came."* The lovemaking that had rocked her world had barely caused a ripple in his.

She cast a resentful glance at his sunlit profile. He drove with one muscled forearm propped on the steering wheel, the wind ruffling his gold-tipped hair. Only a slight squint between his eyebrows betrayed that this was anything other than a vacation to him. As if the future didn't exist. As if last night had never happened.

Miles rolled by. Trucks roared past. They rattled on in silence, the distance between them growing as the sun climbed the sky.

He reached behind his seat, rummaging with one hand until he turned up a battered ball cap. He tossed the hat into her lap. "Put that on. You don't want to burn."

His casual thoughtfulness left her yearning and confused. She fingered the winged P of the Philadelphia Flyers on the front of the cap. There was a certain irony in the logo she wasn't in a mood to appreciate. "What about you?"

"I'm used to the sun. You're not."

She adjusted the visor, shading her eyes so he wouldn't see the vulnerability in them. "Nice of you to make allowances for my lack of experience."

She wasn't referring only to sun exposure. Maybe if she were more practiced, more skilled, better in bed, Iestyn would actually care whether or not they ever had sex again.

Or maybe, she thought drearily, she wouldn't care so much.

Either way, the bite in her voice only made him grin. He returned his attention to the road.

He was so attuned to her physically. So capable of supplying what she needed in the present moment. So absolutely clueless that she was in danger of falling in love with him.

Frustrated, she stared at the passing landscape, low bridges and highway signs, long green medians and endless guard rails. Hamden. Hartford. Worcester.

If she weren't such a coward, she would confront him with her feelings. But that could place them both in an untenable position. More was at stake here than her bruised heart and pathetic pride. She had found him. She had helped him find himself, his true nature, and now she was bringing him home. He *needed* her. She truly believed that.

She blinked fiercely. She had to believe it, or everything she'd risked up to this moment was for nothing.

But she wasn't like him. He lived in the moment, carefree, confident, so sure of himself, while she planned and she worried and she . . .

Slept.

* * *

She was sleeping. Good.

Iestyn figured Lara deserved a rest. She wasn't the type to take things easy. Even riding beside him in the passenger seat, she was revved. He could practically hear her mind turning over, her body coiled tight as an overwound spring.

She needed to learn to relax.

The tangle of traffic smoothed out after Boston. New Hampshire passed in a blur of lottery billboards and liquor warehouses set against a background of pines. In the sunlit fields, flocks of birds gathered and rose as if it were already fall.

As they approached the Maine border, the road curved in a gentle sweeping turn to the right. The thick green girders of a bridge arched against the blue sky and over a broad river. The scent of the tidal inlet rose and smacked him.

The smell of the sea.

His throat clenched. His soul soared. Against the basin of rock, the water shone, deep blue-green and impossibly clear.

Lara whimpered in her sleep. He glanced over. The shadow of the bridge flickered across her face.

Nightmares, he thought. No surprise, after the past twenty-four hours.

He wondered if last night had stirred some old, bad

memories to life. The thought twisted his gut. He'd been as gentle as he knew how to be. But despite her unfeigned physical response, she'd been quick to dismiss the possibility of a replay.

Because of demons, she said.

Or did she regret making love with him?

His jaw set. He couldn't send her back. He couldn't take her back. The girl was demon bait. Not safe with him, but definitely unsafe alone.

Another soft, distressed sound escaped her throat. Without thinking, he lifted a hand from the steering wheel and laid it on her knee. His kind only touched to fight or to mate, acts of passion. But Lara woke something deeper inside him, an urge to comfort, a need to protect. To possess.

Her eyes opened suddenly, brilliant gray.

Their gazes locked. A look burned between them, bright and clear as the sky arching overhead, powerful as the river rushing over the rocks below. Under the brim of her ball cap, her face flushed.

He looked away, unaccountably shaken, to focus on the road.

"I can't believe I fell asleep," she said huskily.

She needed a little rest after yesterday. After last night.

Flashback to her smooth bare legs, her bra-less breasts, her voice saying, *"I thought if I slept with you, we could both get some rest."*

He cleared his throat. "It's the adrenaline."

Her winged brows rose. "I thought adrenaline made you alert. Survival instinct. Fight or flight."

High in the sky, a black speck circled, joined by another and another. Crows, he thought. Or gulls, black against the sun.

"In the short term, yeah." He slid his hand from her

knee, gripping the steering wheel, following the narrowing, winding road away from the Interstate. "But sooner or later, your body crashes. You can't live tensed up all the time."

"Unless being aware of the danger is what keeps you alive."

His attention sharpened. He glanced over at her again. "Are you picking up on something? Some demon thing?"

She moved her shoulders restively. "No. Not exactly."

The back of his neck prickled. "No? Or not exactly?"

She shook her head. "Sorry. It's just a . . . feeling. Not very useful," she added apologetically.

She didn't give herself enough credit. He wanted to chase the frustration from her face, the shadows from her eyes. "A hollow feeling?"

"Not really. More like a—"

He rolled over her. "Because you're probably just hungry."

Her gaze narrowed. "Hungry."

The edge in her voice made him grin. She'd be okay now.

"We've been on the road over five hours," he pointed out. "We need to refuel."

The coastal road was strung with small, bright settlements like lobster buoys in the water. On the outskirts of the next town, he spotted a sign. SHERMAN'S CLAM SHACK. HOME OF THE 24 HOUR BKFST. He pulled into the narrow parking lot that wrapped around the side, out of sight behind an eighteen-wheeler.

A line of crows perched along the low-pitched roof. He tugged on the door, making the bell inside jangle. One of the birds launched noisily into the air.

Lara shivered as she slid past him. What had she said? *"If I go back now, I'll be cleaning birdcages the rest of my life . . ."*

The smell of grilled onions and fried clams, maple

syrup and strong coffee, met them at the door. The walls were paneled, the counters faded yellow linoleum, the floor worn past recognition. A small TV flickered beside the pie case, its volume turned low enough to blend with the hiss of the fryer.

Three men hunched at the counter, an older guy with grizzled brown hair under a red bandanna, a stocky guy with weary eyes in a weathered face, a younger one, muscled, confident, with tattoos poking from beneath his flannel shirt.

All three turned their heads as Lara walked in. Appreciative. Assessing.

Iestyn put a hand at the small of her back, sending a clear signal. *Mine.*

The young guy continued to stare until Stocky gave him a nudge.

Iestyn steered Lara to a booth between an elderly couple and a family—father, mother, toddler, kid—occupying a table of dirty plates and wadded-up napkins.

Iestyn sat Lara with her back to the counter, slid in where he could watch the door. Lara craned to look over her shoulder.

"Babe," he said mildly. "Take a menu."

"I want to see his tattoo."

He shot a glance behind her at the young guy, who was back to watching Lara with narrowed, intense eyes.

"I'm sure he'd be happy to show you all his tattoos. But then he might want to inspect yours."

"I don't have any . . . Oh." She flushed and twisted back around.

Too late.

Young Guy started forward and was blocked by Stocky.

Shit. No time to retreat. No room to react. Iestyn got to his feet as the grizzled man in the bandanna approached their table, uncomfortably aware of the kids in the next booth, the mother dipping her napkin in her water glass to wipe the toddler's hands and mouth.

"Haven't seen you in here before," Bandanna Man said.

And you never will again, Iestyn thought.

"Just passing through," he said easily.

"What do you want?"

Lara opened her mouth.

"Short stack, two eggs over easy, and coffee," Iestyn said quickly before she could speak. "Milk, no sugar."

"What?"

He sighed. "We're not looking for trouble. Just breakfast."

He could see the waitress, a wide woman with a shock of peachy curls, waiting with her pad by the coffeepots, as obviously deadened to disputes as she was to peeling linoleum or the crumbs the kid in the next booth was grinding into the floor.

Bandanna Man shifted his weight, clearly ill at ease. "You're not looking for . . ."

"No trouble," Iestyn repeated. "We just came in for something to eat."

The man jerked his chin in Lara's direction. "What about her?"

"She's with me," Iestyn said firmly, flatly. "Why don't you move on so this nice lady can take our order."

* * *

The man in the red bandanna loomed over their table, exuding menace and testosterone.

Lara tensed. Beneath the bacon and onions, something simmered. Not a smell. An absence of scent and warmth, of light and life. It pressed her chest like a lack of air, muffled her senses like a hood.

For a moment she could not breathe.

The family in the next booth collected themselves and left, the ten-year-old dragging his feet, the mother clutching the toddler in her arms.

Iestyn sat perfectly still, doing nothing, everything about him open and relaxed, his face, his voice, his posture. *Mr. No Problem.* Except she knew him well enough now to see the muscle ticking beside his mouth, to feel the coiled tension in his long, lean body.

Maybe the man in the red bandanna felt it, too. Because after three . . . four . . . five agonizing heartbeats, he turned away.

"Have some water," Iestyn said.

She blinked at him.

He pushed a sweating glass across the table. "Drink some damn water. You look ready to pass out."

His blunt command was easier to bear than sympathy would have been.

She drank and felt the muscles of her throat relax. "You're taking care of me again."

A corner of his mouth quirked up. "As much as you'll let me. What do you want?"

"Whatever you want," he'd said to her last night.

"What can I do for you this morning?"

Her face burned. She dropped her gaze to the straw lying on the table. Absently, she picked it up, rolling it between her fingers. "I just ask, and you'll give it to me?"

"If it's on the menu."

The waitress swept in to take her tip and their order.

When she had left, Lara said, "No, I meant . . . That's what you said last night. 'Whatever feels good to you.' "

Iestyn sipped his coffee, watching her over the rim. "So?"

"So." Her throat felt dry. "I just wondered how far you're

prepared to go to make me feel better. Or do I already know the answer?"

He set down his mug with a clunk. "You think last night was . . . what, a pity fuck? You think I got it up because you were there and I felt sorry for you?"

She shredded the straw's paper wrapper, unable to meet his eyes. "It occurred to me I didn't give you much choice."

"Christ. I was trying to be nice."

She twisted the shreds of paper into little pellets, dropping them into the butter dish. "Exactly."

"No. Not exactly. Not at all." He leaned forward, lowering his voice. "Look, last night you needed somebody. Last night, I wanted you. One doesn't have anything to do with the other."

Lara sat stiffly as the waitress returned with their food, pancakes, eggs, and bacon for him, English muffin and orange juice for her.

Her heart beat a little faster. *"Last night, I wanted you."*

Was it possible he was sincere?

"I didn't mean to insult you," she said when the woman had gone.

"You can't insult me," Iestyn said. "Hell, I've slept with women for less reason before. But give yourself a little credit."

"Credit for what? Throwing myself at you?"

"For putting yourself out there. For doing the right thing. For being smart and determined and loyal and brave. And hot," he added. "You are incredibly hot. *And* you let me have sex with you, which makes you perfect."

Her laughter gurgled out before she could stop it.

He grinned. Their eyes locked. A warm jolt of energy shot clear down to her toes and settled around her heart.

"Even when sex isn't on the menu, you're damn near perfect," he said softly.

She reached blindly for her English muffin, yearning and confused because he was still giving her what she wanted, telling her what she wanted to hear, and even though he was smiling, teasing with her, his eyes were deep and earnest, like he almost believed what he was saying, and for a moment—*oh, God*—he made her want to believe it, too.

He sat across from her, eating pancakes as calmly as if he hadn't just electrified her emotions and shorted her brain. She was dimly aware of stools scraping and people moving behind her. The bell over the door jangled.

She watched his hands on his knife and fork, a sailor's hands, lean and brown and strong, and remembered him touching her breasts with exquisite gentleness, gripping her hips to help her find her rhythm as they moved together. Her head swam. Her heart pounded in her chest as if she'd run a mile. She was stunned by her reaction, unnerved by her vulnerability.

If she was not careful, he could break her heart.

"You have butter."

Disconcerted, she stared at the ruins of the butter plate, decorated with paper confetti. "Sorry. Did you want some?"

His smile was warm and slow. "You have butter . . ." He angled his head, studying her face. "Here."

He reached a hand across the table. His thumb traced the corner of her mouth, lingering on her bottom lip. The pad of his thumb was rough and tasted pleasingly of salt. She sucked it into her mouth.

He inhaled sharply. His gaze darkened and dropped to the front of her T-shirt, where her nipples peaked against the soft cotton. "And there."

She glanced down, and yes, okay, there was a tiny crumb glistening with butter on the front of her shirt.

She looked up to meet his eyes, black as midnight,

brilliant as suns. The heat in them sucked all the oxygen from the room and left her light-headed.

"Want me to take care of that for you?" he offered, his voice husky.

Yes.

She was dry-mouthed, dizzy with excitement. "No."

Touch me.

He smiled again crookedly. "You keep looking at me like that, babe, we won't need to have sex to call in trouble."

Her hands tightened on her napkin. *Skies.* He was right. She tamped down the excitement rising in her blood, the arousal humming like static along her skin. She needed to think.

"I'm going out to the Jeep," she said. "To get a clean shirt."

"I'll go with you."

She shook her head decisively. She needed perspective. Distance. She couldn't think when he was near. "I'll be fine. I'll only be a minute."

He scanned the diner and then her face. Nodded slowly. "If that's what you want. I'll settle up."

She slid out of the booth, striding past the now-empty counter, her heart pounding as if she were running away.

Which, of course, she was.

She shoved open the door, disturbing the birds that had now settled onto the parking lot. She rounded the side of the building, passed the truck. A crow flapped from the Jeep's roll bar to the ground, cocking its head to watch her. Creepy thing.

But she had more on her mind than a bunch of stupid birds.

The bags were in back, behind the driver's seat. She sidled between the Jeep and the big eighteen-wheeler, shivering in the truck's shadow. An odd, stale quiet stole over her. Like walking into a dead zone, like being shut into a closet. Leaning into the open door of the Jeep, she snatched the plastic Walmart bag from the back. Turned.

Three men stepped from behind the truck to block her way. Flannel shirts. Red bandanna. Tattoos . . . The men from the diner.

Her senses, which had been numb and dumb, crackled back to life. Her heart thumped in panic.

Fight? Or flight?

* * *

"Everything all right?" the peach-haired waitress asked as she rang up their order.

"Fine," Iestyn assured her.

It was, wasn't it? Lara had just stepped outside a minute to fetch a shirt, to catch her breath, to set a little distance between them.

He didn't blame her. This thing—connection—between them spooked her. Spooked him, too. Not the sex. Sex came easy for him and his kind. But the intimacy.

He'd never been tangled up in a woman so fast. He'd liked her looks from the start, those clear gray eyes and the little frown between them, that fall of mink brown hair and the angle of her chin. But it was the whole messy package that appealed to him, her fascinating bundle of nerves, spine, and determination.

He frowned at the curling dollar bill taped over the register. He wanted her, sure. But for the first time with a woman, he wanted more. Her safety. Her happiness.

It made him antsy, knowing this time he couldn't walk away without leaving a piece of himself behind. No wonder she needed a minute to herself.

She sure was taking her own sweet time, though.

He threw another glance at the door. The windows were too high, too narrow to see out.

Too much time. Where the hell was she? His neck crawled. Thrusting money at the waitress, he headed for the door.

"Wait! Your change."

The crows in the parking lot yammered like gulls.

"Keep it," he said, and broke into a run.

* * *

Black birds ringed the parking lot like spectators at a boxing match. Or vultures.

Iestyn's heart jack-hammered. The three men from the diner had Lara trapped between a big rig and the Jeep.

At least this time none of her attackers was possessed by a demon.

That he knew of.

A chill chased over his skin. Briefly, he met Lara's gaze, blazing in her pale face. "Get inside."

She opened her mouth to argue before she figured out his order was for the benefit of their audience. Pressing her lips together, she took two jerky steps toward him.

Tattoos took the toothpick from his mouth and pitched it to the ground. "I say she stays."

"Let her go," Iestyn said evenly.

The stocky man with the weary eyes met his gaze. "Or what? You'll call the cops?"

Duck into the diner, leaving her alone? Risk having the cops run a make on their stolen Jeep?

"We don't want trouble," Iestyn said again.

Tattoos laughed.

The man in the red bandanna crossed his arms over his chest. "Then call off your spies."

Spies?

"I don't know what you're talking about," Iestyn said.

"Call 'em off, or your girlfriend's going back to Heaven ahead of schedule."

But Lara was easing between the Jeep and the truck, retreating toward the diner, securing herself space and a wall at her back. *Smart girl.*

Iestyn started circling with Bandanna Man and the stocky guy, hoping to buy time to let her get away, get inside, trying to keep one eye on Lara and the other on his new dance partners, watching their hands, watching their eyes. Hoping nobody had a knife or, Jesus, a gun.

Tattoos realized Lara was slipping away and made a grab for her. The flock of birds burst from the ground, a feathered explosion of black wings and raucous cries.

Lara dropped out of sight behind the Jeep.

Fuck.

Bandanna Man swung. Iestyn grabbed his arm, blocking his punch, spinning him into the back panel of the truck. Metal shook and clanged. Iestyn muscled in, but the second man jumped him from behind, driving a fist into his kidneys. Pain erupted. Pain and rage. Bandanna staggered around, pushing off the truck, and the two men converged on Iestyn in a blur of knuckles, boots, sweat.

The world swam in a red haze of hate and fire. He jammed his knee up into a groin—grunt, *good*—jabbed his fist into a gut. Bandanna folded, but the other guy kicked Iestyn from behind, hard in the back of his knees. Instant collapse. They went down in a tangle of arms and legs, stocky guy on top. The blacktop scraped Iestyn's back as meaty hands dug for his throat.

The heth blazed. Burned.

Stocky Guy froze, his face twisted in surprise.

Iestyn heard fabric rip, heard Lara cry out, and a bubbling gush of fire and fury surged through his veins, washed his brain. Power, fierce and unfamiliar, filled him. Possessed him. He bucked, throwing off his assailant, rolling with him over the hard ground.

A voice—not his voice—hissed in the back of his mind. *Die, son of air.*

Rage flooded him. Hate consumed him. He pinned the son of a bitch to the ground, straddled the struggling body on his knees. Leaning his weight on his forearm, crushing the man's throat, Iestyn reached with his free hand for his knife.

"Iestyn! *No.*" Lara's voice, ringing in his ears.

He tugged the blade free.

"Stop!" Lara's touch on his shoulder.

He growled and shook her off.

"Iestyn, please!"

Her voice, clear, calm, insistent, reached through the blaze of pain and rage crackling inside his head.

He eased slightly on his enemy's windpipe, feeling the flood of hate ebb. The man gurgled, his chest heaving as he dragged in precious air.

Iestyn tightened his grip on his knife.

"It's all right." Lara's small hands alternately tugged and patted his arm. "Let him up. They're flyers."

15

IESTYN'S HEAD WAS RAGING, HIS LIMBS ON FIRE. Lara's voice trickled in his ears like water, abating the fury that infected his blood.

He didn't understand her words, but he trusted that voice. Trusted her. Only her.

He turned his head so her hair brushed his cheek. She stooped over him, her dark hair falling around them, her gray eyes wide and anxious. He inhaled her scent, creamy sweet as lilies at night.

Lara.

Unbloodied.

Unhurt.

His gaze shot behind her to her attacker, standing back beside the man in the red bandanna, their hands uncurled and empty at their sides. The younger man's shirt was ripped at neck and shoulder, exposing his tattoos. *Lara's doing?*

The tightness in Iestyn's chest relaxed a notch.

"Come on." Her smile encouraged him. "Stand up."

He didn't stand. Couldn't. But he sat back on his heels, clutching the knife, adrenaline and something unnamed, foreign, still burning in his blood.

Lara gestured to the men behind her, performing introductions like a nice child at a party. "These are Fremont and Max, flyers out of . . . Where did you say you were from?"

The man in the bandanna, Fremont, wiped blood from his mouth, casting a wary look at the roofline. Crows perched in a solemn black line against the sky, like priests at an execution. "We didn't say."

Awkward pause.

Lara cleared her throat. "And the man you're sitting on is Soldier."

The young guy rubbed the tattoo on his neck and then the bruise rising on his jaw. Iestyn observed his battered face with satisfaction. Too bad Lara hadn't broken his neck.

"Where are you from?" the young man asked.

"Rockhaven," Laura said.

A grunt from the ground. "I thought I recognized the work."

Iestyn blinked down at the man he'd been trying to kill a minute ago. His ears rang. His hands trembled. He shook his head slightly, to clear it. "What . . . work?"

The man called Soldier pulled on the neck of his T-shirt, exposing a white scar circling his throat and a square purple burn mark just under his collarbone. "The glass. I wore a heth once. Took me by surprise, seeing one on you." His smile was sharp as glass. "Or you wouldn't have thrown me."

Iestyn's simmering rage flared, quick and hot. "Don't bet on it."

Lara touched his shoulder, in warning. Reassurance. "Soldier saw the birds and thought we were Guardians sent to bring them in. But now that we know we're in the same boat—"

"How do we know?" Iestyn interrupted. "We don't know anything about them."

"You've seen Soldier's neck. And Max wears the runes," Lara said. "I saw them when I, um . . ."

"Kicked me in the head and tore my shirt," Tattoos said dryly. He grinned, which made him look even younger and much more handsome. *Cocky son of a bitch.*

The young man turned his head, revealing the blue quartered circle inked into his neck. "The tet for luck." He pushed up his right sleeve. "The taw for protection." He rolled back his left, where a simple circle adorned his inner wrist. "The ayin for sight."

"Fat lot of good that did us," Fremont muttered. "You thought they were demons."

Max flushed. "I said they could be. There is a taint."

"It's this one," Soldier said. "He's not one of us."

"He's selkie," Lara said. "One of the children of the sea."

"Where's his sealskin, then?" Fremont asked.

Irritation ignited in Iestyn, running along his veins like a match set to paper. They knew him. They knew what he was. But they were talking about him as if he were deaf or stupid. As if he wasn't there.

"Lost," he growled.

Soldier met his gaze. Held it. The flyer's eyes were faded blue, like worn denim. "Convenient."

"Not for him," Lara snapped.

Her quick defense delighted him. Her hand still rested on his shoulder, her little finger barely brushing the back of his neck above the collar of his shirt, that small touch of skin to skin soothing and inflaming him.

"We're trying to find his people," she continued, "so they can help him."

"Going to World's End, are you?" Fremont asked.

Iestyn went very still. His pulse pounded in his head like the sea. World's End.

Lara's fingers dug into his shoulder. "Where?"

"The island. That's where you fish folk hang out, isn't it?"

"How do you know?" Iestyn forced the words from his raw throat.

"Because we stay the hell away, that's why. We've got enough trouble. We don't need to borrow any more."

Iestyn's head felt stuffed with cotton, his thoughts hazy, his mouth dry. "What kind of trouble?"

Soldier's eyes narrowed in suspicion. "I thought you were one of them."

"I've been . . . away. Demon trouble?" he persisted.

"Maybe. What do you care? I thought your lot didn't take sides." Resentment simmered in Soldier's voice.

Iestyn shrugged. "Things change."

He'd changed. The balance of power was shifting, sliding. Anything—everything—could have changed in seven years.

The thought seeped like ice through his veins, cooling the fire that seethed inside him.

"Can you help us?" Lara asked.

The three men exchanged glances.

"No," Fremont said.

"Why not?" Iestyn demanded.

Soldier ignored him, speaking to Lara. "Well, for starters, he's still crushing my ribs."

Lara's full, soft lips flattened in irritation. *With which one of them*? Iestyn wondered.

"Iestyn, get off," she ordered.

Reluctantly, he complied, offering a hand to the man on the ground.

Soldier brushed him aside, climbing unaided to his feet. "I don't need your help."

"Fine. I don't need yours either." Iestyn drew a ragged breath, holding on to his temper with an effort. "But she does."

Lara's brows snapped together.

"What kind of help are we talking about?" Fremont asked before she could speak.

Iestyn's head throbbed. *Everything could have changed in seven years.* He had no right to drag her with him into whatever trouble awaited on World's End.

"Your protection," he said.

Max's face split in a grin. "Absolutely."

"Absolutely not," Lara said. She rounded on Iestyn. "What are you thinking? You need me to find your people."

His people. Assuming he was even merfolk anymore. Assuming they would take him back, take him in, without his pelt.

"Not anymore." He hooked his thumbs in his front pockets and turned to Fremont. "Where is this World's End?"

"About three hours north by road, another hour or so on the boat. You can take the ferry from Port Clyde."

"Thanks."

"I'm not leaving you," Lara said.

She couldn't depend on him. He must not depend on her. He steeled his heart against the look in her eyes. "You belong with them."

"I'm not a flyer," she said flatly.

Another silence.

"Then they'll take you back," he said. "To Rockhaven, if that's what you want."

To fucking Axton, he thought. His jaw clenched. *Stupid.* It's not like he could offer her another option. Selkie or sailor, he didn't have the kind of life he could share with a woman.

Fremont scratched under his bandanna. "Now, hold on. We didn't agree to anything yet."

"You don't want to go back there," Soldier said.

"There are other communities," Max said unexpectedly. "Other schools."

Iestyn felt a quick clutch in the pit of his stomach. But it was the option he'd wanted for her, wasn't it? Freedom and a future away from the stifling walls of Rockhaven. He looked at Lara. "Is that true?"

She nodded slowly, her eyes dark with doubt. "I've heard of them. Amherst in England, Amarna in Egypt. But . . ."

"You'd be safe there," he persisted. "Right? With other nephilim."

"If they'll take her in," Soldier said.

"If anybody will take her," Fremont said. "Travel's risky."

Lara regarded him with disdain. "Don't worry. I wouldn't go with you to the end of the parking lot, let alone out of the country."

The knot in Iestyn's gut loosened. Like it made a difference whether she was three hundred or three thousand miles from here. Either way, he'd never see her again. "It will have to be Rockhaven, then."

"I don't like it," Soldier said. "It could be a trap. A trick, to get us to the school."

"Don't be paranoid," Lara said.

Exasperation clawed Iestyn. He was trying to protect her, damn it. Trying to do the right thing. Why couldn't she shut up and go along?

But he knew. She'd told him last night. *"I'm getting pretty tired of other people deciding what's best for me."*

He made an effort to soften his voice. "You'll be safe with them. Safer than with me."

Her brows lifted. "Will I?"

Wouldn't she?

What did he know about them, after all? They were flyers, drifters, outlaws. He had too much in common with them to trust them. They didn't care about her the way he did. He was willing to fight for her. To die for her, if need be.

But not to stay.

Sooner or later, Lara would go back to her old life, and he would get on with his.

Such as it was. The thought chilled him.

If she'd just go, leave now, it would save both of them time and heartache.

"Safer than on your own," he amended.

Something flashed behind her eyes before they cooled. "You're not responsible for my safety. Or my choices."

"I'm not waiting around with my thumb up my ass while you two make up your minds," Fremont said.

Lara shot him another of those cool gray looks. "So, leave. We're not stopping you."

He wagged a meaty finger at her. "Now, little girl, you can't come with us if you won't be nice."

Her face turned sheet white. "I'm not your little girl," she said through her teeth. "And I'm sick of being nice."

She looked at Iestyn, her chin lifted in challenge. But it was her mouth that got him, soft and vulnerable. "Whatever I want, you said. What if I want to stay with you?"

His blood pounded. The question rippled through him like the echo of a dream, resurrecting memories and images of last night. Lara, sliding into bed beside him. Lara, holding him close as he dreamed. Lara, rocking above him in the dark, her hair like glory and her eyes like stars.

He met those eyes, and he was lost.

Maybe he'd been lost from the moment she'd found him. Pretty Lara Rho with her composed face and snug skirt, striding down the sun-bleached dock and into his life.

He didn't need her.

But damn him to Hell, he didn't want her to go. He couldn't lose her. Not now.

Maybe not ever.

The thought should have terrified him.

He bared his teeth in a grin. "Then I guess I'm stuck with you."

* * *

Lara smiled back, relieved and triumphant. "As long as you realize it."

Iestyn's grin sharpened.

She felt a quick quiver of caution. What was she doing, dismissing the chance to return safely home? What would she do when this adventure was over, when Iestyn was gone?

But she silenced the whisper of doubt. She was not a victim or a child. She would figure it out. In the meantime, he wanted her with him.

At least for now.

Fremont shuffled his feet. "Guess you'll be leaving us, then."

"Not yet," Lara said.

Iestyn shot her a quick look. "You want to change your shirt?"

"No, I—"

"You need to hit the road now," Fremont said. "We can't leave until you're gone."

"Why?" Lara asked.

"Trackers," Fremont said.

Iestyn glanced at the roofline. “The birds?”

“Guardian spies,” Soldier said.

“We’ve only got your word for it that they’re not after us,” Fremont said. “I want to watch them follow you out of here.”

“We need something from you first,” Lara said.

The youngest flyer, Max, gave her a tomcat grin. “Name it.”

Iestyn stiffened beside her. But she was too focused on his future to worry about his feelings right now. She turned to Soldier. “You wore a heth once, you said.”

The flyer eyed her warily. “So?”

“How did you remove it?”

He shook his head. “You don’t want to mess with that. You could get hurt.”

Her gaze dropped to the puckered scar around his throat. “That’s why I need you to tell me how to do it. I don’t want to cause him any pain.”

Soldier snorted. “It’s not him you should worry about. You want to be careful, girl. He’s not like us. Once that heth’s off, there’s no telling what he’ll do.”

“I’m not an animal. I don’t need a fucking collar,” Iestyn said.

Soldier’s weary blue eyes met his. “That’s a matter of opinion.”

Iestyn’s muscles bunched. She squeezed his arm, willing him to keep quiet.

“Please,” she said to Soldier. “Tell us, and we’ll go.”

He held her gaze a moment and then shrugged. “It’s your funeral. You can’t cut the cord without breaking the charm first.”

“Break it, how?”

“Any way you can. Shatter it. Melt it.”

“While it’s on my neck,” Iestyn said.

Soldier rubbed his scar. “I didn’t say it would be easy,

only that it could be done. If you have the strength and the stomach for it."

"If you have the balls," Max said. He looked at Lara. "You could still change your mind, sweetheart. Come with us."

"Fuck you," Iestyn said. He looked down at her, his eyes molten gold. "We're leaving. Now. Together."

She blinked at his sudden about-face. She almost didn't recognize this hot-eyed, cold-voiced stranger. But she trusted him. "Fine."

Taking her hand, he towed her to the Jeep. If the vehicle had had a door, she thought, he would have slammed it. The engine choked to life.

Iestyn backed out of the parking space, narrowly avoiding the three flyers behind the truck. His face set in grim lines as the Jeep lurched onto the road, picking up speed.

Lara twisted in her seat, pushing her hair from her eyes. The sky was crossed with phone and utility lines, but between them she could see black specks like flies in a spider's web. Misgiving snaked down her spine. "They're following us."

"Not for long."

"I meant the birds."

He flashed her a look. "So did I."

The Jeep tore up the old coast road, changing lanes, weaving in and out of traffic. Motels, restaurants, outlet stores streaked by. The wind whipped Lara's face and rattled the bags in back. She bit her lip, one eye on the quivering needle of the speedometer. The last thing they needed was to be picked up for speeding in a stolen Jeep.

The buildings thinned.

"Hang on," Iestyn said.

He veered hard onto a wooded side road past split rail fences and straggling stone walls, rutted driveways and rusting mailboxes.

Another sharp turn. Lara clutched the roll bar as Iestyn drove the Jeep over a ditch and under the trees, crashing, bumping, bouncing through the brush, light and shadow dancing crazily overhead. Her knuckles turned white.

The Jeep lurched and jolted to a stop deep under the cover of a broad, black pine. He turned off the engine. In the sudden silence she could hear the rasp of his breathing and the beating of her own heart.

The scent of spruce wrapped around them.

Iestyn turned his head. In the tree's shadow, his eyes gleamed like the eyes of an animal, unreadable and intent. "Come here."

Tension thickened the air like the smell of broken bracken.

Lara licked her lips. His gaze dropped to her mouth. "What about the birds?"

"They'll follow the road."

"And the demons?"

"What about them?"

She blinked. "They could be . . ." *Here?* A trace like burning leaves at the back of her palate. A hint of something decaying on the forest floor.

"Miles away," he finished for her.

The sun slanted through the branches of the pine, sculpting his body in sunlight and deep blue shadow. He stretched one arm along the back of his seat, sinewy, graceful. Denim pulled taut over his hard thighs and his hard . . . Well.

Her cheeks flushed. Her heart pounded.

The bruises on his face, the hint of beard roughening his jaw, made him look disreputable. Dangerous. But it wasn't terror that scrambled her pulse.

Cupping the back of her head, he pulled her slowly toward him. His breath seared her lips. His mouth hovered, just out of reach. She made a small, impatient sound deep in her throat, and he kissed her. Not roughly, with none of the suppressed violence that had quivered in him since the parking lot. But slowly, thoroughly, taking possession of her mouth, using his tongue and his teeth. Blinded, she closed her eyes.

His left hand covered her breast. "Your heart is racing," he whispered against her lips.

He filled her head like a day at the beach, hot, salty, golden. "Adrenaline," she managed to say.

He twined his fingers in her hair. "Fight? Or flight?"

The tug on her scalp, the pull on her senses, rippled along her nerves. She didn't want to fight him. "Are you giving me a choice?" she asked, half-seriously.

"You always have the choice."

She attempted a smile. "Not if you're holding my hair."

He twined it around his fist. "Maybe I'm afraid you'll run away."

Was he kidding? She'd just dismissed her last, best chance to go home. Every mile, every decision, separated her more irrevocably from everything and everyone she knew at Rockhaven.

"I'm not the one who's leaving," she said.

"What does that mean?"

Let it go, she told herself.

But of course she didn't. "You're the one on your way to World's End."

"That was your idea."

"Because you need to find your people."

"I'm not like you. I don't need others of my kind to survive."

"It's more than a matter of survival." She struggled to explain the precepts she had lived with for the past thirteen years. The nephilim spent their entire earthly existence aspiring to the perfection that had been theirs before the

Fall. "Only your own kind can see you as you really are. Without their vision, how can you become your best self? The self the Creator intends you to be."

His golden eyes were unreadable. "And you think your masters at Rockhaven see you as your best self."

She opened her mouth. Closed it again. "At least they know me there."

"Well, they don't know me on World's End."

She realized with a shock of sympathy that she wasn't the only one venturing into the unknown on this journey. She had admired Iestyn's confidence, envied his ability to go with the flow. But really, he was as cut-off, as alone in this, as she. More so, because of the seven years he had lived without sight or memory of his own kind.

"Someone there will know you," she reassured him. "This Lucy Hunter. You must have friends who survived. Family."

"I have no family."

She knew nothing of the merfolk's social structure. But he was an elemental, one of the First Creation. "You were born on the foam?" she asked.

"No, I am blood born. My mother is—was—selkie."

Her heart squeezed. "Did she . . . die in the attack?"

Iestyn shrugged. "I do not know."

"I'm so sorry."

"I should have said, I do not know her. She did not want me. I was conceived in human form, so all the time she carried me she could not go to sea. She gave me to my father as soon as a nurse could be found. I do not remember her, and I doubt that she remembers me."

Lara bristled on his behalf. How could a mother not love her child?

But of course it happened. She herself had Fallen trying to save one of those unloved, unwanted children.

"At least you knew your father wanted you," she said.

"My mother paid him to take me. And Prince Conn paid him to give me up. Most children of the sea are fostered in human households until they near the age of Change," he explained. "My father was sorry to lose me just as I grew big enough to help around the farm, but the prince gave him enough gold to hire many men."

As he spoke of his childhood, his speech thickened and slowed. He had a faint burr. Scottish? Welsh?

"Your father was human," Lara said slowly, testing the idea.

Iestyn nodded. "Prince Conn told me my father had finfolk blood, but that could have been because of my eyes. The color," he explained. "I have finfolk eyes."

"You have beautiful eyes," she said.

He smiled faintly. "Fish eyes."

"Who told you that?"

He shrugged.

She frowned. "Is that why your mother didn't want you? Because your father wasn't selkie?"

"I doubt she gave my sire a thought once he rolled off her." He met her shocked gaze and smiled faintly. "The children of the sea don't do commitment."

A chill brushed her. "They don't marry? Ever?"

"We take mates," he offered. "But even among humans, how many couples are together after five years? Or fifty? What kind of relationship could last five hundred?"

No stabilizing influence in his life, she realized with a trickle of cold. No lasting relationships. This was what Simon had warned her about. Iestyn was a child of the sea, restless, rootless, his loyalties and affections as transient as the tides.

She swallowed. "So you went from your father's farm to . . ."

"Sanctuary. Conn collected us, all the fosterlings, and sheltered us until we could take our proper place and form in the sea."

She had a flash, a vision, of round towers and green hills and cliffs rising above the sea, of a great empty hall and a smoldering red fire. "Like Rockhaven. A school."

"A castle."

She raised her eyebrows. "Very romantic."

"It was bloody cold," Iestyn said. "We slept with the dogs. And ran as wild."

She frowned. "But who took care of you?"

"Everyone. No one. It wasn't a . . . tame childhood."

For some reason, she remembered the tawny raptor on Moon's arm, watching her with wicked, golden eyes.

Lara suppressed a shiver, asking lightly, "The Lost Boys in Neverland?"

"More like *Lord of the Flies*." Iestyn met her surprised look and grinned. "I do read. Plenty of time for that at sea."

"So you must have had a teacher."

"Eventually. Miss March." He smiled as if the memory was a pleasant one.

"Maybe you'll see her again," Lara offered. "The flyers said there were merfolk on World's End. Maybe she survived."

"No. She was human. She died almost sixty years ago."

Lara jolted. "I forget that you're immortal."

"*Was* immortal," he corrected her deliberately. "Before I lost my sealskin. I'm demon bait now."

Their eyes met.

Her lungs emptied. "Because of me."

Iestyn shook his head. "I'm alive because of you. But we could die tonight. Tomorrow, we might never see each other again. I can't promise you a future. I can't promise you anything."

We could die . . .

Her heart thumped. "Then give me now."

He watched her with slitted golden eyes. "Is that enough for you?"

Yes.

No.

"If that's all I can have."

"Lara." His tone was unusually serious. "I don't want to hurt you."

"You will." She steeled herself to accept it. "You can't help yourself."

Frustration darkened his face. "What do you want me to say? Tell me what you want."

Tenderness and impatience tangled within her.

This wasn't about her. Not only about her, not anymore. This journey they were on together was taking her farther and farther from the person she had been. But she would not beg. And she would not take the next step alone.

She turned his question back on him. "What do *you* want?"

"You," he answered simply. "I feel like I've spent my whole life waiting for you."

Her eyes blurred. As easily as that, he restored her confidence and destroyed her defenses.

She smiled at him through the mist. "Then take me."

16

IESTYN'S BLOOD DRUMMED IN HIS EARS LIKE A roaring wind, like the crashing sea.

Lara should have left him when she had the chance. Instead, she was putting herself in his hands. Literally. What the hell was she thinking?

"Take me."

Heat surged in his veins. A cold sweat trickled down his spine.

For seven years, he'd drifted, a nobody answerable to no one, responsible for no one but himself. Because of Lara, he knew who he was. What he had been. Her choices had gotten them this far.

But they had left her world behind. With every mile, they traveled closer to his.

Where they went from here was up to him. She was his responsibility now. Her safety, her satisfaction, depended on him.

He looked into her misty gray eyes and his vision contracted suddenly as if he were sighting the stars through a sextant, plotting his course by her light. All he could see was Lara.

He was no angel. Maybe he would never be what she needed. But in one area, at least, he could give her what she wanted.

Sex was part of his world. He could take responsibility for sex without any problem at all.

"Not here," he said.

Her shining eyes dimmed slightly—*with disappointment*?—before she nodded, once more in control of herself and the situation.

"You want to wait," she said, which was a reasonable assumption. The only reasonable course of action.

But maybe she'd had enough of being reasonable at that school of hers. Maybe she was tired of playing it safe, playing by the rules. Maybe she was sick of being in control. Last night he'd let her make the choice, make her move, set the pace, take the lead.

Today they'd try sex his way.

"No," he said.

"We *need* to wait," she amended.

"If a tree falls in a forest and no one's around to hear, does it make a sound?"

She frowned. "Is that a joke?"

He grinned, tickled by her prim tone. "Nobody's around to see us. Nobody can hear. We can do whatever we want."

"Not without attracting attention. The energy released when we make love—"

"How long did it take the demons to track us the last time?" he interrupted.

Her gaze met his. "Hours."

"So we'll be miles away by then." He jumped from his seat and walked around the hood of the Jeep, stripping off his shirt on the way. She watched him, her eyes huge. With doubt . . . or arousal?

Smiling, he held out his hand.

Her throat rippled as she swallowed.

"Do you trust me?" he asked softly.

"Yes," she answered without hesitation.

He waited, hand extended.

She bit her lip. Lacing her fingers with his, she let him help her from the car.

His lower belly tightened. *Progress.*

He used their clasped hands to tug her closer. The branches of the spruce formed a scented tent over and around them, the needles a dense carpet underfoot. Cupping her jaw, he laid his mouth on hers, kissing her with slow, moist deliberation until her lips parted and clung, until she slipped her tongue into his mouth and made him dizzy, kissing him back, tilting her hips in silent urging.

For a second—okay, a couple of seconds—he considered giving her what she thought she wanted, pictured her with her legs around his waist and his hands on her ass and his cock buried deep inside her.

But he could do more than she could imagine. She deserved better. He wanted to show her something else, take her someplace she wouldn't go on her own.

He stroked her lightly up and down, his hands just brushing the outside curve of her breasts. Her heart thudded against the hell of his palm.

"I want you," he said.

"Yes."

"Naked."

"Um . . ."

He slid her T-shirt up her narrow ribcage.

She crossed her arms. "We're outside."

"Under cover." He eased the hem up. "Anyway, I took off my shirt."

"It's not the same." But she lifted her arms to help him.

"That's what makes it fun." He tugged the shirt over her head.

Her breath caught. So did his. He stopped with her arms still trapped in her shirt so he could stare. With her arms pulled back, her breasts thrust forward like a ripe, warm offering, small and firm with pale, pink crests. They beaded under his gaze.

"I don't have these." He touched one with his finger, making the pink tip contract.

One dark, winged brow rose. "Nipples?"

"Breasts. Beautiful breasts. Beautiful Lara."

Her skin was the color of cream. He lapped her like a cat, curling his tongue around her pretty peaks, sucking her into his mouth.

A flush spread over her chest. Her fingers winnowed through his hair, scratched lightly at his scalp, as his mouth tugged at her breasts.

"You taste so good," he murmured. He flicked open the top button of her jeans. The muscles of her warm, smooth stomach jumped. He thrust his hand into her waistband. "I want to lick you all over."

She trembled as he found what he was searching for, rough curls, hot, slick flesh. He withdrew his hand. Holding her gaze, he tasted his fingertips.

"Sweet Heaven." She shuddered and shut her eyes.

"Ssh." He soothed her, pulling her close, letting her feel how she affected him, assuring her without words that she wasn't in this alone. "Do you trust me?"

"I guess. Yes."

He spread his T-shirt onto the hood of the Jeep. Retrieved the condom from his jeans pocket. "I won't do anything you don't want me to do."

He pulled her back into his arms, her back to his chest, the hard ridge of his erection nestled against her sweet rump, her arms still trapped between them. She sighed and leaned her head against his shoulder. Her soft exhalation stabbed his heart. He pressed a kiss to her temple before stripping her shirt from her arms so she wouldn't feel constrained in any way. With his arms around her, he slid down her zipper, the sound loud in the stillness. She sucked in her breath. But she didn't object as he worked pants and panties over the curve of her butt and down her long, smooth thighs. Keeping one hand on her hip for reassurance, he dealt with the condom. His belt buckle rattled as he shoved down his jeans.

And then he bent her over the warm metal hood of the Jeep and covered her from behind.

Lara jerked like a startled pony. "Iestyn."

God, she felt good, warm and good against him. His heart thundered. He kissed her ear. "Do you trust me?"

"Ye-es. But . . ."

"Let me show you." He nuzzled her shoulder. Her skin was like velvet. "Let me take you where you want to go."

Her breathing quickened. He concentrated on that, on the subtle signals of her body as he fit himself over her, as he slid a hand under her, holding her steady for his intrusion. He nudged between her thighs and she rose on tiptoe, angling her hips to receive him. *Oh, baby.* He almost lost his breath. His mind. She was already wet, ripe, ready.

Fisting his cock, he stroked her slowly up and down, working himself into her, just a little. Just enough.

Never enough.

"Is this what you want?"

She writhed and pushed back against him, telling him *yes* over and over, *yes*, in the arch of her back, *yes*, in her wet welcome, *yes*, in the tight, hot clasp of her body.

Yes, I want you.

Yes, I trust you.

Take me.

* * *

The world fell away. There was only this, only Iestyn, his hot, urgent voice in her ear, his hard, insistent body at her back, his knowing hands . . .

He covered her, animal, intimate, and intent, filling her. Stretching her.

Lara tightened in wicked anticipation, on edge with excitement. She had never felt like this before, never been like this, wanting, needy, naked, raw. His clever hands pressed with devastating accuracy right where she needed him most, and she made a choked sound in her throat and hitched against him, pushing back, the heat and the need coiling inside her.

Another stroke of his broad head against her sensitive flesh. "Is this what you want, Lara?"

Oh, God, she was melting, she was dying, she was burning up. She closed her eyes, unable to bear the sweet agony. "You know it is."

He made a low sound, approval or triumph. "Then take it," he said, and slammed his full length into her.

Dark suns exploded behind her closed lids. She cried out, her hands curled, her body clenched in pleasure. He eased from her, a slow, wet caress, and drove in again, jolting her against the hood of the Jeep.

Blindly, she tried to reach back, to touch him. Her fingers curled into his flanks. Bent forward, she was powerless to hurry or control him. She could only accept him, all of him, as he surged into her, his breathing ragged, imprinting her with his scent, his body, making her feel him in every muscle and nerve.

She absorbed the heavy, driving thrusts, taking him again and again. She wanted, *needed* . . . Surely it was impossible to want this much and survive. Her back arched. Her muscles constricted around him. His fingers bit into her as he plunged hard and deep, and she ground her teeth on his shirt and came and came, exploding under and around him, helpless to do anything but feel.

His hands clamped on her hips. She felt the deep, hard spasm of his body, the hot release of his breath against her nape as he shuddered and was still.

Quiet, except for the rasp of his breathing, the thud of her heart.

Slowly, she became aware of small, inconsequential things. The rustle of leaves. A crick in her back. The wetness between her thighs.

She sighed and opened her eyes. Sunlight slanted through the trees, illuminating the floating motes above the forest floor. She'd just had car sex, she thought wonderingly. Naked outdoor car sex with a selkie.

Bria would have been proud.

Iestyn withdrew from her body, the dragging friction setting off aftershocks in her sensitive flesh. She shivered. He dragged her up, tucking her head under his jaw, cradling her against his body. His chest was warm and damp.

She turned her face into his neck and closed her eyes. Should she say something? What could she say? Usually she was better with words than with feelings, but his assault on her senses, her own carnal craving, had left her speechless, sore, and unsettled.

And oddly free of regrets.

Iestyn raised his head and framed her face with his hands. "I was rough with you."

Sudden moisture sprang to her eyes. She could handle rough. His tenderness threatened to destroy her. "Are you apologizing?"

He watched her carefully. "Do I need to?"

"No, I liked it. It was nice." She winced at the woefully inadequate word. "Different."

The laughter sprang back into his eyes. "Different good or different bad?"

"Different for me," she clarified. "I'm not usually so . . ." *Shameless? Fearless?* "Physical."

"Different for me, too." He stroked her hair back from her face, tucking a strand behind her ear. His golden eyes were warm, searching. "You're different."

More than anything, she wanted to believe him. "I bet you say that to all the girls."

"Only you. Two lost souls," he murmured.

She swallowed the sudden lump in her throat. "We're not lost. Maybe we don't know exactly where we're going, but we're here now. Together. For the first time in my life, maybe that's enough."

* * *

Zayin's vision fractured. Splintered. The world below him broke like a shattered kaleidoscope, escaping its ordered patterns, the mosaic of field and forest, rock and road, fragmenting. Falling apart, as his spirit was falling apart, bright, broken slivers of his soul.

"Zayin."

His heart pounded, *a dozen hearts.* His wings flailed, *an explosion of wings.* He—*they*—tumbled down, down, in a bright avalanche of shards, piercing, blinding . . .

"Jude."

Pain burst in his skull, rocked his head, jerked him back into his heavy, human body. The ground spun and solidified under him.

He gasped, dragging air into his inefficient lungs, and felt the cold, hard floor beneath his shoulders, the weight of his bones. He opened his eyes.

Mews mistress Moon knelt over him, scowling, her long hippie hair hanging down around her face.

Jude blinked as shadow returned to his sight, obscuring his bright bird vision. "I lost them."

"I thought I was going to lose you." Moon rolled to her feet and went to the sink of the small keeper's room, leaving him lying on the cold linoleum floor. "Next time you decide to have an out-of-body experience, do it with your lady doctor in attendance."

He flexed his fingers, restoring flexibility to his hands and wrists. "You know I can't."

Miriam's unquestioning loyalty to Simon made it impossible for him to trust her completely. He was rarely vulnerable, even in sex. But spirit casting left him open. Weakened.

"You'll end up in the infirmary anyway," Moon said darkly. "Twelve crows, was it, this time? The spirit isn't meant to divide into that many pieces. You left me with hardly anything to call you back."

"You should be grateful for the excuse to hit me." He rubbed his jaw where the imprint of her hand still burned. "Anyway, I had a wide area to cover."

She turned, a glass of water in her hands. "Here."

He raised one eyebrow. "No cookies and orange juice?"

"Fuck off." But she supported him up with one arm behind his back, guiding the glass to his lips as he drank. "What did you see?"

"Flyers." He swallowed. "They thought I was spying on them."

"There's a shocker. What about our runaways?"

"Still headed north." He sifted through his scattered memories, picking through images and snatches of conversation from the parking lot, reconciling his human knowledge with the crows' perceptions. Dizzied, he closed his eyes. "World's End."

"Where's that?"

He opened his eyes. "Maine, I imagine."

Cautiously, he sat up. His spine popped and stretched. Birds' vertebrae were fused for flight. The return to his human body left him feeling heavy and unsupported.

"You'll go out again," Moon said. "After them."

"I must."

Simon wanted the girl. And Jude wanted Simon in his debt.

Moon's round face creased. "This boy . . ."

"Is irrelevant. He's an elemental. A *hostile* elemental," Jude added for emphasis.

"You see enemies everywhere."

He climbed painfully to his feet, leaning on a table for support. His head swam. "Because we have no allies."

"Heaven has no allies. We're on earth now. Maybe we should put more faith in those who have been here the longest, the fair folk and merfolk. God's creatures, Jude."

It was an old argument between them. One he'd given up on winning.

He glanced at her over his shoulder. "Simon thinks the boy is possessed."

Moon's blue eyes clouded. "And if he is?"

"It makes no difference. Unless he kills the girl. In which case, I will avenge her murder, and Simon can thank me for that."

Moon sniffed. "Sometimes I really don't like you very much."

"So you've said."

Their eyes met, dark with memories and—at least on his part—regret.

A faint flush rose in her cheeks. "You replaced me quickly enough."

"A lesson I learned from Simon."

She shot him a questioning look.

"Keep your friends close," Jude explained. "And your enemies closer."

"And you, of course, see enemies everywhere," Moon said again dryly.

He did not smile. "I don't fuck all of them."

"Such self-restraint."

He did not defend himself. In truth, he used sex the same way he used everything else.

The nephilim did have enemies. Everywhere. He did what he must to ensure their survival. He played a long game with high stakes against incredible odds. Lara Rho was just another card to turn to his advantage.

Assuming he could find her.

"I'm going to Maine," he said.

* * *

Iestyn had never sailed into Port Clyde before, but he recognized the sights and smells of a working harbor. Beyond the kayaks, tourist cars, and ice cream shops, the waterfront moved with the rhythm of the seasons and the tides.

By three o'clock, sturdy fishing boats ruffled the blue water, chugging in to offload their catch behind the general store. The air was rich with salt and fish, sharp with diesel oil.

He joined Lara, waiting in line to board the ferry between a couple of hikers and a little girl with a pink backpack. Something about Lara—the way she looked or the way she stood, the turn of her head or the pucker of her brows as she squinted into the sun behind him—lodged like a fishbone in his throat. His chest swelled. He couldn't speak. He could barely breathe.

"We're here now," she'd told him. *"Together. For the first time in my life, maybe that's enough."*

But what if it wasn't enough? he wondered with a sliver of panic. For her. For him.

She smiled at him, relaxed, expectant. "Did you find parking?"

He cleared his throat, rubbed at the burn itching beneath his collarbone. "A couple blocks over."

He'd left the Jeep behind a hardware store with the key in the ignition. In Newark, in Norfolk, in Montevideo, the vehicle would vanish within the hour. Even in Maine, he figured it would disappear eventually.

She raised her brows. "You know the ferry lot only charges five dollars a day."

"We don't know when we'll be back." *If I'll come back.* He pushed the thought away. Concentrate on the moment. Live in the moment. They crossed the metal ramp behind a woman dragging a shopping cart. "We can't leave the Jeep in the parking lot, pointing at the ferry like a bloody arrow," he said.

She nodded in comprehension. "Because of the crows."

"The crows and the cops." He lowered his voice. "They'll run the plates on an abandoned vehicle."

Lara's eyes widened. "I didn't think of that."

Of course not. His conscience winced. She was a rule follower, not a law breaker.

"I hope you got rid of the license plates," she said.

He grinned, his conscience relieved. What a miracle she was. "Tossed them in a Dumpster."

"Good." The approval in her tone, the trust in her eyes, caused that funny swelling in his chest again.

They found a place on the upper deck with the hikers and a cable repairman toting a plastic utility bucket.

The deck shuddered. Machinery groaned. Iestyn's pulse leaped as the ferry pushed into the waters of the harbor under the gleaming eye of the squat lighthouse, past boats tethered to round white mooring buoys. A curving line of jagged rocks like a broken jawbone slid away to starboard.

He inhaled, tasting salt, baring his teeth to the wind. Christ, it felt good to be on the water again. Too damn bad he was on this floating parking garage instead of under sail.

But even the stink of fuel and the engine's vibration couldn't diminish his pleasure. The sea was what he knew, where he belonged.

He glanced at Lara, standing beside him, her cheeks flushed, her eyes shining. A wandering sea breeze played with her hair.

With everything she'd been through these past two days, she still took his breath away. She had entrusted herself to him. Her body. Her safety. Her future.

Confusion caught him under the ribs, sharp as a cramp.

How could he ever leave her?

How could he ask her to stay?

17

THE WORLD SHIFTED UNDERFOOT AS THEY MOVED farther and farther from shore.

No turning back, Lara thought. Every step toward their destination severed her further from her old life and brought Iestyn nearer to his. And when he was gone . . .

But she couldn't let herself think about that. Those worries belonged to the future, and she was determined to stay in the here-and-now for as long as she could.

She watched him brace beside her at the rail, his strong legs set against the chop of the waves, the wind molding his shirt to the hard planes and muscled curves of his body. The stitches along his hairline were barely visible. In the slanting afternoon light, he burned like a seraph, his hair fired to sunlight, his skin like liquid gold.

A great wave of lust and longing seized her by the throat. She took a deep breath and held it until everything settled and was still again.

She would not regret this, she told herself fiercely. Whatever happened.

She could admire and enjoy him without possessing him. Like admiring a sunset or an eagle or anything wild and beautiful and beyond her grasp.

Iestyn turned his head, smiling down at her, the light in his eyes and on his hair, and her heart—her foolish, female, human heart—quite simply tumbled at his feet. He tucked her against him, her back to his chest, his jaw by her ear, and held her while time and the world slipped away.

Water churned under the prow. Lumps of land rose and fell from view. His heart thudded against her shoulder blades, her breathing slowed to match his breath, until it seemed they shared one heart, one breath, one flesh. She covered his hands where they linked around her waist, trying to hold on to him. Hold on to the moment.

Until the arms around her stiffened and his heart changed beat.

"Iestyn? Iestyn."

He didn't respond.

* * *

"Hold on!" Iestyn shouted, his heart hammering in his chest.

A wall of water reared on the horizon, gray and terrible as a ghost army, spears of debris held aloft by dirty crests. Foam spewed and flew as far as the eye could reach.

He tightened his grip on the ship's wheel, his palms burning. Sweating.

"We have to Change." Roth thrust the sealskin bundled in his arms at Iestyn. "Now."

The heavy pelt thumped to the deck. Iestyn's pelt. Every

instinct he possessed screamed at him to grab it and go, flee, dive. Abandon ship.

Madagh barked, barked, barked, the deep, frantic sound echoing Iestyn's own terror.

He swallowed the greasy panic in his stomach, prayed he wouldn't disgrace himself. "You go. The prince trusted me to see the boat to safety."

"Prince Conn would not ask you to die for his boat."

"His boat, no. Maybe his dog."

Kera stumbled over the rope Iestyn had used to tie himself to the mast. "Don't be stupid," she snapped. Her eyes glittered. With tears? But selkies did not cry.

Roth growled. "Not stupid. It wasn't his idea to turn around."

"He agreed. We all agreed. I thought we could help."

Kera was a talented weather worker. But her magic could not turn the demon tide. The wall of water thundered toward them under the sun-washed November sky.

The bow hit the first deep trough and pitched. Spray shot up on both sides. Madagh's claws scrabbled furiously for purchase on the wooden deck. Kera lunged for the rail as the ropes binding Iestyn dragged and held.

Chafed and burned.

The wrinkle on the horizon swelled. Another wave.

No, land. Another island rising from the slate blue sea.

Iestyn drew a shuddering breath, struggling to get his bearings.

Lara stirred in his arms, her slight weight anchoring him to the present. "World's End."

Journey's end.

He could not speak. His heart still pounded. His throat burned.

* * *

Iestyn's arms around her were ridged like ropes. His breath rasped.

Lara turned, her own heart quickening in sympathy, a drawn-out, distant roaring in her head like the approaching tide. "Another flashback?"

She should have expected it. Last night had triggered one, too. Iestyn's past was crashing in on him, his future rushing in on him like the wave in his dreams, inexorable, inescapable.

"Are you all right?" she asked.

He nodded, his pupils wide and unfocused.

"It's natural for you to be upset," she said gently. "You must feel like you're losing your cohort all over again."

His gaze narrowed on her face. "What?"

"Your friends." The sturdy boy, the sulky-mouthed girl in his dream. Lara kept talking, saying anything, really, determined to banish that black, blank look from his eyes. "I know when Bria left, I . . . What's wrong?"

"Nothing. I'm fine."

"Really? Because you look terrible." Sweat beaded his upper lip. Beneath his tan, his face was gray. "Maybe you should sit down."

"I'll be fine," he insisted, irritation roughening his voice.

She slid her arm around his waist. He resisted leaning his weight on her. But when she nudged him to the seat on deck, he lowered himself heavily onto the bench.

The cable repairman shifted over to make room. "What's the matter with him?"

Iestyn ignored him, closing his eyes, all his golden vitality drained away. His head dropped back, exposing the long, strong column of his throat. Just above the neckline of his shirt, his skin was red and inflamed.

She frowned. Redder than before?

Gently, she inserted two fingers under the edge of the fabric. Iestyn jerked from her touch, baring his teeth like an animal in pain.

Her heart wobbled. Shifting to block the cable guy's vision, she slowly, carefully peeled back the collar of Iestyn's T-shirt.

Her stomach lurched. Her vision blurred. She blinked to clear it. The skin around the heth puffed, fresh blisters bubbling on already raw flesh.

"I think he's had too much sun," she said to the cable guy. She moistened her lips. "Would you mind . . . Could you get us some water?"

"I don't need anything," Iestyn said.

"Water? Sure." The man pushed to his feet, leaving his bucket under the bench. His boots clanged on the metal stairs as he descended to the lower deck.

"How long has it been like this?" she asked Iestyn.

"Started . . . When the island came in sight."

Men. "Why didn't you tell me?"

He raised his lashes and looked at her. "Because I'm okay. I'm breathing, aren't I?"

Worry made her sharp. "Barely."

Incredibly, his dry lips twitched in a shadow of his customary smile. "Beats the alternative."

Yes, it did. But she didn't know what to do for him now. Forcing air into his lungs wouldn't relieve his pain.

"We need to take it off. The heth."

His lips tightened. "Not now. Your friend with the bucket will be back any minute."

She stared at him helplessly. She had to do something to relieve his pain. What would Miriam do? Or Simon?

Burns were common at Rockhaven. The factory workers called the process of blowing, pressing, and casting glass "taming fire." Jacob was always complaining of first-degree burns from pausing too long at the furnace or glory-hole, second-degree burns from handling hot glass. The first, best treatment was to plunge the burn in water.

Which she didn't have. She glanced at the ocean tumbling out of reach before she stooped and blew gently on Iestyn's inflamed skin.

"What are you doing?"

"Trying to help."

"I'm not a steak dinner, babe. You're not going to cool my meat by blowing on it."

She ignored his innuendo, focusing instead on the angry red swelling below his collarbone. "Do you have a better idea?"

"Yeah. Ignore it," he said.

"And it'll go away?"

Their eyes met, the memory of last night vibrating in the air between them, the feel of him in her hand, hot satin over stone.

"Eventually," he muttered.

But an idea had sparked. "There's a sign for water."

His brows drew together. "A sign."

She nodded. "A rune. Mem."

Like the letter M with an extra uptick at the beginning. She traced it in her mind, sort of a wave shape. Inside her, power squiggled, rising and falling with each line, a surge of possibility, a downstroke of intent.

What should be . . .

She touched a single fingertip to his throat. The contact

kindled a quiver low in her belly, a tingle in her fingers and her toes. Down and up and . . .

His hand, warm and strong, covered hers. She jumped.

"No spells," he said flatly. "No magic. I don't want the demons tracing us here."

Her heartbeat quickened. "Then we shouldn't have had sex."

Their gazes locked. Held.

A corner of his mouth curled. "That was worth it."

Warmth flooded her face. "So is this," she insisted. "So are you."

He looked unconvinced.

"Anyway, we're in the middle of the ocean," she said. "What are they going to do? Swim after us?"

All those years, the sea had protected him. Until she found him and brought the demons down on them both.

"At least let me try," she said.

Slowly, his grip on her hand relaxed. She breathed a sigh of relief.

What can be . . .

Water was not her element. But she traced the sign of it carefully on his skin, standing between his thighs, conscious of his blood pulsing below the surface, the ebb and flow of his breath. She imagined water, glasses and buckets and tubs full of water, quenching, cooling, soothing.

Iestyn's skin sizzled. Heat flared.

She gasped. But Iestyn reached up and covered her hand with his, pressing her fingers deep into his blistered skin. His thought swelled and supported hers. *Water.* Briny, cold, and clear, erupting from the rock to race rejoicing to the sea, bursting from the Creator's mind, the deep salt dark, moving, utterly free. *What must be.* Power flowed, his magic, hers, pouring out of her into his flesh.

He shuddered, a deep, hard spasm like orgasm, his grasp on her hand almost painful. The reverberations shivered from his body to hers, every tremble and quake echoed deep inside her, the aftershock of power like the release after sex.

Lara sagged.

Iestyn wrapped his arms around her, almost as if he were protecting her from something. For long moments, neither of them spoke. The ship engines rumbled. A seabird cried and plummeted into the water.

"That did it," Iestyn said finally, his voice muffled. His warm breath seared her breasts.

She eased away from him, far enough to see his face. "Do you feel any better?"

He laughed.

She caught herself grinning foolishly back at him. "You know what I mean."

"I'm good." He pulled down the collar of his shirt to show her the burn. Still red, but the frightening blisters had subsided. His gaze was steady on hers. "We're good. We're more together than we are apart."

Her heart thrummed. "It's magic."

"It's more than magic."

He cupped the back of her head and drew her down for his kiss. She trembled as their lips met, as his mouth nudged and searched and caressed hers. He kissed her as if he were inside her, as if he knew her, soul kisses, sweet, wet, consuming.

She pulled back, dazed.

He smiled into her eyes. "We're good together."

"For how much longer?" The words escaped before she could snatch them back.

So much for her determination to live in the here-and-now. Annoyed with him, with herself, she said, "Forget it. I shouldn't have asked."

He opened his mouth, but before he could say anything, she heard boots climbing the metal stairs. She sprang back. The cable repairman emerged from the lower deck, approaching them with a curious look and a bottle of water.

"Thank you so much," Lara said.

Iestyn dug for his wallet to repay him.

The cable guy tucked the money into his front shirt pocket. "Ferry's pulling in," he observed with a nod toward the approaching dock. Green metal towers and concrete pilings overshadowed a strip of parking lot. "You need any help? Like on the stairs?"

"I'm fine. This helps." Iestyn raised the water bottle. "Thanks."

"No problem." The repairman picked up his bucket and, after another busy glance between the two of them, clomped down the stairs.

Vibrations rose from the deck through the soles of Lara's feet as the ferry chugged and churned into the harbor. A broken line of weathered gray buildings climbed the hill overlooking the water. A big white house stood on the crest of a cliff. There were gulls everywhere.

Lara shivered, reminded of the crows.

Iestyn offered her the bottle.

She shook her head.

He drank. "You have every reason to ask," he said, capping the bottle.

"But no right."

He rubbed his jaw, looking out at the water, where strings of buoys bobbed against the blue. "You ditched your people, you left your home and your job, to get me out of there. To bring me here. That gives you the right to ask me any damn thing you want."

"I guess I wondered where you see this going."

Us going.

"That depends on what we find here."

"That's a nice, noncommittal answer."

A trick of reflected light made his eyes appear to gleam. "After three days together, you want commitment."

Yes.

"Of course not." She swallowed the lump in her throat. He was male. And merfolk. What did she expect? "Just a little communication." To start.

He nodded slowly. "You want things clear."

She nodded, relieved.

"I get that. You're an angel. Everything's light or dark for you, black or white."

"I'm not asking you for promises," she began. *"I don't make promises,"* he'd told her thirty-six hours—a lifetime—ago.

He made a rough sound. "This isn't about promises. It's about guarantees."

The ship jolted into dock.

"I don't understand the difference."

"Because in your world, if you do the right thing, you get rewarded. Follow the rules, and everything will be fine. My world, the real world, isn't like that. I can't tell you everything's going to be all right because I don't know."

Hurt bloomed in her chest. Swam in her eyes. But when she blinked, it wasn't impatience she saw in his face. It wasn't irritation that ripped that ragged edge in his voice. It was doubt.

Sympathy moved in her, for the boy he had been, for the man he had become, struggling to steer an honorable course without compass or bearings.

"I don't need guarantees," she said gently. "I'll settle for good intentions."

The first car rumbled off the ferry.

Iestyn smiled wryly and stood, carrying the plastic bags that held all their worldly possessions. "Paving the road to Hell?"

"I don't believe that."

"Babe, you're living proof of that. We both are. We've both made what we thought were the right choices for the right reasons. You turn back the ship, or you tie yourself to the fucking mast. You try to save something, a dog, a kid, a sailor you found hanging in the rigging. You put yourself out there, take a stand. And you fail." His voice rang with quiet intensity. "You Fall."

Beneath the sunlit surface, his eyes were deep and bitter as the sea.

Her heart wrenched with pity. This was what he believed. This was why he was drifting. Lost. Not because he was selkie, but because he had lost faith in himself and his choices. Even his loss of memory was another layer of defense between him and what he perceived as his failure.

"So we're not perfect," she said, preceding him to the stairs. "We don't have perfect knowledge. Sometimes we make bad decisions. And maybe sometimes things happen as part of a larger plan, and we just can't see it yet."

"What happened to you as a child wasn't part of any plan."

Oddly, the fury pulsing in his voice made her own pain and anger easier to accept. But then, she'd had years of therapy that made it possible to say, "What happened to me as a child wasn't my fault. Or God's will. I don't blame myself or Him for the actions of one sick, evil man." She drew a steadying breath as they emerged into the sunlight of the lower deck. "But sooner or later, my choices led me to you. This may not be the reward I was looking for at the time I expected it. But I think I was always meant to find you somehow. To bring you back where you belong."

* * *

"Lara." Iestyn stopped, at a loss for words. Her confidence shook him. Her strength awed him.

"I don't have your faith," he said quietly. "But I admire the hell out of you."

Somehow she had taken her Fall from grace and the trauma of her childhood to forge herself into the woman who stood before him, brave, clear-eyed, and strong.

He didn't deserve her.

"Whatever brought us together—choice or chance or God—I'm grateful." He rested his hand at the small of her back to steer her across the ramp to the dock. "But I don't know if I belong here. I don't know where I belong."

She looked back at him, her smile misty around the edges. "That's why we came, isn't it? To find out."

She made it sound so simple. His gut churned. He scanned beyond her to the ragged line of rooftops climbing above the parking strip. World's End wasn't Sanctuary. No seals played in the harbor, no castle stood upon the hill, no shimmer of magic hung like mist around the rocks.

But despite his words to Lara a moment ago, something tightened his chest and his throat. Longing. Anticipation.

A woman swung down from her landscaping truck—CORA'S FLORAS was painted on the side—to sign for a pallet of mulch being offloaded from the ferry. Iestyn caught a flash of blond braid beneath her cap and stiffened like Madagh spotting a hare.

Lara glanced over quickly. "Is that her? Lucy Hunter?"

He took a second, longer look. Sure, there was a resemblance, but . . . This woman's face was too full, her eyes too green. "No."

"I thought I recognized her," Lara said. "From your dream."

She was a Seeker, Iestyn remembered. "You didn't pick up some kind of vibe?"

Regretfully, she shook her head. "Only with you. Usually I need physical contact to identify the presence of another elemental."

His mind stumbled on that *only with you* before he grinned. "That's your plan? Walk around the island groping people?"

"I don't have a plan," Lara admitted ruefully. "I was sort of hoping that when we finally got here, it would be like the return of the prodigal son."

He raised an eyebrow. " 'Father, I have sinned against Heaven and in thy sight'?"

Her laughter bubbled, surprising them both. "I was thinking more along the lines of killing the fatted calf."

"Hungry, are you?"

Her cheeks turned pink. "I'm fine. Don't worry about it."

She was brushing him off. Just the way he'd brushed aside her concerns on the boat.

He hadn't given a thought to where they would eat tonight. Where they would sleep.

For years, he hadn't bothered to plan ahead. Hadn't needed to think about anyone but himself. The fact that he was now, that he wanted to now, was something else he'd have to think about. Later.

"I'll take you out to eat as soon as we find a place to stay," he promised.

She glanced around the emptying wharf. "Shouldn't we stick around here? In case someone shows up with the WELCOME SELKIES banner?"

"Berth first. Search later."

"It's the middle of the season," Lara said. "It might be hard to find a vacancy."

He regarded the picture postcard view, the parked cars and storefronts staggering up the hill, the snapping flags and spilling window boxes. She had a point. He didn't know much about vacation rentals. But he knew rich people. Yacht people. There would be a room somewhere, for a price.

He nodded at the big white elephant overlooking the harbor. "So we'll start at the top."

* * *

The Island Inn was undergoing renovations, red-haired Kate Begley told them when she finally answered the bell at the front desk.

She was a younger woman, wiry and energetic. Judging from the paint in her hair and under her nails, she was doing at least some of those renovations herself.

"I'd hoped to have more of the guest rooms open by now. But we do have a king suite available on the third floor," she said, regarding them over the top of her little black glasses. "Private bath, great ocean view."

"How much?" Iestyn asked.

Her gaze flickered to the plastic Walmart bags in his hand. "The suite lists for three fifty-five a night. But I can let it go for three hundred."

He winced inwardly, doing the mental calculations. Beside him Lara had the fine-boned, fragile appearance of an angel in a stained glass window, her skin pale and transparent, every shadow showing. After all he'd put her through, she deserved the best the inn could offer. The best he had to offer.

He still had most of his roll from his last job. He could swing at least a couple of nights.

"One fifty cash in advance," Lara said.

They both regarded her with varying degrees of surprise and respect.

"We came in on the four o'clock ferry," Lara said, suddenly looking a lot less unworldly. "It's highly unlikely you're going to see any more late drop-ins tonight. You can either leave the room empty or take our money."

"Two hundred," Kate Begley said. "That includes breakfast in the bar in the morning. Our dining room's closed during renovations. But I can set you up with coffee, bagels, fruit, stuff like that."

Lara looked at Iestyn.

"That'd be great," he said. "What about dinner?"

"Antonia's on Main Street is very good. A lot of the locals eat there."

Iestyn peeled a couple big bills off his roll. "You're not a local?"

Kate's face set. "I am for now."

It was an opening. He dived right through. "It must be hard moving into a place like this where everybody knows everybody else."

"I don't plan on staying." She wiped her hands, fished a key from a cubby. "My parents bought this place ten years ago. I'm just trying to turn enough of a profit to sell."

Iestyn ran his tongue over his teeth. "So, I guess you don't know Lucy Hunter."

"Hunter . . . I know Caleb Hunter. The chief of police," Kate explained in response to Iestyn's lifted brow. "And the chef at Antonia's is a Hunter, too. His sister-in-law, I think. Regina."

Memories scuttled like crabs on the sea bottom, stirring him up.

Caleb Hunter.

Regina Hunter. "His sister-in-law, I think."

Which meant . . . The connections pinched at Iestyn with razor-sharp claws. Which meant . . .

"Dylan's wife." He forced the words from his thick tongue.

Kate Begley shrugged, pushing two keys across the counter. "Maybe. I haven't met her husband."

Iestyn's head pounded. He couldn't breathe.

Lara slipped her hand into his arm. He looked down at her, abruptly recalled to the present.

"Thanks." He pocketed the keys. "Antonia's, you said?"

Kate's glasses glinted as she nodded. "Order the swordfish. Or the lobster fra diavolo."

The stair carpet was covered in plaster dust. An empty utility bucket sat out on the second floor landing. But their room was large and clean, with a thick white comforter on the bed and thin white sheers at the windows framing a spectacular view of the harbor.

As soon as the door closed behind them, Lara asked, "What was that about?"

Iestyn crossed the window and stood looking out at the sea. "It appears we have a lead."

"The police chief. Caleb Hunter?"

"Yes."

"He's selkie?"

"No." Iestyn jammed his hands in his pockets. "But his brother Dylan is."

"How does that work?"

"Their father was human. Their mother was the sea witch Atargatis. Halfbloods are more often human than not. It is one of the reasons the merfolk are dying out."

The sun was slipping in the sky, staining the water rose and gold.

"I thought the children of the sea were immortal," she said.

He turned to face her. "As long as we stay in the sea. Or live protected by the magic of Sanctuary. But we pay for that immortality with a low birth rate."

A pause while she digested that. "So Dylan Hunter is selkie."

"A selkie warden, one of the sea lord's elite."

"You know him?"

"I did."

He remembered the day Dylan's mother brought him to the prince's court on Sanctuary, a sneering, black-eyed boy with a chip on his shoulder and a shield around him even Griff's patient teaching could not dent. Dylan had been younger than Iestyn then. Dylan's determination to grow up, the time he spent away from the magic of Sanctuary, had quickly aged him beyond the others.

Still, it had been a shock, Iestyn recalled, when he learned the sullen youth had been made a warden on the human island of World's End.

He could practically hear the *click, snap, pop*, as Lara's busy mind made the connections. "So if Caleb is Dylan's brother, then their sister is . . ."

"Lucy Hunter."

Her smile broke like dawn. "But that's wonderful! You're almost there. We're almost done."

"We're not done."

She nodded seriously. "Of course not. We still have to find him. Her. But . . ."

"We're not done," he repeated. His heart pumped, panicked for the first time by the end of a journey. "I'm not finished with you yet."

When she stared at him, wide-eyed, he crossed the room to her and pulled her into his arms.

18

HE WAS DESPERATE FOR HER.

Her taste. Her smell. The wide, soft curve of her lower lip. The fine, shining core of her, like tempered steel.

He pressed his lips to her shoulder and felt her tremble, pressed a kiss to her throat and heard her sigh. The quiet exhalation stirred his soul like wind on the water, moving him to the depths.

"Lara." He stopped, at a loss for words.

"I'm not asking you for promises," she'd said.

But he wanted to make them.

"Ssh." Her fingers winnowed his hair, brushed his jaw, her touch as light as air. "Kiss me."

How could he think when she looked at him from under those dark winged brows, her big eyes shining with trust and need? How could he speak?

So he kissed her, hoping that would be enough, trying to tell her without words all the longing that bloomed in his heart, soft, tender kisses to her temple, her cheek, her mouth.

When her fingers found the edge of his shirt and the hot skin underneath, he stepped back and ripped it over his head.

Her eyes widened and then narrowed. She reached for the burn that still throbbed below the hollow of his throat.

But he didn't need her healing now. He needed her with him, in this room, in this moment, all of her with him. Catching her hand, he pulled her to him, coaxing her shirt up, inch by inch.

Her skin had the thick, creamy texture of lilies. Her scent swam in his head. He pushed her jeans down, frowning at the faint shadows that marched along her hip. Bruises. He'd bruised her with his hands, his fingertips.

Sinking to his knees, he kissed each careless mark and then the curve of her belly and then the silky dark thatch between her thighs. Her legs trembled. Her hips arched in silent invitation. He pushed her back to lie on the bed, licking into her, sipping from her skin, drinking her heady response. She moved with him and against him, against his mouth and hands, her body fluid and restless as water, until everything that was in him gathered like a flood, and he surged from the floor, rising over her, crawling to get to her, dying to be inside her.

He dug a condom from his discarded jeans—*almost the last one, maybe the last time*, the finality of it beat in his blood—and covered himself with shaking hands.

She lay back, watching him, as he nudged her thighs apart and found his place between them. Everything he was, everything inside him, he gave to her, pleasure flowing through him, tenderness brimming inside him, and it almost didn't matter where they went from here, what they did, who they found. If this was love, he was fathoms deep and drowning.

When he sank into her, he was already home.

* * *

She wanted to take him inside her, hold him inside her, absorb him through her skin. Every kiss, every stroke, pulled her deeper into something sacred, something holy, a sacrament of flesh and love.

She loved him.

But she would not force her words on him and risk his puzzled disbelief. He did not want her guarantees.

And so she gave him herself instead, her body, loving him with everything in her, everything she'd held inside, pouring herself into their union, feeling his pleasure rise and build and crest. Until the wave that took him swamped them both, carrying her away, leaving her heart stranded on an unfamiliar shore.

She hugged him tightly while their ragged breathing smoothed, while their rapid heartbeats slowed, while their bodies cooled, sealed together by sweat and sex.

A finger of sunset stole through the pretty white curtains and lay across the bed.

She could never go home again.

* * *

"Have you thought what you're going to say to him?" Lara asked as they climbed the hill toward the center of town, a two-block stretch of parked cars, telephone poles, and gray-shingled houses.

A few family groups wandered the dusk, peering in the darkened windows of picturesque storefronts. Island Realty. Lighthouse Gift Shop. An amorphous group of teenagers blocking the sidewalk in front of Wiley's Market shuffled to let them by. One of the boys muttered a comment as they passed. One of the girls laughed. With a pang, Lara thought of Bria.

It was all very ordinary, she supposed. It was like nothing she knew. She had never been part of a family. She had never been like those teens, chafing against the restrictions of a parent's love, experimenting with freedom within safe distance of home.

Maybe she was going through some kind of delayed adolescence.

She stole a glance at Iestyn. He looked at home here, with his sun-streaked hair and easy, waterman's stride.

There was more to her flight from Rockhaven than teenage rebellion. More to her feelings for him than a dizzy infatuation with sex.

He could belong here. Her heart swelled with hope and loss. He could make a life here.

For a moment, she let herself imagine it, Iestyn, working on the water during the day, coming home at night to a gray-shingled house and a couple of children with golden eyes . . .

He slanted a look down at her. "Say to who?"

She pulled her thoughts back together, embarrassed to be caught dreaming over a future that didn't belong to her. "Dylan Hunter. Have you planned what to say?"

"Besides hello?"

"I'm sure you have questions, but I think it's important to explain about the amnesia because . . ." She caught him grinning at her and broke off. "What? It's good to be prepared."

"It is if you know what you're preparing for. We don't." He caught her hand, making her jolt with surprise and pleasure, adjusting his steps to hers. Anyone looking at them would think they were any couple strolling to dinner.

But they weren't.

"Relax," he murmured. "We'll make it up as we go along."

"I don't know if I can," she confessed.

He stroked her knuckles with his thumb, tiny circles she felt in the pit of her stomach. "You're doing fine so far."

She had a feeling he wasn't just talking about their search for Lucy Hunter.

The red awning of Antonia's Ristorante stretched over the sidewalk, glowing from the lights outside and in. The bell over the door jangled as Iestyn opened it for Lara to precede him inside.

Red vinyl booths and crowded four-top tables, a scarred wooden floor, and an open pass-through window. Voices hummed. Dishes clattered. Smells floated on the air, a rich broth of garlic, onions, clams.

Lara inhaled appreciatively and heard Iestyn suck in his breath behind her.

She turned at once, her nerves jumping, but he only opened the door wider, stepping back to let an older couple leave.

Inside, a few tables were clearing. A black-haired busboy who couldn't be more than fifteen stopped with a tray full of dishes.

His face lit with pleasure when he saw them. "Zack! Man, why didn't you tell me you were . . ." His dark eyes flickered. His face flushed. "Sorry. I thought you were somebody else."

"Who?" Lara asked.

The boy jerked one shoulder in a shrug. Apology. Dismissal. "Sit anywhere," he said. "Hailey will take your order."

They found a booth near the kitchen, with a view of the chalkboard menu.

"Zack?" Lara repeated quietly when they were seated.

Iestyn rubbed at the front of his shirt, over the burn. "Who knows?"

"You don't recognize the name?"

He shook his head.

Their waitress—young, blond, with a face full of freckles—arrived at their table. "What'll you have?"

"Do you have bottled water?" Lara asked.

"This isn't the Galaxy. You can drink out of a glass here." Iestyn smiled. "You can even order wine."

Wine was a bad idea. Wine belonged to celebrations and candlelit dinners, the whole ordinary dating world she'd never really been part of. But just for tonight, she was tempted to go with the flow, to pretend they were out to dinner to enjoy each other's company, to imagine that they could have a future together.

"I'm not finished with you yet."

She swallowed. "Maybe . . . a glass of white?"

"A bottle of the pinot grigio," Iestyn said. "A bottle of Sam Adams. And the swordfish for me."

"I hear the lobster fra diavolo is good," Lara said to the waitress.

"Well, yeah, it is, but . . ."

"I'm not making it," a raspy female voice shouted through the pass. "You can have the steamed lobster or the clam linguini."

Lara bit her lip, wavering between offense and amusement.

"She'll have the lobster," Iestyn said.

"One swordfish, one lobster." A strong-featured Italian woman, with one of those faces that looked the same at forty and at sixty, appeared briefly in the pass, her mouth a hard red slash, her dark eyes snapping in satisfaction. "Coming up."

"Cole slaw, fries, or baked potato with that?" their waitress asked.

"Cole slaw, I think."

When their waitress was gone with their order, Lara met Iestyn's eyes, resisting the urge to giggle.

"If that was Dylan Hunter's wife," he said, "more has changed than I thought."

"Don't mind Nonna." The busboy appeared with a basket of bread and a bottle of olive oil. "Mom's out of the kitchen tonight, so she's feeling feisty."

"Nonna?" Lara repeated.

His smile was quick and charming. "My grandmother Antonia."

Antonia's Ristorante.

Lara squeezed her hands together under the table. "So the regular chef—your mother—would be Regina Hunter."

The boy drizzled oil and herbs onto a thick white plate. "That's right."

"Your father is Dylan Hunter."

"So?"

"Where is he?" Lara asked.

The question earned her a measuring look from those big, dark Italian eyes and another charming smile. "At work."

"What kind of work does he do?"

The boy's smile faded.

Iestyn's foot pressed hers under the table. "Good bread."

"Glad you like it," said the boy and escaped.

Lara frowned. "Why did you stop me?"

"Because you were scaring him." Iestyn's long, strong fingers tore a hunk from the loaf of bread. "And because I want to enjoy our dinner."

She didn't understand him. Everything inside her was alight and alive with impatience. If this was the end, she wanted to get there as quickly as possible. *Minimize the pain*, she told herself. *Like ripping off a bandage.* "Don't you want to find them? Dylan? Lucy?"

"We will find them." He dipped the bread into the olive oil. "Tomorrow."

She stared at him, frustrated. "But we're so close."

He offered her the bread across the table. "Lara, I've been gone for seven years. We've been searching less than two days. Another night won't make any difference."

Reluctantly, she reached for the bread. He pulled it back, holding it teasingly away from her mouth until she leaned forward to eat from his hand. As her lips closed around the bread, he added softly, with intent, "Especially if it means I get to spend that night with you."

Her gaze met his.

She almost choked, bathed in golden heat.

"Another night won't make any difference."

Oh, but it could. How long could she be with him, how many times could she lie with him, and still survive a separation?

And yet how could she resist this chance to know him better? To make love with him one more time?

Deliberately, she picked up her wineglass. "So," she said. "Tell me how you learned about wine."

He narrowed his eyes at her obvious change of subject, but he played along, telling her about the yachts he'd crewed, the jobs he'd handled, the places he'd been.

Their lives could hardly have been more different, she reflected, listening to his stories about a delivery to Bahia, a race in Key West. In thirteen years, she'd rarely left the walls of Rockhaven. Yet he seemed genuinely interested in her life there, encouraging her to talk about her job in the school office.

"It might seem like busywork to some," she said. "But I like the routine. I like being organized."

His eyes gleamed. "I noticed."

Under his subtle prodding, she told him things that should have bored him silly, details about living in the dorms, minor infractions after lights out, stories about Bria.

"You must miss her," he said quietly, and tipsy with wine and attention, Lara blurted out a truth she had barely admitted to herself.

"I hated her. She was the person I was closest to in the whole world, and she left me. She didn't care enough to try to talk to me, she didn't tell me she was going. And then I wondered if she left because of me. Because she knew I resented her for having the courage to do all the things I wasn't brave enough to try."

"Bullshit," Iestyn said.

Lara blinked. "Excuse me?"

"First, you're one of the bravest people I know." He reached across and took her hand, holding it in his warm, strong clasp. "Second, your friend didn't leave because of you. She left because she had to, because of something inside her that couldn't be there anymore. Maybe she really cared about you." He looked down at their fingers, joined on the table; up into her eyes. "Maybe she was afraid if she told you, you'd talk her out of it."

* * *

They were among the last customers to leave the restaurant. They walked back to the inn along roads without streetlamps under stars pulsing raw and real overhead. So many stars, undimmed by human light, Lara could almost imagine herself in Heaven.

In the near darkness of their room, he undressed her,

revealing her pale body in the silver light that slipped through the window. He laid her back on the soft white bed, spreading her legs wide, easing inside her.

Her sore muscles tensed against his blunt intrusion.

"Sorry," she whispered.

He kissed her, stroking her hair back from her face. "It's all right. You're all right. You're perfect."

"I guess I'm not used to . . . *Oh*," as he slid carefully deeper, as her tender flesh yielded around him.

"I'll go slow," he whispered wickedly, and he did, teasing her with his hands and his body, making her tremble, making her moan and clutch at him with anxious hands.

He pressed deep inside her, holding himself still inside her, until she shimmered with impatience, until she twined her legs around him, pushing her hips against him, nudging in restless rhythm, *I want, I want, I want*, until his control broke and he gave it to her, stroking into her, thrusting into her, driving deep and hard.

She came so hard she saw stars. With a groan, he plunged once, twice, again, before he finally let himself go and followed her into oblivion.

Afterward they lay in silence, her head on his shoulder, his hand in her hair.

Lara closed her eyes, holding thought at bay.

Iestyn kissed her forehead and got up and went into the bathroom. The light shone under the door, dimming the glow from beyond the curtains.

He was gone a long time. She lay motionless, listening to the sounds of running water, a muffled thump, almost glad for the respite. Not for her body, but for her heart. She could handle a little soreness from their lovemaking. She was unprepared to deal with these extremes of emotion, the delight and the pain of loving him so much.

But after a while, a niggle of discomfort made itself heard over the twinges of her muscles and the ache of her heart.

What was taking him so long?

Plucking his T-shirt from the floor, she pulled it over her head and followed him into the bathroom.

Iestyn stood leaning over the sink, looking at himself in the mirror, his back to the door.

She met his eyes in the glass. Around his throat, the angry red line of the heth burned. New blisters puffed and oozed on his skin.

She inhaled sharply, taking in the lines of pain on his face, the open tube of burn ointment on the sink. "You should have called me."

"I thought you were asleep."

"Then you should have woken me up."

"Why?"

"Why?" Her voice cracked. "To help you. To do what I did before."

"How many times?" he asked wearily.

"As many times as it takes. Until your burn gets better."

But the burn wasn't getting better. It was worse, had been worse since they were on the ferry to the island, and they both knew it.

Iestyn scrubbed his hand over his face, a tired gesture that made her heart contract. "I'm not bothering you every half hour because of a damn necklace."

"Then we need to take it off," she said steadily.

"How?"

"Soldier said . . ." She struggled to concentrate with the image of his raw, wet wound seared into her brain. "Any way we can. It's glass. It can be fractured."

"I've tried," he said. She recalled the muffled thump. "It's not so easy."

"You said yourself we can do more together than we can apart," she reminded him.

He turned to face her. "Unless I don't know what the hell I'm doing."

"I do."

She wasn't a chemist. She wasn't an artist or a magic worker. Simon had never recommended her, Zayin had never recruited her, to work in the factory. But she had a good memory. She'd taken theory classes with the rest of her cohort. For years, she'd listened to Jacob and David argue about glass over breakfast, lunch, and dinner. She could do this. They could do this.

She hoped.

"The spell is in the bead," she explained. "If there are flaws in the glass, if we put the right pressure on the flaws, the bead will crack. The spell will be broken."

"Just like that."

She bit her lip. "It's worth a try."

His eyes warmed as he looked at her. "Yeah, it is. Tell me what you need me to do."

"Sit down?" she suggested.

He sat on the closed lid of the toilet, his large square knees jutting into the confined space.

She swallowed. "Do you want to put on some clothes?"

"Will it make a difference?"

"Probably not. Okay." She looked into his steady eyes and felt the knot of nerves in her stomach relax. Taking a slow breath, she tried to imagine What-should-be.

Iestyn, free.

He held her hand. The way they did before. *Yes.*

She closed her free hand on the heth. The bead was smooth and strong, hot against her clenched palm. She felt the power collecting in the pit of her stomach, at the nape of her neck, from her hand joined to Iestyn's hand, felt the pressure building, moving up from her gut and down her arms. Her heart pounded.

But there was no place for the power to go. The bead was smooth and black and impenetrable. Their combined magic slid off the polished glass surface.

Her palm burned as if she held a live coal. She gasped and dropped it.

Iestyn tightened his grip on her other hand. "Easy."

"I'm sorry," she said.

"You're doing great. Is there a sign for this?" he asked. "Like there was for water?"

She stared at him, considering. "Well . . . *Heth* means 'wall.'" She thought. "Or 'fence.' A spell of binding and containment."

"So all we need is a door," he joked.

A way in. A crack. An opening.

She felt a glimmer of hope. It was worth a shot.

"You'll have to hold on to me," she said. "I need both hands for this."

Wordlessly, he wrapped his arms around her waist. She took another deep breath that did nothing to settle her stomach and grabbed the heth again, trying to remember the ancient symbols.

What can be . . .

Daleth, door. *He*, window. She pictured the runes in her mind, scratching them into the surface of the glass, probing it for weakness.

Iestyn, free.

Daleth, door, *he*, window, over and over again like a madwoman scribbling on the walls of her cell. A great surge of power pushed from her heart and her stomach, from Iestyn's arms around her waist, ripples of power flowing through her veins, racing along her nerves, shooting into the heth.

What must be.

Free.

And power *exploded* under her hand, red hot, white hot, scalding, boiling out of control.

Glass cracked.

Sharp pain cut across her palm. Blood dripped between her fingers. The room stank.

Lara shuddered. She uncurled her bleeding hand, and the shards of the heth fell dully to the bathroom floor. She touched her other hand lightly to Iestyn's hair, willing him to look up and reassure her.

"Well, we did it," she said shakily.

"Oh yes." He raised his head and smiled a terrible smile, and his eyes were not Iestyn's eyes, and his voice was not Iestyn's voice. "We certainly did."

19

HE WAS LOSING HIS MIND.

Losing control. Of his voice, his arms, his . . . self.

Christ. The word lashed like a bright crack of lightning along his abused nerves.

Iestyn sat trapped on the toilet seat, trapped in his unresponsive body, fat, fiery ripples of power coursing through his veins and along his bones, coiling in his heart and bowels, as the demon burrowed and twined deeper, farther, into its host.

"Iestyn?" Shock in Lara's voice.

Horror in her eyes.

Freed from hiding, the demon who had been held captive by the heth's power tightened his borrowed arms around Lara's hips, enjoying her panicked struggle to be free—*free, free, after days of concealment, of confinement*—savoring the soft, yielding flesh of her belly against his stubbled jaw. His cock swelled. Twitched. He wanted to turn his face and bite her, fuck her, eat her, have her, while she jerked and bled and moaned.

No.

No.

Iestyn loosed his arms.

Lara stumbled back a step, reaching behind her for the support of the tiled wall. "Iestyn, what's wrong? What happened?"

Silly bitch. He could smell her fear. She knew. She had to know.

Iestyn exerted control, fighting for his voice. "Get away from me." A guttural growl.

"What is it?" Shaking, Lara stood her ground. "Let me help. Let me help you."

"Can't." The word burst from Iestyn's throat. "*Go.* Now."

"What happened to you?"

Angels and their fucking explanations.

A great wave of love and despair swept over him. His head throbbed. He couldn't think. The demon hammered iron spikes into his brain, punishment for his disobedience. He could feel his skull splitting, his mind yielding, his identity failing and falling away like ice chunks dropping from a glacier, caving into the sea. *Lost . . .*

"Demon. *You may call me Cudd.*" Iestyn shivered. Had he said that out loud? He licked his lips. "Inside me. In Norfolk."

Lara's back pressed the wall. "How?"

Cudd fed on her disbelief, fed on her fear.

"You know what they say." The demon jerked Iestyn's mouth into a grin. "Lie down with dogs, get up with fleas. He really shouldn't have passed out on a dead man after our little alley fight."

"But in the car . . ."

"Wasn't I clever?" *Spinning, weaving, plotting, planning,*

biding his fucking time. "Or perhaps you were just very dumb. We wanted to get inside Rockhaven. Inside the wards. Our merfolk friend's shields provided the means. And you provided the way."

Iestyn heard the demon's words coming out of his mouth, his throat. He flailed inside his head, trapped inside his own body. He couldn't move. His strength was drying up. Like a beached whale, beyond help or hope of the sea.

"Zayin . . ." He forced the name through stiff lips. *Damn him, curse him, eat him.* "Bound it."

The demon's spite flared. *Like being in a box, blind, deaf, dumb. Hate it. Hate him. Hate.*

Iestyn spasmed and went rigid.

Cudd shook his borrowed body like a dog, once more in control. "But I'm here now. I'm free. Thanks to you. The merfolk aren't quite as attractive a target as the nephilim, of course. But still, my master will be pleased."

"Why?" Lara asked.

Why didn't she run? *Run*, thought Iestyn.

"Their wards have been nearly as inconvenient as yours. I must reward you for that. Although perhaps you won't enjoy your reward. You're such a *good* girl, Lara," the demon crooned. "But that just makes it more delicious for me."

Her face went white.

"No," Iestyn said simply and stood.

This son of a bitch would not touch her. *He* would not touch her.

Not while he lived.

"Go," he said clearly. "Get away."

Her eyes narrowed. "I can't leave. You need me."

Need you to be safe, he thought. *Need you to go.*

"Get help. Get . . ." He searched through the haze of pain, the stink of decay and death rising from his brain. "Dylan."

But instead of moving away, she took a step toward him. "There's no time."

No time, he accepted. No guarantees, no hope.

"Iestyn." Another step closer. He could smell her hair, sweet as lilies over the stink of blood. He clenched his fists. "Do you trust me?"

He met her eyes, deep shining gray like the sea at sunset or the sky at dawn.

"Yes," he said.

* * *

Lara's heart slammed against her ribs. Her stomach was trying to crawl up her throat.

She didn't kid herself she knew what she was doing. But Simon wasn't going to rescue her this time. Rescue them. She knew the damage a thwarted demon could inflict on a reluctant host, wreck his body, scramble his brains. She couldn't run away and let that happen. Not to anybody. Not to Iestyn.

Her knees shook.

Maybe, if he believed in her, it didn't matter so much that she had so little faith in herself. Maybe together . . .

She thought she understood what had happened. By opening himself to Lara, by allowing her to tap his elemental energy, Iestyn had left himself vulnerable to the demon trapped inside him. When their conjoined magics shattered the heth, Cudd had rushed along the open channels of power to take swift possession of his host. With the demon already lodged inside him, Iestyn could not tear free of Cudd's control. Not alone.

A frisson of uncertainty shook her spine. She was drained and sore, tired and afraid. She didn't have the training or the power for what she was about to attempt. She didn't have an anchor.

She didn't have a choice.

Framing Iestyn's face in her bloody hands, she pressed her mouth to his mouth. A fetid whiff of demon made her pause. But under it, she could taste Iestyn, his flavor, rich, salty, reassuring.

What must be . . .

Closing her eyes, she poured out her soul, spirit casting into his body.

* * *

Hot. Bright. Like swallowing the sun.

Light burst in Iestyn's skull, burned behind his eyes. He could not see. An enormous ball of gaseous energy seethed inside him. It radiated from the center of his chest, shoving aside his internal organs, spleen, liver, lungs. He was stretched full, what was left of his mind and will stretched as thin as the latex of a balloon.

If he so much as breathed in, Iestyn thought, he would pop.

His boundaries wavered. He could not feel the limits of his body, could not find his fingers and toes.

But he felt Lara, moving inside him, offering up her strength for his use, giving shape to his body, giving form to the brightness. Lara, breathing with his lungs. Lara, seeing out of his eyes.

He squinted. Focused.

And saw Lara's body crumpled against the wall, her black hair spread on the white tile.

The sight snapped him back to himself.

What had she done? Was she dead?

But he could feel her with him. Inside him. With the demon.

He was in the bathroom. *They* were. Lara and the demon, inside his body, naked, in the bathroom.

He looked at the shell of her body, motionless on the floor. *Not dead, not dead.* But empty. She had emptied herself for him.

A dull throbbing filled his head, like feet rushing up the stairs, like fists pounding at the door, like the beating of his own heart.

Cudd raged inside him like a fever, evil, virulent, shooting out lines of sticky fire. But the demon was no match for them, for Iestyn's strength and Lara's words and their combined power.

"Unclean spirit!" Iestyn shouted as the door to the suite burst open. "I cast you out!"

And the fire ripped from his brain and heart and loins and erupted into the room.

He barely noticed.

He crawled across the floor to Lara. She looked like Hell. Like death. Her face was the color of melted wax, her lashes dark against her pale cheeks.

"Lara."

A wind whipped through the open door. The fire shrieked and shot toward the ceiling. Heat singed his legs. Iestyn threw himself over Lara's limp body, wrapping protectively around her to shield her from the reaching, greedy flames.

Someone shouted, a deep command.

The fire flickered and died.

Shaking, Iestyn pulled Lara's body into his arms, cradling her against his naked chest. One blood-streaked hand slipped to the tile, fingers curled upward like the petals of a lily. He pressed his lips to her brow, her cheek, her unresponsive mouth. *Not dead, please God, not . . .*

"Lara." A cry from his heart. A prayer, breathed against the smoke and silence.

When her eyes opened, he buried his face in her hair.

Footsteps crossed the outer room. A light flicked on, slanting across the threshold.

"Well, well." A male voice, vaguely familiar, almost amused. A man's legs in the corner of his vision. "Somebody's been having fun."

Stunned, Iestyn raised his head.

And saw Dylan Hunter standing at the bathroom door.

* * *

They made, Lara was forced to admit, quite an impression. Lucy Hunter's brother Dylan, lean and dark, with brooding black eyes and a pirate's ponytail. And Morgan Bressay, the finfolk lord—she wasn't quite sure what finfolk were, and no one bothered to explain—with Iestyn's eyes in his brutal Viking face. The wardens of World's End.

Under any other circumstances she would have been even more impressed.

At the moment she was mostly just exhausted.

She'd managed to stay alert and more or less on her feet during the introductions. But after Iestyn had dragged on his jeans and settled back against the headboard of their bed, she'd allowed herself to be coaxed against his side.

Now she drifted, safe and deliciously warm, his chest for her pillow, his arms holding her close, the murmur of masculine voices rising and falling around her like the sound of the sea.

"—must have triggered the wards."

"—could account for your burn."

"—knew . . . a breach somewhere."

Iestyn's fingers feathered gently through her hair. She closed her eyes. Just for a moment, she promised herself.

They were silent awhile, or maybe she dozed.

"—what to do with her," someone was saying.

She stirred.

"—be here without Lara." Iestyn's voice was firm.

"The angel," Dylan said dryly.

"Fallen angel," Morgan said.

A knock at the door. Lara opened her eyes. And caught them staring at her, these strangers who knew Iestyn. She was suddenly conscious of the fact that she was lying practically across his lap wearing nothing but his T-shirt. She tugged the hem down over her thighs.

"That would be my wife," Morgan said and went to open the door.

Elizabeth Bressay had sleek brown hair, intelligent brown eyes, and a reassuring manner. She cleaned and irrigated Lara's hand, applied ointment and a butterfly closure.

"There doesn't seem to be any sensory or vascular damage," she said. "But we'll want to keep an eye on it for infection."

Don't ask, Lara told herself. *It doesn't matter.* And a moment later heard herself say, "I'm sorry, but are you . . ."

"A real medical doctor?" Elizabeth smiled. "Yes."

"She wants to know if you are one of us," Morgan said over his wife's shoulder.

Lara flushed.

"Oh. I see." Elizabeth glanced from Lara to Iestyn and back again. But whatever she saw, she kept to herself. "No, I'm human. Quite ordinary."

"Not ordinary at all," her husband murmured.

A look passed between them, intimate as a kiss, before Elizabeth turned back to Lara. "Date of last tetanus shot?" she asked briskly.

"I'm not sure," Lara confessed.

"Well, stop by the clinic tomorrow and we'll take care

of that. You, too," she said to Iestyn. "Although Lucy can do more for you than I can."

Iestyn's face was suddenly raw and young. "Lucy."

"Yes, didn't they tell you? Men." Elizabeth shook her head. Smiled at Iestyn with maternal warmth. "Lucy and Conn are on their way here. To World's End. We're expecting them tomorrow."

* * *

Lara stood with Iestyn on the private dock that jutted out from the fingers of rock and the shelter of pines.

Dylan and Regina's house perched on a patch of short, sandy lawn above the bay, a traditional New England saltbox with a sturdy central chimney. The spare lines of the house were softened by tubs of blooming flowers and curtains blowing in the open windows. Cars and trucks parked haphazardly in the drive. Three boats were tied to the dock. Cats and children wandered underfoot, of both sexes and various ages, from teenagers to toddlers. She did her best to sort them out, to keep them straight, to match siblings to spouses to children, but they flowed together, sweeping around Iestyn and Lara in a warm, welcoming, undisciplined wave, merfolk and human.

For a people with a low birth rate, there certainly were a lot of them.

Confused and overwhelmed, Lara stuck close by Iestyn's side, the one familiar face in this sea of friendly strangers. She had always thought of him as someone fundamentally alone. Like her. Hadn't he done his best to make her see him that way?

Two lost souls.

She bit her lip, the tiny pain a counterpoint to the pang at her heart.

She knew all about the importance of community. All along, she'd wanted to restore Iestyn to his own kind, to the protection of his people.

But what they'd actually found was different. Unlike the nephilim at Rockhaven, the people in this house weren't bound together by the need for self-preservation or some quest for self-improvement. It was disconcerting to realize that Iestyn had more than a community willing to reclaim him. This was a family waiting to embrace him.

Any doubt she might have harbored about that disappeared when the last boat tied at the dock and three passengers disembarked.

Lara squinted, her heart quickening as she recognized the figures from her dream. Iestyn's dream. *A man with eyes like rain, a girl with hair like straw, a dog . . .*

"Is that . . ."

Conn ap Llyr, the sea lord, and his consort, Lucy.

Iestyn stiffened beside her. Under her hand, his arm muscles were rigid. His face was white with emotion.

"Go on," Lara murmured and released his arm. "Go see them."

With one bright, backward glance like a boy's, he left her, striding down the sun-bleached dock, not quite running to meet them.

The dog, a massive, graying beast, barked.

The woman raised her head. Lara was close enough to see the emotions flit across her face. Shock. Relief. Delight.

Lucy held out her arms and Iestyn went into them.

* * *

He was taller than Lucy now, Iestyn realized. The top of her head almost clipped his chin before she hugged him tight.

"Iestyn," she whispered. And again, as if she couldn't believe it, *"Iestyn."*

He adjusted his arms around her, her face warm and wet against his shirtfront. She was crying over him, which made him feel really good and bad at the same time. Awkwardly, he patted her back, looking over her head to meet Conn's gaze.

The sea lord regarded their embrace, his cool, austere face as unreadable as always. His silver eyes blazed with unidentifiable emotion.

Iestyn's throat tightened. His heart clenched like a fist in the center of his chest. Everything he had done and failed to do in the past seven years crashed on him like a wave.

"Sorry about the boat," he blurted out.

Lucy lifted her head from his chest. "The *boat*? Honestly, Iestyn—"

Conn did not waste time on scoldings or reassurances. He reached Iestyn in one quick stride and pulled him into his arms, holding him hard in a wordless embrace.

Tears burned Iestyn's throat. Closing his eyes, he bowed his head to the prince's shoulder.

Finally—*finally*—home.

* * *

Lara blinked back tears. She could feel the force of their connection. She recognized the love in the woman's welcome, the naked look in the prince's eyes.

Her heart softened and yearned. But she kept away, wistful and more than a little envious, unwilling to intrude on their private moment.

"Here." A thin woman with chopped black hair thrust a tray at Lara. Her hostess, Regina Hunter, mother of Nick, Grace, and . . . Lara's mind fumbled. *Jacob? Noah?*

Regina smiled warmly. "Come have some wine while

they get through the big reunion scene. They'll come up to the house when they're ready."

Grateful for direction, for a distraction, Lara followed Regina into the large, surprisingly modern kitchen. The sleek refrigerator was covered in children's artwork. Pots steamed on the massive stove. Lara recognized the brusque restaurant cook cutting watermelon at the kitchen table. The dark-eyed busboy stood beside a teenage girl with a halo of soft black curls, slicing bread on the counter.

"My mother, Antonia," Regina introduced them. "My son, Nick. And the pretty girl with the knife is Elizabeth and Morgan's daughter Emily."

Antonia nodded at Lara. "We met," she said in a smoker's rasp, low and surprisingly sexy. "Welcome to chaos."

"You run the restaurant," Lara said.

"The restaurant and the town. Ma's the mayor," Regina explained.

A pair of dark-haired children burst through the screened back door, heading for the refrigerator.

"Hold on," Regina ordered.

The little girl—seven? eight?—turned on her with black, beseeching eyes. "But, Mom, Calder's starving."

"Good. It's almost time to eat." Regina handed her a platter of deviled eggs and gave a tray of delicately browned crab cakes to the boy. "Take these outside. You can come back in to tell me when the coals are ready."

The children thumped outside.

"Have a glass of wine," Regina said. "Or a beer."

"I'm fine," Lara said. Out of place and slightly out of sorts in the midst of this cheerful family whirlpool, but otherwise all right.

"I'll have a beer," Nick said.

His mother narrowed her eyes. "In your dreams, pal."

"Is there anything I can do to help?" Lara asked.

She didn't cook. But she wanted to fit in.

Regina poured her a large glass of white wine. "Relax. Enjoy."

Lara sipped, but she couldn't relax.

The teenager, Emily, glanced over her shoulder. She was slim and dark-skinned and very, very pretty. "You could give me a hand with the crostini," she said kindly.

Lara smiled. "I can if you tell me what to do."

Under Emily's careful supervision, she assembled appetizers, spreading little rounds of bread with something black that smelled delicious. Focused on her task, she only gradually registered the conversation around her.

"No big deal if I can't take algebra," Nick was saying. "I'm not a brain like Em."

"You're no dummy either," his grandmother said.

"But it's first period," Nick protested. "When winter comes, I'll miss half the classes anyway."

Lara knew most teens were too sleep-deprived to concentrate first thing in the morning. But . . .

"Why when winter comes?" she wanted to know.

"We take the ferry to school on the mainland," Emily explained. "When the ice is bad, we can't get across until later in the day."

"It's not safe for the boats to travel in the dark," Regina said.

Lara frowned. "You don't have your own school?"

"K through nine. No high school," Antonia said.

"We've got the numbers. Almost thirty now," said Regina.

"The budget the way it is, the state's consolidating schools," Antonia said. "They don't want to open another way out here."

"A lot of kids board off the island during the school year," said Emily.

"Or drop out." Nick shrugged. "I can make more money lobstering over the summer than a teacher makes in a year."

"If that's what you want to do all your life," his mother said.

"What if you developed a high school magnet program?" Lara asked. "Or learning enrichment based on, oh, ship building or marine studies or something. That would help your student retention rate and attract families and money from off island."

Antonia shot her a sharp look. "You a teacher?"

"No, I . . ." Lara hesitated, her world shifting underfoot. What was she now?

"She's an administrator," Iestyn said.

He was there, leaning against the doorjamb, regarding her with warm, golden eyes.

She shook her head, ignoring the bump of her pulse. "I worked in an office."

"The headmaster's office. You know stuff."

His obvious pride made her flush with pleasure and embarrassment. "I know a little. Bookkeeping. Grant writing."

"See?" He smiled, making her heart flop foolishly. "Stuff."

He strolled forward and gave her a warm, firm kiss that did nothing to steady her shaky heart. He smelled like sunshine and the sea.

Regina hummed in interest.

"I need to talk to you," Iestyn said.

"Wait your turn," Antonia said.

"Go." Regina took the knife from Lara's hand. "Eat, drink, enjoy yourself."

Lara looked from Emily's bright, curious face to the unfinished crostini. "But . . ."

"Go on. You're a guest."

A guest, Lara thought as Iestyn took her hand, his grip hard and steady, and practically dragged her out to the porch. *Of course*. That's exactly what she was.

That was all that she was. She swallowed, stricken.

Iestyn swung her to face him. The sun slanted under the porch eaves, illuminating his handsome face, tipping his hair with gold. "Why did you disappear like that?"

"I didn't disappear." She was proud of the way she kept her voice even. "You saw me, I was right here, I—"

He cut her off. "I wanted you to hear."

"Hear what?"

"Good news. The best." He lifted her up and seated her on the rail of the porch, trapping her between his long, muscled arms. He nuzzled her jaw. "You know Lucy is a healer, right?"

"I . . ." Lara inhaled, dizzied by his closeness, dazzled by his bright expectation. "Did you show her your burn?"

"What? Oh, yeah." He eased back.

Lara shivered, deprived of his warmth, as he tugged down the neck of his T-shirt, exposing his throat.

She stared at the smooth white scar, faint against his tan. "You're healed," she said stupidly. "She healed you."

She pushed back his tawny hair. Even his stitches were gone, his head wound healed as if it had never been.

Lucy had done for him what Lara could not.

Iestyn shrugged, revealing in a single, careless gesture how little the pain and trauma of the past few days had affected him. "She *is* the *targair inghean*. But the thing is, she says I'm finfolk. Part finfolk anyway."

A sliver of ice worked into Lara's heart. "I don't understand." But she did. Or was afraid she did.

"There are two kinds of merfolk," Iestyn said. "Selkie, like Dylan, who shed their sealskins to take human form on land. And finfolk, like Morgan, who are total shape-shifters, who can take the form of any creature of the sea."

Morgan. Lara summoned a vision of the big, brutal Viking with the sea foam hair and golden eyes.

Iestyn's eyes.

"He looks like you," she said slowly.

"Actually, I look like him," Iestyn said. "My mother was selkie. When I Changed for the first time, I took seal form, so I always figured that was it for me. But I guessed I had finfolk blood, on my da's side. Because of the eyes."

"You told me your father was human."

"He was. But Conn thinks maybe Morgan's sister Morwenna could have been his grandmother."

Lara's head spun. "So, Morgan is your . . . uncle? Great uncle?"

"Something like that."

"Wouldn't he have known?"

"I don't think he cared. He and his sister were estranged after she married a human. None of her children could Change. Morgan probably never even thought about grandchildren." Iestyn shook his head impatiently. "Anyway, that's not the point."

The sliver in her chest dug deeper. "What is the point?"

"I told you." Iestyn took a deep breath. "I'm part finfolk. Lucy told me that with her help, I can learn to Change."

Lara stared at him, her mouth dry, her heart beating up in her throat. She had wanted to restore him to his people. She had hoped to restore him to himself. Apparently she had succeeded beyond her wildest expectations.

"That's . . ." She sought for a word. "Wonderful."

"It's everything. Lara." Iestyn gripped her arms, the sunlight in his eyes and on his hair, his face lit with joy. "I can go back to sea again."

* * *

"It's everything." The words rang in Lara's head, dogged her footsteps, as she trudged back alone to the hotel. *"I can go back to sea again."*

A bitter little breeze blew, kicking the shining surface of the water into running caps of foam.

She was not running away, Lara told herself, pausing on the bluffs to watch a bird fold its wings and plunge into the sea. She was merely taking some time to herself to think. To regroup. No one would even notice she was gone.

She pulled a face. If she were honest with herself, that was part of the problem.

Her problem.

She climbed the drive to the inn under storm-weathered trees, over rolling green lawn. She was genuinely glad for Iestyn. How could she fail to be glad? She loved him.

But he'd never said the words to her. It was unlikely now that he ever would. She would have to find a way to live with that.

Or live without him.

Wearily, she climbed the stairs to their room. The door was unlocked. Kate Begley, she wondered, making the bed?

She almost turned away. She really wasn't in the mood for company. But the prospect of the cool, white room, of peace and solitude, beckoned too strongly. With a little sigh, she pushed opened the door.

Jude Zayin sat in the rocker by the window, his big, broad-shouldered body dwarfing the chair. Crowding the room.

He looked up at her entrance, his dark face unreadable.

Her heart stopped.

"Hello, Lara," he said. "I've come to take you home."

20

IESTYN WANDERED AROUND THE CORNER OF THE house, beer in hand, a vague unease ruffling his mood like wind at the edge of a sail. The scent of the salt wood and saltwater blended with the aroma of charcoal-grilled fish. The tables set under the trees were set with food and surrounded by the Hunters' extended family.

He liked it all, the view, the smells, the mingling of merfolk and humankind. And felt slightly removed from the scene at the same time. He hadn't been to a lot of family picnics in the past seven years. Or before then. But he felt instinctively that something was missing.

Lara.

A war of badminton was being waged over a net strung between two trees. Four players of varying heights and skills competed on either side. Iestyn watched as a small girl in a pink dress dropped her racket and burst into tears. Her father—Caleb Hunter, Lucy's brother—scooped her onto his shoulders and resumed play, the delighted child now wrapped like a hat around his head.

Iestyn grinned. But Lara wasn't there to meet his eyes, to share a smile and the moment.

His sense of dissatisfaction grew. He scanned the yard, searching for her.

Conn and Lucy sat in camp chairs overlooking the ocean, Madagh drowsing beside them.

Iestyn dropped to a crouch at their feet, scratching the hound's graying muzzle. "Hey, boy. Remember me?"

The old dog rolled to his back, wriggling like a pup, his thin tail whipping the pine needles.

Iestyn's throat tightened. He scratched the hound's wiry belly. "I thought you would have replaced him by now," he said to Conn.

The sea lord lived forever. His dogs did not. But there was always a dog, always a deerhound, always named "Madagh"—hound—at the prince's side.

Conn smiled his wintry smile. "This one has led something of a charmed life. As, apparently, have you."

"Yeah." Iestyn realized, to his horror, that his eyes were wet. He focused hastily on the dog. "I guess I hoped . . . I thought Roth and Kera might have made it."

"We don't know that they did not," Conn said. "I have never stopped searching."

"I never stopped hoping." Lucy reached out and squeezed Iestyn's forearm. His right arm, the one she'd healed seven years and a lifetime ago, after he stood with her against the demons. "For seven years, I've asked myself if I could have made another choice that would have saved Sanctuary. What happened to you was my fault."

Silence descended on the hill above the sea.

"You must not blame yourself," Conn said. "I have never blamed you. It was my decision to send the younger ones away."

Iestyn cleared his throat. "It wasn't your fault," he said to Lucy. He turned to the prince. "Or yours. It was our decision to turn back. My choice. My responsibility."

What had Lara said? *"Sometimes things happen as part of a larger plan, and we just can't see it yet."*

"None of us figured the ship would go down. Nobody could have predicted I'd turn up now, after all this time. Maybe it was an accident. Or luck." He shrugged. "Or maybe it was something else."

"Destiny," Conn said.

He met the sea lord's eyes. "Maybe."

Lucy smiled. "And here you are, safe and back with us again."

Back among his own kind, she meant.

Back where he belonged.

Iestyn smiled, but a vague dissatisfaction still gnawed his gut.

"The question is, where will you go now?" Conn said.

He had no idea. His lack of direction had never bothered him before. *We flow as the sea flows.*

But something was missing. Something was wrong.

Lucy tipped her head. "Won't you come with us? To Sanctuary."

Iestyn pictured the green hills and round towers, the magic island set like a jewel between the swaying kelp forests and swirling sky. The work of rebuilding was done, Lucy had told him earlier. Everything was as it had been. He could go home again. He waited for the rush of relief, the sense of homecoming.

And was surprised to hear himself say, "No."

"Ah," Conn said.

The wind whispered from the sea, stirring Lucy's hair.

"It's the girl, isn't it?" she said. "Lara."

Iestyn ducked his head, feeling about fifteen again. Lucy had been his first love or at least his first serious crush. He suspected she knew it. He was sure Conn did. How could he tell them he was reconsidering his future based on his feelings for a girl he'd known less than a week?

"She saved my life," he said.

"She also put you in danger," Lucy said.

"Not deliberately."

"We have never allied with the children of air," Morgan said. The finfolk lord strolled from the cover of trees like a shark emerging from the shadow of the rocks. His hair gleamed pale in the sunlight.

My great-uncle, Iestyn thought, Lara's words fresh in his mind. He could see the resemblance, a trick of coloring, a similarity in build. But he didn't feel the connection.

"Because we were neutral in Hell's war on Heaven and humankind," Conn said.

"Aren't we neutral now?" Iestyn asked.

"Alliances change," Morgan said. "The demons no longer disguise their enmity. Your affinity with this girl now could tip things in our favor."

Conn raised his eyebrows. "Another shift in the balance of power?" he inquired softly.

Morgan met his gaze. "Why not? I liked the look of that heth. We could use something like that."

The undercurrents of the conversation sucked at Iestyn, leaving him edgy and off balance. "Lara didn't make the heth," he said.

"But she understands how it was made. How it works."

Morgan directed another look at Conn. "It would be interesting to learn what else she knows. What else she can do."

Iestyn gritted his teeth. Lara had run with him rather than let him be used by the nephilim. "Forget it. I won't let you use her."

They all regarded him with varying degrees of affront or surprise.

"The pup has grown teeth," Morgan murmured.

"Your concern for the girl does you credit," Conn said. "But her appearance now has implications for us all. We'd be fools not to take advantage of her knowledge."

"Only if she agrees," Iestyn said. "If she stays."

The thought that she might not stay struck at his heart.

"Why wouldn't she stay?" Morgan asked. "She's obviously in love with you."

Was she?

Iestyn's throat tightened. He gulped his beer.

Was love enough to make her stay?

"Unless you don't love her," Conn said, watching him closely.

Iestyn stared morosely at the bottle in his hand. "She'll never believe it. Not now. Not if she thinks I'm using her."

"But you've told her how you feel," Lucy said.

"No."

No promises. No guarantees.

Conn raised his eyebrows. "Then you should."

Iestyn's jaw set stubbornly. Lara had told him straight out that she was tired of other people telling her how to live her life. "She ought to be able to decide what she wants for herself."

"And how can she do that if she doesn't know that you love her?" Lucy asked.

"She should understand her options," Conn said.

"She deserves the words," Morgan said. He glanced toward the picnic table, where his wife Elizabeth chatted with Margred Hunter. "Women need words."

Iestyn's chest felt tight. Lara had been so careful not to ask him for promises.

But he could make them, because the words mattered. Because she mattered.

He wanted her. He trusted her. But he hadn't trusted his feelings until now.

He regarded the three under the trees, his prince, his friend, his only living blood relative.

"I need to talk to her."

"She's gone," Morgan said.

Iestyn's blood drummed in his ears. "What?"

"Dylan saw her headed back to the inn. I came to tell you."

Conn's gaze narrowed. "Problem?"

Uneasiness gripped Iestyn. That sense of something off, something wrong, swept over him.

"I don't know. I have to find her."

* * *

Lucy watched Iestyn stride down the hill with the quick impatience of the boy she once knew.

But he wasn't a boy any longer.

She sighed, remembering. Iestyn had been her first friend on Sanctuary, a gawky adolescent with a kind heart and a flashing smile. Seeing him all grown up made her feel . . . old.

She listened to the ocean's long-drawn-out lament, the cries of the seabirds drifting over the water like the voices of lost children.

"You are disappointed," Conn said quietly.

She turned her head to find him watching her, his silver eyes impenetrable.

She didn't understand. "Disappointed?"

"That he is not returning with us to Sanctuary."

She shook her head. "No." She roused herself to give a better answer. Conn was forcing himself out of his customary reserve to communicate. To talk about her *feelings*, poor man. He was trying. They both were.

"I was just thinking how much he's changed. Iestyn."

"He is older."

She attempted a smile. "Aren't we all."

"Not you."

The magic of Sanctuary kept her from aging. In physical years, she was probably younger than Iestyn now.

Her throat tightened. "I feel about a hundred."

"You are as fresh and young as spring," Conn said. "And more beautiful than the day I met you."

"Oh." He took her breath away. Tears welled in her eyes. "You don't have to say that."

"Women need words, Morgan tells me. And it gives me pleasure to say them."

He knelt before her on the grass.

"Conn." She was shaken. Embarrassed. He was a proud man. Prince of the merfolk, lord of the sea. And at any moment, anyone could look over and see him kneeling at her feet. "What are you doing?"

"Something I should have done long ago." He took her hands. Her fingers trembled in his strong clasp. "Lucy, my love. My heart. Will you marry me?"

The earth whirled and settled around them. She swallowed the ache in her heart, the lump in her throat. One of them had to be practical. They had duties. Obligations. "What if I can never give you children? You need an heir."

"I need you. I will always need you." He looked up at her, his silver eyes blazing. "Recommit to me, Lucy. Here, in a church, in the sight of God, according to the custom of your people. Take me as your husband. Will you?"

Her tears washed her grief away. She forgot pride and obligation, forgot whoever might be watching. All she could see was Conn's eyes, Conn's face, full of heat and love and tenderness.

She felt an overwhelming rush of love for him.

"Yes," she whispered. "Yes, please, I will."

He rose to his feet and pulled her into his arms, kissing her fiercely. The sun sank to the surface of the sea, trailing banners of scarlet and gold.

* * *

A fist closed in Lara's chest. She didn't trust Zayin, not for a moment. But she couldn't bring herself to believe that the Master Guardian would actually hurt her.

She edged backward toward the door, feeling with her foot for the threshold, keeping her eyes on him.

"Please." Zayin sounded more derisive than angry. "Don't put me to the trouble of coming after you."

Again. The unspoken word echoed between them.

"What do you want?" she asked.

"We've been worried about you," Zayin said. "Simon in particular."

"I'm fine. You can tell him so."

"Tell him yourself. Come home with me."

Home. A vision of Rockhaven rose in her mind, glossy and sharp as a photograph, the strong, stone walls, the jewellike windows, everything she'd once loved, everything that was permanent and safe.

She shook her head without speaking.

"Frankly, I'm relieved to find you alive," Zayin said. "This room stinks of demon. Demon and fish."

Shocked, she met his gaze.

"You do know he's possessed," Zayin said. "Aqua Boy."

Lara sucked in her breath. "You *knew*?"

"I knew he was a danger to you."

"Not anymore. Iestyn cast the demon out."

Zayin stared at her, arrested. "He did."

"We did." The memory of it straightened her spine. "Together."

"Well." Zayin leaned back in the chair, his big body deliberately relaxed. "It appears we underestimated you."

"So you see . . ." She exhaled. "You don't have to worry about me. I can take care of myself."

"Possibly. But then you have an obligation to protect others. *Scire, servare, obtemperare*." His smile was dark and joyless. "The only way to regain the perfection of Heaven is through the Rule."

"Do you really believe that?"

Black eyes flickered. "Simon does. And you are Simon's disciple, are you not?"

Her chest felt tight. She didn't know what she was anymore. What she believed. "I can't go back to the way things were."

"No one would expect it. You've changed," Zayin said, with an assessing look. "Other things can change. If you came back of your own volition, Simon would welcome you with an open heart and open arms. We need you, Lara. What you have learned, you can teach to others."

His words tore at her soul. More than physical safety, she craved emotional security. Simon's praise and approval, a valued place at Rockhaven, were all she'd ever wanted.

The burden of freedom, the weight of fear, pressed on her heart. Her lips felt numb. She heard herself say, "What about Iestyn?"

"What of him?"

"I can't just leave him."

Zayin glanced around the empty room. "And yet he is not here."

A flush heated her face. "He'll be back."

"For how long?" Zayin asked.

She stared at him, stricken, seeing Iestyn's face, alight with joy. Hearing Iestyn's voice, bright with hope. *"With her help, I can learn to Change . . . I can go back to sea again."*

Zayin pressed his advantage. "Let it go, Lara. Let him go. He's free to be with his own people now. And you can be safe with yours."

"So you're asking me to trade a chance at happiness for . . . What? Security?"

"I'm telling you. Give up your infatuation with this boy for a guaranteed future."

But there were no guarantees outside of Heaven. Iestyn had said that. The only thing certain was change.

Lara gnawed the inside of her cheek. She *had* changed. She was more confident now, more sure of herself and what she wanted. She didn't need to look to Simon for approval anymore or to the nephilim for safety and acceptance.

She had to trust herself. She trusted Iestyn. She wanted him, wanted what they could be together.

Zayin stood, big and dark and alien in the charming white room. Despite herself, Lara's heart gave a little bump.

"We've both wasted enough time here," he said. "I'm taking you back."

"No, you're not," Iestyn said.

Lara's head jerked around to the door. "Iestyn."

"Hey, babe." He smiled, but his eyes were cold. "We missed you at the party. You should have stuck around."

Her eyes blurred. Her heart pounded. But a combination of pride and hurt and honesty held her back. Made her say, "I wasn't sure you wanted me."

He winced. "I guess I deserve that. Stay. Let me make it up to you."

"You don't have to—"

"You're too late," Zayin interrupted. "She's leaving."

"Not with you, asshole."

"You can't stop her." Zayin looked Iestyn up and down. "And you definitely can't stop me."

Iestyn bared his teeth in a grin. "I've killed demons, church breath. Angels don't scare me."

Violence boiled up in the room, quick and hot as steam.

"Stop it, both of you." Lara stepped between them, facing Zayin. "What I do and where I go is my choice."

"Not after I get through with him," Zayin promised darkly.

"But then you'd have to go through us," a male voice announced from behind them.

Zayin's black gaze switched over Lara's shoulder. "Who the hell are you?"

Bewildered, she turned.

Morgan and Dylan stood shoulder to shoulder in the doorway backing Iestyn. They could hardly have appeared more different, she thought dazedly: Dylan, dark and lean, Morgan, broad and fair, Iestyn with his sun-streaked hair and hammered gold eyes. But at that moment, they were as close as brothers, united in her defense.

Her eyes sought Iestyn. He held her gaze, smiling crookedly. "I told you we missed you. I missed you. I came to get you back. Whatever it takes."

A wave of relief, of reassurance and love, crashed over her. She started to shake.

Sometimes you didn't need words and guarantees.

Sometimes one look said everything and one act, one gesture of faith, was enough.

"Don't be a fool," Zayin growled. "Do you have any idea what you're giving up?"

She lifted her chin. "I think so. I can go with you and follow the Rule. Or I can stay with him and follow my heart."

Zayin stared at her, his eyes black and blank and opaque as always. "Simon will never understand. Will never accept your decision."

She felt a quiver of anxiety, a flutter of regret. But she held his gaze without hesitation or apology. "What will you tell him?"

A corner of Zayin's mouth turned up in a barely perceptible smile. "That I couldn't find you, of course." He bowed his sleek dark head, in acknowledgment of defeat. "I wish you joy of your decision."

He stalked toward the door. Morgan and Dylan stepped aside to let him pass. As his footsteps faded down the hall, the tension leaked from the room.

Dylan cleared his throat. "We'll just see him as far as the ferry."

The two wardens followed him down the stairs.

Lara shivered in reaction. "Well." She swallowed. "I'm glad that's over."

"Not over yet," Iestyn said and then he was there, solid, warm, and real, wrapping his arms around her, driving away the cold.

She melted into him. Her heart began a slow pound in her chest. "There's more?"

"There has to be. For me, at least." He took her hands, holding them palm to palm between both of his as if he were praying. He kissed her fingers, his face serious.

Nerves knotted her stomach. "You don't have to say anything," she said. *Don't let go.* "You don't have to feel obligated to me because I chose to stay."

He shook his head. "I'm not obligated. I want to be with you."

She smiled at him wryly. Tenderly. "Yesterday you said we barely know each other."

"I know what I feel." He held her closer, her head against his chest. "I know that without you, I'm lost."

"Not anymore," she mumbled into his shirt. "You're back where you belong now. You can go back to the sea."

"I belong with you. We belong with each other." His voice was sure, his heartbeat strong and steady. She could feel her body softening, adjusting to his, all of her pressed against all of him, breasts, belly, thighs. *Heaven.* "Give me time to prove it to you."

All her doubts were dissolving away. But she eased back within the circle of his arms to look him in the eye. "How much time are we talking about?"

His grin flashed. "Five years? Fifty? Five hundred?"

"You want me to wait for you that long?"

"I want you to stay with me. Be with me. Here on the island. They need you. I need you. I love you, Lara, by God I do." His voice shook. His arms tightened around her.

"I love you," he repeated, resting his forehead against hers. "If you don't want to live here, we'll go someplace else. Just don't leave me."

Hope welled inside her. "You love me." She tested the words in her mouth, tasting their sweetness.

His arms tightened in frustration. "How many ways do I have to say it for you to believe me? Give me a chance. Give us a chance."

"A leap of faith?" she murmured.

"If you'll take it, I swear I won't let you down."

She wrapped her arms around his neck, leaning her weight against his hard, sheltering body. "I believe in you. In us. I love you, too."

"Thank God." He cradled her face in his hands, tipping her head back to kiss her, her eyes, her nose, her cheek. Her mouth. Joy flooded her soul.

"You know, you could come with me," he murmured after long moments had passed.

Lara surfaced reluctantly. "Come with you where?"

"When I go to sea. You could come inside me."

She blinked. "You mean, spirit cast? Under water?"

He grinned down at her. "Why not? You said yourself we can do more together than we can apart."

The possibility teased her. Tempted her. She felt no fear. Only wonder that they had two worlds and all of their lives to explore.

"Let me share my world with you, Lara," Iestyn said in unconscious echo of her thoughts. "My life with you."

She smiled, twining her arms around his neck. "Why not?" She threw his challenge back at him. "After all, there's more than one way to fly."

He laughed and covered her mouth with his.

Beyond their window, the bright sky blended into the shining sea.

TURN THE PAGE FOR A SPECIAL PREVIEW OF THE FIRST IN VIRGINIA KANTRA'S NEW CONTEMPORARY ROMANCE SERIES SET ON DARE ISLAND, NORTH CAROLINA.

COMING SOON FROM BERKLEY SENSATION!

1

MATT FLETCHER DIDN'T GO LOOKING FOR TROUble. Most times, it just found him.

The angry echoes of last night's argument had stirred up old ghosts, old frustrations and resentments. But a day's hard work on the water had settled him and given him a chance to think things through. Sweat and salt cured everything in time.

Now, with a full fish box in the stern and four sunburned, satisfied passengers on deck, he turned the *Sea Lady II* toward home. The twin diesels chugged as he eased the boat through the long rock jetties that hunched like shoulders at the neck of the harbor. Water churned, attracting a flock of greedy gulls that cried and hovered in his wake. The smell of fish, fuel, marsh grass, and mud thickened the air. The August heat pressed down, flattening the inlet like glass. Sunlight flashed on the fractured surface.

Braced on the bridge, Matt navigated the forty-five-foot

Lady past bobbing boats, narrow slips and a thicket of masts and fishing rods, heading for the bleached wooden dock and weathered shack that served as office for his tiny charter fleet. With Joshua back in school and unable to crew, Matt had been forced to leave the original *Sea Lady* in dock and bring his father, Tom, along as mate. It hurt leaving a boat behind, losing business this late in the season.

But his passengers, doctors from Raleigh sporting khaki shorts and expensive haircuts, wanted the kind of amenities the *Lady II* could provide. They hadn't balked at the full-day offshore rate, and they'd pay to have their catch cleaned, too, three big yellowfin, two dozen dorado, a cooler full of steely-faced wahoo.

A good day all around.

Fishermen learned to accept what the sea gave and what the sea took away. A captain pitted his boat and equipment, his experience and skill, against the whims of the ocean, the season, and the weather. Sometimes you did everything you could do and still came home empty-handed.

Matt was grateful for the good days.

Water lapped the pier as he revved the diesels, swinging the *Lady II* around in a tight arc to back without a bump into the slip. A pelican launched from the wharf, settling expectantly in the water.

Matt's father secured the lines. At six-two and sixty-four, Tom Fletcher resembled one of the pilings that lined the wharf, gray, tall, and spare. He wore a United States Marine Corps baseball cap, the red bill faded with sun and age.

"I was a Navy corpsman," one of the doctors offered as he jumped onto the dock.

"Nothing against the Navy." Tom handed up the man's backpack, jacket, and cooler. "The Marines need bus drivers."

A brief pause before the offended doctor decided to laugh.

Matt grinned. It was customary to tip the mate on a charter fishing boat. But twenty-five years as a career sergeant major hadn't taught the old man the value of keeping his mouth shut. Dad wouldn't get a tip from *that* ex–Navy man.

Along the waterfront, gawkers had gathered to compare the day's take from the different boats. Tourists. Matt didn't mind them. True, they crowded the island so that a man sometimes couldn't talk with his neighbors until after Labor Day. But the tourist tide in summer kept the island economy afloat the rest of the year.

He scanned the small crowd, trying to pick the potential customers from the merely curious.

His gaze snagged. Caught.

A young woman stood at the end of his dock, her long blond hair bundled into some kind of ponytail, a V of pink skin at her throat, a flutter of skirt at her knee. Nice legs. Too young. And as tall, cool, and appealing as a long-necked bottle of beer.

For a moment his mouth went dry.

Matt shook his head, amused by his reaction. He wasn't about to break his dry spell with a pretty young thing dressed like a model in a J.Crew catalogue.

No harm in looking, though. He studied her from the bridge. She wasn't a native. He'd have recognized her. Or the average tourist on vacation. She looked more put together somehow, like a real estate agent or his ex-wife's lawyer or somebody attached to one of the doctors. A daughter, maybe, or a trophy wife, although Matt didn't spot any big chunks of jewelry on her. No ring.

His father opened the fish box in the stern and began tossing up the catch. Fish flew in a rainbow arc, blue, gold, glittering silver, all their angry energy transformed by death to pale, stiff beauty.

But the girl wasn't watching the show. Her deep brown eyes fixed on his father. Her chin lifted. Her soft mouth firmed.

Matt recognized the determination in her gaze and felt a tightening in his gut, a familiar tension at the back of his neck.

Trouble.

* * *

Allison Casey stood on the dock under the weathered FLETCHER'S QUAY sign, a bead of sweat running between her breasts to soak into her bra.

After two years of teaching in the Mississippi Delta, she had been ready for a change.

She'd loved her students, was enthusiastic about her subject, and had learned to embrace the tight-knit rural community and the rhythms of the South. But she was sick of bugs the size of house pets and thirty-six students per class. She was tired of her parents' complaints that she lived too far away.

So when her Teach For America stint was up, she had applied for the job on Dare Island, North Carolina, eight hours closer to her family in D.C. Better pay. Smaller class sizes.

Same damn heat.

She shifted her weight in her ballet flats, resisting the urge to peel off her tissue-thin sweater. She knew she looked only a little older than some of her students. She had to present a professional appearance.

Especially when she was meeting with a parent.

Not, she thought, one of the four men standing on the dock arguing over who got to take home the tuna. Men like her father, with perfect capped teeth and an air of entitlement.

She squinted into the sun sinking toward Pamlico Sound. Maybe the one on the bridge?

Her gaze skated over him. From a purely female, personal perspective, he was certainly worth looking at. Hard muscle packed into a faded T-shirt and jeans. Damp, dark, curling hair jammed under a baseball cap. A lean, watchful face with a hint of pirate stubble.

He didn't look like any high school father she'd ever seen. And she wasn't here to drool over the scenery.

She dragged her gaze away to focus on the older man tossing fish into a large plastic garbage can. Now *he* looked the way she imagined a boat captain should look. Like Ahab in *Moby-Dick*, all "*compacted aged robustness.*" Minus the scar and the peg leg, of course.

She lifted her chin. "Mr. Fletcher?"

He spared her a quick glance from faded blue eyes before hauling the garbage can over to a long metal table under the shade of wooden roof. "Yep."

She followed him. So did a dozen gulls, hopping, hovering, swooping, and lighting on the roof and in the water.

"I'm Miss Casey." She had to raise her voice to be heard over the squawking birds. "Joshua's Language Arts teacher. I have to tell you how much I'm looking forward to working with your son."

Captain Ahab Fletcher flipped the dead fish out on the table, smooth as a blackjack dealer in Vegas. Out came a knife. *Cut, cut, cut,* down the row of heads. *Cut, cut, cut,* along the spines and bellies. "No, you don't."

Allison straightened to her full five feet and ten inches. Last year, she had motivated, coaxed, and bullied one hundred and twenty-seven underachieving students into scoring at a basic or proficient level on the English II graduation exit exam. She could not be deterred by a little thing like dead fish or a bad attitude.

"Actually, I make it a point to talk to all my students' parents at the beginning of the school year."

"Then you want his dad. Matt!" he called over her shoulder. "Josh's teacher is here to see you."

Her stomach sank at her mistake. She fixed a smile on her face and turned, determined to remain pleasant. Professional.

And came face-to-face with the solid chest and drool-worthy shoulders of the man from the boat. Of course. Because nothing beat getting off on the wrong foot with a parent like embarrassing yourself in front of a really hot guy.

She cleared her throat. "Mr. Fletcher?"

"Call him 'Captain,'" the older man suggested.

"Dad." The quiet tone held warning. Blue eyes, dark and level, met hers from under the brim of his cap. "I'm Matt Fletcher. What can I do for you?"

"Allison Casey. Joshua is in my Language Arts class." She hesitated, aware of the crowded wharf behind him. "Is there someplace we can talk privately?"

The senior Mr. Fletcher snorted.

Matt Fletcher's mouth tightened. "We're kind of busy right now," he said politely enough. "Is Josh all right?"

She noted, and appreciated, his concern for his son. "He's fine," she said. "Have you spoken with him today?"

Matt tugged off his cap, wiping his forehead with the back of his arm. He smelled, rather pleasantly, of sweat and the sea. "We've been out on the water since five this morning. What did he do?"

"Nothing." And that, of course, was the problem. "I was actually hoping to talk to you about Joshua's progress. We've been in class now for almost two weeks and he has yet to open his mouth. Or, as far as I can tell, a book."

He regarded her without expression. "He's not giving you any trouble, is he?"

"He's very respectful," she assured him. If a total lack of interest in her subject matter could be called respect. "But I am *troubled* because he's a bright boy who's obviously not living up to his potential."

"We've heard that one before," the older Fletcher said.

Matt sighed. "Look, I appreciate you coming by, but I can't do this now. I've got customers to deal with and a boat to hose down. I need a shower and I want a beer."

"Of course," she said rather stiffly. "I'm sorry to have bothered you at work. But when I called the number on file, your wife said I should come down to the harbor to talk to you."

"I'm not married."

A pause.

Like things couldn't get any more awkward.

"Josh's mother is out of the picture," Fletcher Senior said. "That was my Tess you talked to. Josh's grandmother. You want that boy straightened out, you should let her know."

"Josh is my son," Matt said flatly. "I'll talk to him."

Allison knew parents who were too overwhelmed by the struggle to survive to focus on their children's education. And parents like her own, too self-absorbed to see beyond their own needs and convenience, who only wanted perfect, perfect children to accessorize their perfect, perfect life.

She wondered which category Matt Fletcher fell into.

"It's important to begin the school year on the right foot," she said earnestly. "I'm very excited about having Joshua in my classroom. But communication is key to his success."

"I said I'll talk to him. Tonight."

"After your beer?"

She'd meant it—hadn't she?—as a sort of a joke. An acknowledgment of his long day, an attempt to smooth things over.

Matt Fletcher gave her a hard look. "That's right," he said briefly. "Now, unless you're buying, you'll have to excuse me."

KEEP READING FOR A SPECIAL PREVIEW OF

Delaney's Shadow

BY INGRID WEAVER

COMING IN AUGUST 2011 FROM BERKLEY SENSATION!

HE CAME BACK TO HER IN A DREAM. YET EVEN AS Delaney sensed his presence in her head, the watchful, grown-up part of her knew he couldn't be real. This couldn't be happening. He was the boy of make-believe.

"Max?" Her lips mouthed the name. She hadn't spoken it aloud since her childhood. It belonged to the past, to the girl who used to sleep in this ribbons-and-bows room, to the days of laughter in the kitchen and bees in the roses and sheets snapping in the sunshine.

She couldn't remember when he'd first appeared. It seemed as if Max had always been with her, in some corner of her mind. Whenever she'd needed him, he would show up, the skinny little boy with dark hair and a crooked front tooth.

Oh, the times they'd had, the games they'd played. Racing along the lane, their arms extended like airplane wings, they would fix their gazes on the horizon and pretend to soar. Or quietly, so quietly, they would creep past Grandpa's room to the attic for rainy afternoon treasure hunts. There had been safaris in her grandmother's garden, elaborate banquets on the playroom floor, and gleeful, giggling slides down the curving oak banister.

But the best times, the very best ones, had been when he'd taken her to their own special world, the place they made up together, where nothing bad happened and nothing ever hurt.

She breathed his name again. Max. He'd been her partner in mischief, her secret confidante, the imaginary friend she had created to become her playmate. The first time she'd insisted on setting a place for Max at dinner, Grandpa had banged his cane on the floor and had told her to quit making up stories or by God she would turn out as flighty as her mother. Grandma had just winked at her and slid an extra plate beside the butter dish.

But then Delaney's mother had died, and her father had returned for her. They'd moved to the city. She'd tried to bring Max, too, but there hadn't been a banister or extra plates in the apartment, and Mrs. Joiner said that imaginary friends weren't allowed at school.

And eventually Delaney had stopped believing. She'd grown up and left Max behind.

Yet if she'd left him behind, how could he be here?

It was a dream, she reminded herself. And unlike the other ones, this dream wasn't filled with images of twisted metal and death.

Why hadn't she realized it before? Max would be able to keep the nightmares away. He could do anything.

"Max," she whispered.

His presence strengthened until the air around him seemed to reach out in a welcoming smile. He stood in the shadow beside the bedroom doorway. A stubborn, wayward lock of hair hid one eye, but the other sparkled in a conspirator's grin.

What would they do today? Where would they go? What games would they play?

It didn't matter. As long as he kept her safe from the nightmares.

She had always felt safe with Max.

He shuffled forward, his sneakers making stealthy squeaks against the floor. As usual, he wore jeans that looked a size too large, the denim hanging loosely from his hips. His T-shirt bore a smear from the mud pies she'd made him the morning she'd left Willowbank. He had the same hopeful smile, the same live-wire sizzle of energy, that clean, fresh-air feeling of sunshine and summer breezes . . .

The watchful, grown-up part of her stirred once more, but she kept her mind focused on Max. He was a part of the past that it didn't hurt to remember, part of the days of innocence, when life stretched out before her in endless possibilities, and pain was no worse than a skinned knee. Sleep hadn't been something she dreaded then.

She splayed her fingers, reaching toward him. "Let's play, Max."

His image wavered.

"No, Max. Stay!"

Like a shadow glimpsed on the edge of vision, like the dream he was, the little boy faded.

She fought the return of consciousness. "Not yet," she urged. "Not yet."

Through the open window came the cheerful lilt of a robin, as persistent as an alarm clock. Against her closed eyelids, Delaney could feel the tentative warmth of sunrise.

The presence that was Max trembled, then silently flickered out.

Sighing, Delaney rolled to her back and opened her eyes.

Something was wrong. Where was the shelf with her dolls? What had happened to the lacy canopy that sheltered her bed?

It took a few moments for her brain to catch up with her senses. Books lined the shelf, not toys, and a dieffenbachia filled the corner where there had once been a rocking horse. The dolls and the lace were gone. They had been packed up decades ago, along with her fairy-tale books and her frilly socks. The canopy bed had been replaced by a cherrywood four-poster. A matching, grown-up-sized dresser stood beside the plant. Her grandmother had redecorated the house when she'd converted the front half into a bed-and-breakfast.

Delaney sat up and raked her hair off her face. Instead of the typical sleep-tangled lengths, she felt stubby chunks slide between her fingers. There was another one of those moments of puzzlement. What had happened to her hair? She slipped her hand beneath the neckline of her nightgown. Scar tissue ridges as fine as stretched crepe paper slid beneath her palm. The burns no longer hurt. She could barely feel her own touch.

Full wakefulness hit her, bringing a spurt of panic. It had been more than six months since the accident. The changes to her life were so enormous, she still had trouble absorbing the full scope of them. She understood what had happened to her body, just as she was aware of what had happened to her husband. The doctors at the clinic had explained it. So had the police. But it wasn't the same as *knowing.*

Maybe today would be the day that she actually remembered.

After all, she had remembered Max, hadn't she?

Ah, Max. She'd had such a vivid imagination when she'd been a child; her make-believe friend would have been able to help her.

Too bad she'd grown up and was beyond all that.